Morris Gleitzman was ░░░░░░░░░░░
to Australia with his fa░░░░░░░░░░ ░
worked as a frozen-chick... ...uwer, fashion-industry trainee,
department-store Santa, TV producer, newspaper columnist
and freelance screenwriter. Then in 1985 he wrote his first
novel for young people. Now he's one of Australia's favourite
children's authors, with a large following in Britain and many
other countries. His most successful titles include *Belly Flop* and
Water Wings, also published by Macmillan as a bind-up, *Two
Weeks with the Queen, Bumface, Boy Overboard* and *Once.*

Both *Blabber Mouth* and *Sticky Beak* were adapted for television
when they were first published, and the programme, made for
Channel 4, won an International Emmy.

Rave reviews for *Blabber Mouth, Sticky Beak* and *Gift of the Gab*:

'Gleitzman tells his story brilliantly and with enormous
humour' Julia Eccleshare, *Bookseller*

'A giggle a minute' *Daily Telegraph*

'Funny, fresh and very readable' *Weekend Telegraph*

'Hectic, raucous . . . Ace' *TES*

The Blabber Mouth Collection

MACMILLAN CHILDREN'S BOOKS

Blabber Mouth and *Sticky Beak* first published individually 1992 and 1993
respectively by Pan Macmillan Publishers Australia.
First published in the UK 1993 and 1994 respectively
by Macmillan Children's Books

Gift of the Gab first published individually 1999
by Penguin Books, Australia.
First published in the UK 1999 by Viking

This edition published 2008 by Macmillan Children's Books
a division of Macmillan Publishers Limited
20 New Wharf Road, London N1 9RR
Basingstoke and Oxford
www.panmacmillan.com

Associated companies throughout the world

ISBN 978-0-330-45293-9

1 3 5 7 9 8 6 4 2

A CIP catalogue record for this book is available from
the British Library.

Printed and bound in Great Britain by Mackays of Chatham plc, Kent

Contents

Blabber Mouth

For Chris, Sophie and Ben

I'm so dumb.

I never thought I'd say that about myself, but after what I've just done I deserve it.

How could I have messed up my first day here so totally and completely?

Two hours ago, when I walked into this school for the first time, the sun was shining, the birds were singing and, apart from a knot in my guts the size of Tasmania, life was great.

Now here I am, locked in the stationery cupboard.

Just me, a pile of exam papers and what smells like one of last year's cheese and devon sandwiches.

Cheer up exam papers, cheer up ancient sanger, if you think you're unpopular, take a look at me.

I wish those teachers would stop shouting at me to unlock the door and come out. I don't want to come out. I want to sit here in the dark with my friend the sandwich.

Oh no, now Ms Dunning's trying to pick the

1

lock with the staff-room knife. One of the other teachers is telling her not to cut herself. The principal's telling her not to damage the staff-room knife.

I hope she doesn't cut herself because she was really good to me this morning.

I was an Orange-to-Dubbo-phone-line-in-a-heap-sized bundle of nerves when I walked into that classroom this morning with everyone staring. Even though we've been in the district over a week, and I've seen several of the kids in the main street, they still stared.

I didn't blame them. In small country towns you don't get much to stare at. Just newcomers and old men who dribble, mostly.

Ms Dunning was great. She told everyone to remember their manners or she'd kick them in the bum, and everyone laughed. Then when she saw the letters me and Dad had photocopied she said it was the best idea she'd seen since microwave pizza, and gave me permission to hand them round.

I watched anxiously while all the kids read the letter. I was pretty pleased with it, but you can never tell how an audience is going to react.

'G'day', the letter said, 'my name's Rowena Batts and, as you've probably noticed by now, I can't speak. Don't worry, but, we can still be friends cause I can write, draw, point, nod, shake my head, screw up my nose and do sign language. I used to go to a special school but the government closed it down. The reason I can't speak is I was born with some

2

bits missing from my throat. (It's OK, I don't leak.) Apart from that, I'm completely normal and my hobbies are reading, watching TV and driving my Dad's tractor. I hope we can be friends, yours sincerely, Rowena Batts.'

That letter took me about two hours to write last night, not counting the time I spent arguing with Dad about the spelling, so I was pleased that most people read it all the way through.

Some kids smiled.

Some laughed, but in a nice way.

A few nudged each other and gave me smirky looks.

'OK,' said Ms Dunning, 'let's all say g'day to Rowena.'

'G'day,' everyone chorused, which I thought was a bit humiliating for them, but Ms Dunning meant well.

I gave them the biggest grin I could, even though Tasmania was trying to crawl up my throat.

A couple of the kids didn't say g'day, they just kept on with the smirky looks.

One of them was a boy with red lips and ginger hair and there was something about his extra-big smirk that made me think even then that I was probably going to have trouble with him.

'Right,' said Ms Dunning after she'd sat me down next to a girl with white hair who was still only halfway through my letter, 'who's on frogs today?' She looked at a chart on the wall next to a tank with some small green frogs in it.

'Darryn Peck,' she said.

The kid with the big red smirk got up and swaggered over to the tank.

'Clean it thoroughly,' warned Ms Dunning, 'or I'll feed you to them.'

We all laughed and Darryn Peck gave her a rude sign behind her back. A couple of kids laughed again and Ms Dunning was just about to turn back to Darryn when a woman came to the door and said there was a phone call for her in the office.

'Ignore the floor show,' Ms Dunning told us, giving Darryn Peck a long look, 'and read something interesting. I'll only be a sec.'

As soon as she'd gone, Darryn Peck started.

'I can speak sign language,' he said loudly, smirking right at me. Then he gave me the same finger he'd given Ms Dunning.

About half the class laughed.

I decided to ignore him.

The girl next to me was still having trouble with my letter. She had her ruler under the word 'sincerely' and was frowning at it.

I found my pen, leaned over, crossed out 'Yours sincerely' and wrote 'No bull'. She looked at it for a moment, then grinned at me.

'Rowena Batts,' said Darryn Peck. 'What sort of a name is Batts? Do you fly around at night and suck people's blood?'

Hardly anyone laughed and I didn't blame them. I've had better insults from kids with permanent brain damage.

I thought about asking him what sort of a name Peck was, and did he get a sore knees from eating with the chooks, but then I remembered nobody there would be able to understand my hand movements, and the trouble with writing insults is it takes years.

'My parents'd go for a kid like you,' said Darryn, even louder. 'They're always saying they wish I'd lose my voice.'

Nobody laughed.

Darryn could see he was losing his audience.

Why didn't I treat that as a victory and ignore him and swap addresses with the slow reader next to me?

Because I'm not just mute, I'm dumb.

'Your parents must be really pleased you're a freak,' brayed Darryn. 'Or are they freaks too and haven't noticed?'

He shouldn't have said that.

Dad can look after himself, but Mum died when I was born and if anyone says anything bad about her I get really angry.

I got really angry.

Tasmania sprouted volcanoes and the inside of my head filled up with molten lava.

I leapt across the room and snatched the frog Darryn Peck was holding and squeezed his cheeks hard so his red lips popped open and stuffed the frog into his mouth and grabbed the sticky tape from the art table and wound it round and round his head till there was none left.

The others all stared at me, mouths open, horrified. Then they quickly closed their mouths.

I stood there while the lava cooled in my head and Darryn Peck gurgled and the other kids backed away.

Then I realised what I'd done.

Lost all my friends before I'd even made them.

I ran out of the room and down the corridor past a startled Ms Dunning and just as she was calling out I saw a cupboard door with a key in it and threw myself in and locked it.

The smell in here's getting worse.

I don't think it's a cheese and devon sandwich after all, I think it's a dead frog.

I'm not opening the door.

I just want to sit here in the dark and pretend I'm at my old school with my old friends.

It's not easy because the teachers out there in the corridor are making such a racket scurrying around and muttering to each other and yelling at kids to get back in the classroom.

Ms Dunning's just been to phone Dad, and the principal's just asked if anyone's got a crowbar in their car.

It doesn't sound as though anyone has, or if they have, they don't want to go and get it.

I don't blame them. Who'd want to walk all the way to the staff car park for the least popular girl in the school?

Dad arrived just in time.

I was getting desperate because the smell was making me feel sick and Ms Dunning pleading with me through the door was making me feel guilty and the sound of an electric drill being tested was making me feel scared.

But I couldn't bring myself to open the door and face all those horrified kids.

And angry teachers.

And Mr Fowler the principal who'd skinned his knuckles trying to force the lock with a stapler.

Not by myself.

Then I heard a truck pull up outside.

I've never been so pleased to hear a vibrating tailgate. The tailgate on our truck has vibrated ever since Dad took the old engine out and put in a turbo-powered one with twin exhausts.

There were more scurrying and muttering sounds from out in the corridor and then Ms Dunning called through the door.

'Rowena, your father's here. If you come out now we'll try and keep him calm.'

I grinned to myself in the dark. She obviously didn't know my father.

I took a deep breath and opened the door.

The corridor was full of faces, all staring at me.

The principal, looking grim and holding a bandaged hand.

Ms Dunning, looking concerned.

The other teachers, looking annoyed.

Kids peeking out of classrooms, some horrified, some smirking.

Plus a couple of blokes in bushfire brigade overalls carrying a huge electric drill, and a man in a dustcoat with *Vic's Hardware* embroidered on the pocket holding a big bunch of keys, and an elderly woman in a yellow oilskin jacket with *State Emergency Service* printed on it.

All staring at me.

I don't think anybody said anything. But I wouldn't have heard them if they had because my heart was pounding in my ears like a stump excavator.

Then the door at the other end of the corridor swung open with a bang and all the heads turned.

It was Dad.

As he walked slowly down the corridor, taking in the situation, everyone stared at him even harder than they'd stared at me.

I didn't blame them. People usually stare at Dad the first time they see him. They're not being rude, it's just that most people have never seen an apple farmer wearing goanna-skin boots, black jeans, a studded belt with a polished metal cow's skull buckle, a black shirt with white tassels and a black cowboy hat.

Dad came up to me, looking concerned.

'You OK, Tonto?' he asked.

He always calls me Tonto. I think it's a character from a TV show he used to watch when he was a kid. I'd be embarrassed if he said it out loud, but it's OK when he says it with his hands because nobody else can understand. Dad always talks to me with his hands. He reckons two people can have a better conversation when they're both speaking the same language.

'I'm fine, Dad,' I replied.

Everyone was staring at our hands, wondering what we were saying.

'Tough day, huh?' said Dad.

'Fairly tough,' I said.

Dad gave me a sympathetic smile, then turned and met the gaze of all the people in the corridor.

Mr Fowler, the principal, stepped forward.

'We can't have a repeat of this sort of thing, Mr Batts,' he said.

'It was just first day nerves,' said Ms Dunning. 'I'm sure it won't happen again.'

Dad cleared his throat.

My stomach sank.

When Dad clears his throat it usually means one thing.

It did today.

He moved slowly around the semicircle of people, looking each of them in the eye, and sang to them.

Their mouths fell open.

Mr Fowler stepped back.

The hardware bloke dropped his keys.

As usual, Dad sang a country and western number from his record collection. He's got this huge collection of records by people with names like Slim Dusty and Carla Tamworth—the big black plastic records you play on one of those old-fashioned record players with a needle.

This one was about lips like a graveyard and a heart like a fairground and I knew Dad was singing about me.

Part of me felt proud and grateful.

The other part of me wanted to creep back into the cupboard and shut the door.

Several of the teachers looked as though they wanted to as well.

Dad thinks country and western is the best music ever written and he assumes everyone else does too. They usually don't, mostly because he doesn't get many of the notes right.

When he'd finished, and the hardware bloke had picked up his keys, Dad put an arm round my shoulders.

'Ladies and gentlemen,' he announced, 'Rowena Batts is taking the rest of the day off. Apologies for the inconvenience, and if anyone's out of pocket, give us a hoy and I'll bung you a bag of apples.'

He steered me down the corridor.

Just before we went out the door, I glanced back. Nobody had moved. Everyone looked stunned, except Ms Dunning, who had a big grin on her face.

In the truck driving into town, I told Dad what had happened. He hardly took his eyes off my hands the whole time except when he had to swerve to avoid the war memorial. When I told him about the frog in Darryn Peck's mouth he laughed so much his hat fell off.

I didn't think any of it was funny.

What's funny about everyone thinking you're a psychopath who's cruel to frogs and not wanting to touch you with a bargepole?

Just thinking about it made my eyes hot and prickly.

Dad saw this and stopped laughing.

'OK, Tonto,' he said, steering with his knees, 'let's go and rot our teeth.'

We went and had chocolate milkshakes with marshmallows floating on top, and Dad did such a good imitation of Darryn Peck with the frog in his mouth that I couldn't help laughing.

Specially when the man in the milk bar thought Dad was choking on a marshmallow.

Then we played Intergalactic Ice Invaders and I was twenty-seven thousand points ahead when the milk bar man asked us to leave because Dad was making too much noise. I guess the milk bar man must have been right because as we left, a man in a brown suit glared at us from the menswear shop next door.

We went to the pub and had lemon squash and played pool. Dad slaughtered me as usual, but I didn't mind. One of the things I really like about Dad is he doesn't fake stuff just to make you feel better. So when he says good things you know he means it. Like on the pool table today when I cracked a backspin for the first time and he said how proud it made him because he hadn't done it till he was thirteen.

When we got back here the sun was going down but Dad let me drive the tractor round the orchard a few times while he stood up on the engine cover waving a branch to keep the mozzies off us.

I was feeling so good by then I didn't even mind his singing.

We came inside and made fried eggs and apple fritters, which everyone thinks sounds yukky but that's only because they don't know how to make it. You've got to leave the eggs runny.

After dinner we watched telly, then I went to bed.

Dad came in and gave me a hug.

I switched the lamp on so he could hear me.

'If you ever get really depressed about anything,' I said, 'feel free to use the school stationery cupboard, but take a peg for your nose.'

Dad grinned.

'Thanks, Tonto,' he said. 'Anyone who doesn't want to be your mate has got bubbles in the brain. Or frogs in the mouth.'

I hugged him again and thought how lucky I am to have such a great Dad.

It's true, I am.

He's a completely and totally great Dad.

Except for one little thing.

But I don't want to think about that tonight because I'm feeling too happy.

I love talking in my head.

For a start you can yak on for hours and your hands don't get tired. Plus, while you're yakking, you can use your hands for other things like making apple fritters or driving tractors or squeezing pimples.

Pretty yukky, I know, but sometimes Dad gets one on his back and can't reach it so I have to help him out.

Another good thing about conversations in your head is you can talk to whoever you like. I talk to Madonna and the federal Minister for Health and Miles from 'Murphy Brown' and all sorts of people. You can save a fortune in phone bills.

And, if you want to, you can talk to people who've died, like Mum or Erin my best friend from my last school.

I don't do that too much, but, because it gets pretty depressing.

It's depressing me now so I'm going to stop thinking about it.

The best thing about talking in your head is you can have exactly the conversation you want.

'G'day Dad,' you say.

'G'day Ro,' he answers.

'Dad,' you say, 'do you think you could back off a bit when you meet people from my new school cause I'm really worried that even if they get over the frog incident none of the them'll want to be friends with the daughter of an apple cowboy who sings at them and even if they do their parents won't let them.'

'Right-o,' he says, 'no problem.'

People pay attention when you talk to them in your head.

Not like in real life.

In real life, even if you're really careful not to hurt their feelings, and you just say something like 'Dad, could you wear a dull shirt and not sing today please', people just roll their eyes and grin and nudge you in the ribs and say 'loosen up, Tonto' and 'the world'd be a crook place without a bit of colour and movement'.

He's yelling at me now to get out of the shower because I'll be late for school and the soap'll go squishy and the water always sprays over the top of the curtain when I stand here and think.

How come he knows when a shower's going over the top, but he doesn't know when he is?

I wish I hadn't mentioned Erin because now I'm feeling squishy myself.

It's the soap that's doing it.

It's making me think of the time Erin and me put soap in the carrot soup at our school and watched everyone dribble it down their fronts, even the kids who didn't normally dribble.

This is dumb, it's over one year and two months since she died, I shouldn't be feeling like this.

I tell you what, if I ever have another best friend I'm going to make sure she wasn't born with a dicky heart and lungs.

If I ever have another best friend I'm going to make her take a medical before we start.

If I ever have one.

Dad said today'd be better than yesterday because he reckons second days at new schools are always better than first days.

He was right.

Just.

It started off worse, but.

When I walked through the gate, all the kids stared and backed away, even the ones from other classes.

Then I had to go and see the principal, Mr Fowler, in his office.

He seemed quite tense. The skin on the top of his head was pink and when he stood up to take the tube of antiseptic cream out of his shorts pocket his knees were fairly pink too, which I've read is a danger sign for blood pressure if you're not sunburnt.

'Rowena,' he began, rubbing some of the cream onto his grazed knuckles, 'Ms Dunning has told me what happened in class yesterday and Darryn Peck has been spoken to. I know this move to a normal school isn't easy for you, but that does not excuse your behaviour yesterday and I do not want a repeat of it, do you understand?'

I nodded. I wanted to tell him you shouldn't use too much cream, Dad reckons it's better to let the air get to a graze and dry it out, but I didn't in case he'd studied antiseptic creams at university or something.

'Rowena,' Mr Fowler went on, examining the graze closely, 'if there are any problems with your father, such as, for example, him drinking too much, you know you can tell me or Ms Dunning about it, don't you?'

I got my pen and pad out of my school bag and wrote Mr Fowler a short note explaining that Dad gave up drinking four years ago after he'd had one too many and accidentally spilled seventy cases of Granny Smiths in the main street of our last town.

Mr Fowler read the note twice, and I thought he was going to criticise my spelling, but he just nodded and said, 'That's all, Rowena'.

He still seemed pretty tense.

Perhaps he'd discovered his graze was going soggy.

In class everyone stared when I walked in, except Ms Dunning who smiled.

'Ah, Rowena,' she said, 'you're just in time.'

I went over to her desk and wrote a note on my pad asking if I could say something to the class.

She looked surprised, but said yes.

My hands were shaking so much I could hardly pick up the chalk, but I managed.

When she'd finished writing down all the names, she said 'One hundred metres, girls'.

No one moved.

Then the whole class turned and looked at a girl sitting on the other side of the room.

I don't know why I hadn't noticed her before because she's got the most ringlets I've ever seen on one human head in my life. The colour's fairly ordinary, barbecue-sauce-brown, but the curls are amazing. She must keep a whole hairdressing salon in business just by herself.

Everyone watched as she looked embarrassed and raised her hand.

'Amanda Cosgrove,' smiled Ms Dunning, writing on her list. 'Who else?'

No one moved.

'Come on,' said Ms Dunning, 'Amanda can't run the race by herself.'

Amanda was looking even more embarrassed now.

Must be another new kid, I thought. I wondered what she'd done to make everyone not want to race with her, and whether it had involved jamming something in Darryn Peck's mouth.

She was looking so uncomfortable I found myself feeling sorry for her.

Which must have been why I put my hand up.

'Rowena Batts,' said Ms Dunning, writing down my name. 'Good on you, Ro. Now, who's going to follow Ro's example?'

No one moved.

'OK,' sighed Ms Dunning, 'I'll have to choose some volunteers.'

While she did, and the people she chose groaned and rolled their eyes, the girl next to me scribbled a note and passed it over.

I thought for a moment she'd got it wrong and thought I was deaf, but then I remembered that you're not meant to talk in class in normal schools.

I read the note.

'Amanda Cosgrove,' it said, 'is the 100 metres champion of the whole school.'

I smiled to myself. At least tomorrow people won't be thinking I'm a show-off. And as the rest of the people were dragged into the race, and it's really hard to sulk and run at the same time, I can probably manage not to come last.

My heart didn't sink until several minutes later.

When Ms Dunning reminded everyone that sports carnivals are family events, and she's hoping to see as many parents there as possible.

Since then I've been feeling a bit tense. Nothing serious, my knees aren't pink or anything, but I've got a bit of a knot in the guts. Not Tasmania or anything, but Lord Howe Island.

The other kids keep looking at me a bit strangely, so it must be showing.

Ms Dunning even asked if I'm feeling OK.

I reached for my notepad, then had second thoughts and just smiled and nodded.

I couldn't bring myself to tell her the truth.

That I keep having horrible visions of Dad in the middle of the oval singing to everyone, and everyone backing away.

I thought about not telling him.

I didn't tell him all the way home in the truck.

By the time we got home I felt terrible.

Here's Dad busting a gut moving us here and fixing up the house and knocking the new orchard into shape, all so I can go to a proper school and live at home, and here's me not even inviting him to the first chance he's really had to meet people in our new town.

OK, second chance if you count the conversation he had with the man in the milk bar about how if the man didn't want people to cheer and thump the wall he shouldn't have got a video game in the first place.

I mean, Dad gets lonely too.

He doesn't talk about it, but he must do.

He's left all his friends behind as well, including girlfriends.

All for me.

Even before we left he always put me first. He never invited his girlfriends to stay the night at our place when I was home on weekends because he reckoned it wasn't fair for me to get used to someone when I'd probably never see them again. That was a really thoughtful gesture because I never did see them again. His girlfriends always leave him after a couple of weeks. They're probably married to someone else and just having a fling.

All the things he's done for me, and here's me having unkind thoughts about him.

I mean, who am I to have visions about him scaring people away?

Me, who can clear a classroom in three seconds.

Two if I've got a frog in my hand.

Dad's just a slightly unusual bloke with slightly unusual clothes and a slightly unusual way with people.

I'm the psychopathic frog torturer.

Plus if he found out I hadn't told him he'd be incredibly hurt.

So I told him.

I went down to the orchard where he was spraying and jumped on the front of the tractor.

'Tomorrow's our sports carnival,' I said, 'and parents are invited. If they're not too busy. But if they are it's OK, the school understands, and us kids do too.'

The good thing about talking with your hands is people hear you even when there's a tractor roaring away and a compressor thumping and spray hissing.

The bad thing is people hear you even when, deep down, you don't want them to.

Dad stopped the tractor, tilted his hat back and his face creased with thought.

'Well, amigo,' he said, holding his thumb in the position we invented for when we want to speak with a Mexican accent, 'it's a frontier out here. Enemies all around us.'

He dropped the Mexican accent and used some of the signs we invented last week.

'Weevils,' he said, eyes darting around the orchard like a wary gunfighter. 'Weeds. Mites. Fungi. Moulds. Mildews.'

He spun round and shot a blast of spray at a clump of couch grass. The last people to run this orchard were very slack.

'On the frontier, a bloke can never rest,' he said.

I realised I was holding my breath.

Was he saying he was too busy?

'Except,' he continued, 'when it's his daughter's sports carnival. Then you couldn't keep him away even if a ten foot lump of blue mould had tied him to a railway track. What time does it start, Tonto?'

It'll be fine.

I know it will.

If I keep telling myself that, I'll get to sleep soon.

Tomorrow's just an ordinary old sports carnival and he's my dad and it's the most normal thing in the world for him to go.

It'll be fine.

It was fine.

Mostly.

Sort of.

At least Dad didn't sing.

And when he put his hand down the front of Mrs Cosgrove's dress, he was just trying to be helpful.

I'd better start at the beginning.

I got up really early and ironed Dad a shirt. One without tassels. Or pictures of cowgirls riding horses at rodeos. It had metal corners on the collar, but I hoped people would think Dad was just careful about his shirts fraying.

While he was getting dressed, Dad announced he was going to wear a special belt buckle to bring me luck in the race. I was worried for a moment, but when he came into the kitchen he was wearing one I hadn't seen before—a kangaroo in mid-hop.

I gave him a hug, partly because it was a kind thought, and partly because I was relieved he wasn't wearing the grinning skeleton riding the Harley Davidson.

In the truck on the way into town he played me one of his Carla Tamworth tapes. It was the song about the marathon runner who realises at the end of the race he's left his sweetheart's photo in the motel room so he runs all the way back to get it.

I could see Dad was trying to inspire me.

I wished he'd stop.

'Dad,' I said, 'I'm only in the hundred metres. And I'm up against an ace runner.'

Dad grinned and played the song again.

'What it's saying, Tonto,' he said, 'is that we can do all kinds of stuff even when we think we can't.'

If it was saying that, I thought, it'd be about a girl at a sports carnival who manages to persuade her dad not to upset the other spectators.

When we got to the school oval, the first event was just about to start. Kids and parents were standing around talking quietly, teachers were hurrying about with stopwatches and clipboards, and Ms Dunning was telling Darryn Peck off for throwing a javelin in the boys' toilet.

'Well, Tonto,' asked Dad, 'are we going to stand here all day like stunned fungi or are you going to introduce me to some of your classmates?'

I tried to explain that it wasn't a good time as the sack race was about to start and everyone was very tense.

'You're the only one who looks tense, Tonto,' said Dad. 'You can't win a race with your guts in a knot. Come on, lie down and we'll do some breathing exercises.'

Dad took his hat off, stretched out on the ground on his back, and started taking deep breaths through his nose.

I saw other parents glancing over with puzzled expressions, and other kids smirking.

'Dad,' I said, 'if you don't get up I'm going to drop a heavy metal ball on your head.'

Dad shrugged and got up.

As he did, Ms Dunning came over to us.

'G'day Ro,' she said. 'G'day Mr Batts.'

I explained to Dad who she was.

'G'day,' said Dad. 'Kenny Batts.' He grinned and shook her hand for about two months. 'Ro's told me what a top teacher you are.'

Ms Dunning grinned modestly and Dad turned to me and winked and asked me if Ms Dunning was married.

For the millionth time in my life I was grateful that Dad talks to me with his hands.

But I still wanted to go and bury myself in the long-jump pit.

'I can see I'm going to have to learn some sign-language,' grinned Ms Dunning. Then she excused herself and hurried away because she'd just seen Darryn Peck holding a starting pistol to another kid's head.

'Nice teacher,' said Dad. 'OK, let's mingle.'

As usual I was torn between going off and sitting in the toilets so no one could see I was with him, and sticking with him to try and keep him out of trouble.

As usual I stuck with him.

27

He walked over to some parents talking to their kid.

He'd already said 'G'day, nice day for it', and stuck out his hand when I realised the kid was Amanda Cosgrove, the hundred metres champion.

And Mr Cosgrove had already shaken Dad's hand and was already looking Dad up and down with a sour expression on his face when I recognised his brown suit and realised he was the bloke who'd glared at us as we were being chucked out of the milk bar.

I smiled nervously at Amanda, but she was staring at the ground.

Either that or Dad's goanna-skin boots.

'G'day,' said Dad, shaking Mrs Cosgrove's hand.

Mrs Cosgrove was looking very nervous and gripping her handbag very tightly.

'Nice suit,' said Dad, feeling Mr Cosgrove's lapel and winking at him. 'Bet it cost a few bob. Criminal, the price of clothes these days.'

'I own a menswear store,' replied Mr Cosgrove coldly.

'You'd be right then, eh?' said Dad, giving him a friendly nudge. 'Listen, you might be able to help me out. Last year at a Carla Tamworth concert one of the backup singers was wearing this unreal pink satin shirt with black fringing on the back and a black guitar on the front. I've been looking everywhere for one. You wouldn't have one in stock, would you?'

'We don't stock satin shirts,' said Mr Cosgrove, even more coldly.

Dad stared at him, amazed. 'You should,' he said, 'they're big sellers. I buy one every couple of months.'

Mr Cosgrove didn't look as though he was going to rush out and order a truckload.

Amanda nudged me gently. 'It's our race,' she said softly.

She was right.

Mr Fowler was calling through his megaphone for all the contestants in the hundred metre races. Kids were lining up in their different age groups near the starting line.

I was just about to go with Amanda to join them when I saw Dad staring at Mrs Cosgrove's chest.

Crawling across her dress was a small greyish-brown moth.

Dad took a step closer to her.

'Don't move,' he said.

Mrs Cosgrove froze with fear.

'Codling moth,' explained Dad. 'If you've got any apple or pear trees at home these mongrels'll go through 'em like guided missiles.'

'We haven't,' said Mr Cosgrove.

'I have,' said Dad, and made a grab for the moth.

Before he could get his hand to it, the moth fluttered in through the armhole of Mrs Cosgrove's dress.

Mrs Cosgrove gave a little scream.

'Hold still,' said Dad, 'I'll get it.'

He grabbed Mrs Cosgrove's shoulder and stuck his hand into the armhole.

Mrs Cosgrove gave a louder scream.

Mr Cosgrove grabbed Dad and pulled him away. 'You be careful, mister,' he snapped.

'It's OK,' said Dad, 'I've got it.'

He showed Mr Cosgrove the squashed moth between his fingers.

'You,' Mr Cosgrove said loudly, glaring at Dad, 'are a rude, unpleasant, badly-dressed hoon. Why don't you back off, go home, and leave us in peace?'

Dad stared at Mr Cosgrove, bewildered, and he looked so hurt I felt like crying.

'Amanda Cosgrove and Rowena Batts to the starting line,' boomed Mr Fowler's voice through the megaphone.

Then Dad stopped looking hurt.

He glared at Mr Cosgrove. 'Pull your head in,' he said, 'I was only trying to help.'

He turned to me. 'The bloke's a cheese-brain,' he said with his hands. 'Don't let him spoil your race. Get out there and show 'em your dust, Tonto.'

He glared at Mr Cosgrove again and walked off.

I followed Amanda to the starting line and glanced at her but she didn't look at me.

I stood there while Darryn Peck won his race and crowed about it for several minutes.

I hardly noticed.

I was seeing something else in my head.

Me doing what I should have done ages ago.

Telling Dad to back off and stop scaring people away.

Making him listen.

Sorry about that interruption, it was Dad coming in to say goodnight.

He must have noticed I've been pretty quiet since the race this afternoon because he walked into the room on his hands and he only does that when I'm depressed.

He flipped over onto his feet, or tried to, but landed on his bottom.

He didn't speak for a bit because he was using his hands to rub his buttocks and then to say some rude words. Me and Dad have got an agreement that we're allowed to swear with our hands as long as we wash them with soap afterwards.

'That's life, Tonto,' he said finally. 'Sometimes you try to pull one off and you don't quite make it. Though in my book a dead heat with the school champ's nothing to be ashamed of.'

Then he sang me a Carla Tamworth number the way I like best, with him humming the tune and doing the words with his hands. He doesn't get so many notes wrong that way.

It was the song about the axe-murderer who's a failure because his axe is blunt, but his sweetheart still loves him anyway.

Then Dad gave me a big hug.

'In my book,' he said, 'you're the champ.'

How can you be angry with a Dad like that?

'Today'll be better than yesterday,' Dad promised this morning when he dropped me at the gate, 'partly because fourth days at new schools are always better than third days, and partly because any day's better than a school sports day where the other parents are cheese-brains and the judges are bent.'

He was right.

Completely and totally.

Today is the best day of my life.

It started wonderfully and it's still wonderful.

Well actually it started strangely.

I walked through the gate and who should come up to me but Amanda Cosgrove.

'Nice turtle,' she said.

I stared at her, partly because she was the first kid to come up to me at that school, partly because I didn't have a clue what she was on about, and partly because she was speaking with her hands.

My heart was thumping and I hoped I wasn't imagining things.

Sometimes, when you're desperate for conversation, you think someone's speaking to you and they're just brushing a mozzie away.

She wasn't brushing a mozzie away.

She was frowning, and thinking.

'Good air-crash,' she said.

I still didn't have a clue what she was on about, and I told her.

She seemed to understand, because she looked embarrassed and thought some more.

I wondered if that extra bit of effort to catch up with me yesterday had starved her brain of oxygen and she hadn't fully recovered yet.

'Good race,' she said.

Her hand movements were a bit sloppy, but I understood.

I nodded and smiled.

'You're a good runner,' I said.

She rolled her eyes. 'I hate it,' she said with her mouth. 'Dad makes me do it.'

Normally I'd have been sympathetic to hear something like that, but I was too busy being excited.

Here I was having an actual conversation with another kid at school that didn't involve insults or an amphibian in the kisser.

Then something totally and completely great happened.

'Glue,' she said, with her hands.

She saw from my expression I didn't understand.

She shook her head, cross with herself, ringlets flapping.

'Twin,' she said, then waved her hand to cancel it.

'Friend,' she said.

I stared at her, desperately hoping she'd got the right word.

And that she wasn't asking if I'd seen her friend or her friend's twin or her friend's glue, she was asking if I'd be her friend.

She said it again, grinning.

I grinned back and nodded like someone on 'Sale Of The Century' who's just been asked if they'd like a mansion for $2.99.

Actually I wanted to do cartwheels across the playground, but I didn't in case she thought I was trying to tell her something about a cart.

I asked her where she'd learnt sign language, and she said on the sun.

I suggested she tell me by mouth.

She told me she'd learnt it at a summer school in Sydney, something to do with a project she's doing. Before she could fill me in on all the details, the bell rang.

It was great in class this morning because even though we sit on opposite sides of the room, we were able to carry on talking.

When Ms Dunning said something funny about Captain Cook and hamburgers, I caught Amanda's eye.

'She's nice,' I said under the desk.

Amanda smiled and nodded.

And when Ms Dunning asked Darryn Peck a question about clouds and he rabbited on for several months boasting about how his brother the crop-duster pilot can do skywriting, I caught Amanda's eye again.

'He's a dingle,' I said.

She looked puzzled.

I remembered 'dingle' was a sign Dad and me had made up ourselves, so I tried something different.

She understood 'cheese-brain' and smiled and nodded.

We've just had a great lunch break sitting under a tree on the other side of the oval yakking on about all sorts of things.

She doesn't go to the hairdresser every day, her curls are natural. She told me she wishes she had straight hair like mine, and how she tried ironing it once but her dad hit the roof because he thought something was burning inside the telly.

I told her how Dad bought me some electric curlers for my birthday and tried to run them off the tractor generator to keep his legs warm in winter and they melted.

She's got a younger brother in year two who eats fluff.

I told her how I couldn't have any younger brothers because of Mum dying, and she was really sympathetic.

And when I told her about Erin I thought she was going to cry.

She's really sensitive, which can be a bit of a pain with some people, but usually isn't a problem with people who are also good runners.

She apologised for her dad losing his temper

yesterday and I apologised for Dad's antics with her mum's armhole, and we both had a laugh about how dumb parents are.

Plus we discovered we both like runny eggs.

I told her I'd make her some apple fritters.

Sometimes I had to write things down, and sometimes she had to say stuff by mouth, but the more we yakked the better she got with sign.

She even got the joke about the octopus and the combine harvester, which is only funny if you do it with your hands.

She was about to tell me more about her project, but the bell went.

It was the best lunch break I've ever had.

And now even though Ms Dunning's telling us some really interesting stuff about dinosaurs, I just can't concentrate.

I just want to think about how great it is to have a friend at last.

I wonder if Ms Dunning can see the glazed look on my face?

No problem, I'm sure she'll understand if I explain that I'm just feeling a bit mental because today's the best day of my life.

Cancel that.

This is the worst day of my life, including yesterday at the sports carnival.

No, that's not true.

The day Erin died was the worst day of my life, but at least that one started off badly with her being real crook and everything.

What I hate are days that start off well and end up down the dunny.

Like today.

This arvo everything was still fine.

Better than fine, because during art Amanda asked me if I wanted to go to her place tonight for tea.

Of course I said yes, and Ms Dunning, who I think might be a saint, or at least someone who has an incredibly well-balanced diet, let us ring Dad from the staff room to let him know.

Obviously I can't speak to Dad on the phone, except in an emergency when we've arranged I'll ring him and give three of my loudest whistles, so Amanda explained the situation to him.

'He wants to speak to you,' she said, handing me the phone.

'Tonto,' said Dad's voice, 'are you gunna be OK with that cheese-brain of an old man of hers?'

I wrote on my pad, 'Tell him I'll be fine and I promise no frogs', and gave it and the phone to Amanda.

She looked at me, puzzled, then remembered Dad was hanging on the other end.

'Ro says she'll be fine and she promises no frogs,' she told Dad, then handed me the phone.

'Right-o,' said Dad. 'I'll come and get you at eight. If cheese-brain gives you a hard time, just ring me and whistle.'

Amanda said bye from both of us and we went back to class. I felt a bit guilty not telling her what Dad had said about her dad, but at that time I still thought she was my friend and I wanted to protect her feelings.

I did have a few doubts about Amanda's dad during the rest of the afternoon.

What if he flew into a rage when I walked through the door and said something hurtful about Dad?

Or Mum?

And my head erupted again?

And he was cleaning out a goldfish bowl?

Or a hamster cage?

Or a kennel belonging to a very small dog?

I told myself to stop being silly.

I watched Ms Dunning patiently explaining to Darryn Peck that painting Doug Walsh's ears wasn't a good idea, and told myself I should be more like her.

Calm and sensible.

But I did mention my doubts to Amanda while we were walking to her house.

'Are you sure your dad won't mind me coming?' I asked.

'Course not,' she grinned. 'He'll be delighted to see I've got a community service project.'

I stared at her and felt my guts slowly going cold.

'A what?' I said.

'A community service project,' she said. 'Dad's the president of the Progress Association and they're sponsoring a youth community service drive. It's where kids find someone who's disadvantaged and help them. There's a community service night tomorrow night where we introduce our projects to the other members so they can help them too.'

My guts had turned to ice.

Amanda must have seen the expression on my face because her voice went quiet.

'I thought you could be my project,' she said.

I stared at her while my guts turned to liquid nitrogen and all the heat in my body rushed to my eyelids.

Words writhed around inside my head, stuff about how if I wanted to be a project I'd pin myself to the notice board in the classroom, and if I wanted to be a tragic case I'd go on '60 Minutes', and if I wanted everyone to point at me and snigger I'd cover myself in Vegemite and chook feathers, but I knew she wouldn't understand all the signs, and my handwriting goes to pieces when I'm angry and disappointed and upset.

'No thanks,' I said, and turned and ran.

She called my name a couple of times, but I didn't slow down.

I didn't stop running till I was halfway home and the ice in my guts was stabbing me.

I walked the rest of the way and the trees all pointed at me and whispered, 'Poor thing, she thought she'd cracked it'.

OK, I know trees can't point and whisper, but the insects did.

I decided if I ever make another friend I'll wait at least a week before I get excited.

A week should be long enough to find out if the person's a true friend, or if she just wants me for charity or to borrow money or because she needs a kidney transplant or something.

Dad was surprised to see me.

I must have looked pretty upset because he immediately switched off the tractor and the compressor and was all set to go and pay Mr Cosgrove a visit with a pair of long-handled pruning shears.

I calmed him down and told him about the community service drive.

'Tonto,' he said, his face creased the way it is when he's trying to add up the purchase dockets from the wholesaler, 'sometimes life's a big shiny

'Sorry about yesterday,' I wrote on the board. 'I'll pay for the frog.'

My hands were still shaking when I turned back to the class.

I was relieved to see none of the kids were backing away, and some were even smiling.

'It's OK, Rowena,' said Ms Dunning, 'the frog survived.'

The class laughed. Except Darryn Peck up the back who scowled at me.

'Thank you for that, Rowena,' said Ms Dunning.

I turned back to the board and wrote 'My friends call me Ro', and went back to my seat.

The girl next to me smiled, and suddenly I felt really good. Then I realised she was smiling at somebody over my left shoulder.

'OK, Ro,' said Ms Dunning, 'you're just in time for the sports carnival nominations.'

She explained about tomorrow being the school sports carnival and, because it's a small school, everyone having to take part.

'Right,' she said, 'who wants to be in the javelin?'

I didn't put my hand up for anything because I didn't want to seem too pushy and aggressive, not so soon after the frog. Plus you never win friends at sports carnivals. If you come first people think you're a show-off, if you come last they think you're a dork, and if you come in the middle they don't notice you.

'One hundred metres, boys,' said Ms Dunning and just about every boy in the class stuck his hand up.

And him doing what I've always feared he'd do.

Looking hurt like he did with Mr Cosgrove but ten times worse because it was me, then glaring at me and walking away.

The gun went off and I leapt forward and squashed the picture in my head.

Suddenly I felt so angry I wanted to scream, but of course I couldn't so I concentrated on pounding my legs into the ground as hard as I could.

The kids on either side dropped back and suddenly the only one I could see out of the corner of my eye was Amanda Cosgrove, and then she disappeared too.

I was in front.

Then I saw Dad, up ahead by the finish line, a big grin on his face, eyes gleaming with excitement, jumping up and down and waving his arms at me.

And another picture flashed into my head.

Dad, after I'd won, sharing his excitement with the other parents.

Slapping them on the back so they spilt their drinks.

Digging them in the ribs so they dropped their sandwiches.

Sticking his hand into their armholes until they all ran for their cars and roared away as fast as they could and had serious accidents on the way home so all their kids had to go to special schools and I was the only one who didn't.

And suddenly I could hardly move my legs any more, and as I stumbled over the finish line Amanda Cosgrove was there at my side.

red apple and sometimes it's a bucket of blue mould and disappointment.'

I nodded.

When Dad gets upset he tends to talk like a country and western song, but he means well.

'It's like the time apple scab wiped out all the Jonathans at the last place,' he said. 'I thought the potholes in my heart'd never be repaired, but they were.'

He started to sing 'Highway Of My Heart' by Carla Tamworth.

I squeezed his hand and pretended to listen, but I was thinking of Erin.

Then we went into town and had a pizza and six games of pool, which made me feel better. Dad said he'd never seen me hit the balls so hard. I didn't tell him that was because I was pretending each one was Amanda Cosgrove.

The strange thing was I couldn't sink any.

Then we came home and we've been sitting here since, listening to Dad's records.

I like doing this, because most of the songs are about unhappy people wishing their relationships had turned out better, and that's exactly how I feel about me and Amanda Cosgrove.

I wish I'd never run in that dumb race.

Because then Dad wouldn't have noticed the photo in the local paper.

'Tonto, take a squiz at this!' he yelled, bursting into the kitchen this morning.

When he gets excited he forgets and uses his voice.

I nearly dropped six eggs because the sudden noise startled me. I'd been miles away trying to work out how much batter I'd need to make enough apple fritters for a class of thirty-two kids.

OK, I know you can't buy friendship, but when the other kids think you're a psychopathic frog torturer, a plate of apple fritters might just help them see your good side.

And just because one of them's looking for a project rather than a friend, it doesn't mean they all are.

'Look,' said Dad, sticking the paper in front of my face.

There was half a page of photos of the sports

carnival, and the one Dad was pointing to was of me and Amanda crossing the finish line.

'See,' shouted Dad, 'I said the judges were bent. Look, this clearly shows you yards in front.'

I put the eggs down.

'It's the angle of the camera, Dad,' I said.

'Weevil poop,' he said. 'You're two or three centimetres in front here, easy.'

It made me feel pretty good, Dad being so indignant, but I still wish he hadn't seen the photo.

Because then he wouldn't have seen the public notice on the bottom half of the page.

'Look at this,' he said, 'your school's having a Parents and Teachers Association fund-raising barbecue on Sunday.'

My stomach sank.

I had a vision of Dad at the P and T barbie in his most jaw-dropping shirt, the purple and yellow one, digging people in the ribs and singing at them and sword-fighting Mr Cosgrove with a T-bone steak and undoing all the good that a plate of apple fritters could ever do, even ones that had been fried in olive oil and rolled in sugar.

I raised my hands to tell him I didn't want him to go, but they wouldn't say the words. It just felt too mean, hurting him after what he'd done for me earlier this morning.

He'd come out and found me in the orchard looking for ripe apples and, when I'd told him what I wanted them for, he'd insisted on going round every tree to find the ripest.

I put my hands down and he looked up from the paper.

'Do you think Ms Dunning'll be there?' he asked, flicking his fingers so I'd think it was just a casual enquiry.

'I doubt it,' I replied. 'I think she said something about going mountain climbing in Venezuela on Sunday.'

I should have thought of something a bit more believable.

Then Dad wouldn't have given me one of his winks and said, 'Should be a good day, I think I'll wash my purple and yellow shirt'.

While he rummaged through the laundry basket, I thought frantically.

If I blew up the school, they'd have to cancel the barbie.

I told myself to stop being dumb. When you've injured people with falling masonry they very rarely become your friends. Plus it's really hard to form satisfying relationships in jail because everyone's depressed and tired from tunnelling.

Then I saw it.

An ad on the opposite page for a golf tournament. FEATURING INTERSTATE PROS it said in big letters.

I went over and pulled Dad's head out of the laundry basket.

'There's a really good golf tournament on Sunday,' I told him.

He stared at me.

46

'It's only two hours drive away and it'll be really good fun to watch.'

He continued to stare at me.

'There'll be interstate pros,' I said, trying to sound as if I knew what they were.

'I hate golf,' said Dad.

'I want to go,' I said.

'You hate golf,' said Dad.

'I know,' I said, 'but I like the coloured umbrellas.'

OK, it was a pathetic attempt, I know, but you do things like that when you're desperate.

Dad frowned, which he does when he's thinking, then his eyes lit up and he made the sign for a lightbulb going on.

'Tonto,' he said, and put his hand on his chest, 'cross my heart and hope to lose my singing voice, I promise not to start a ruckus with cheese-brain Cosgrove on Sunday arvo. OK? Now, let's get these fritters done.'

I felt pretty relieved, I can tell you.

Well, fairly relieved.

Well, I did when he said it.

We've just passed Mr Cosgrove's shop on the way to school and Dad's stuck his head out the truck and blown a big raspberry at the window display and suddenly I don't feel very relieved at all.

I made myself stop thinking about Dad as I walked into school this morning with the plate of apple fritters because I wanted to look as relaxed and friendly and approachable as possible.

All the kids rushed over, excited and curious to see what was on the plate, and I gave them a fritter each, and they gobbled them up, and they all said how yummy they were, and about six kids begged me to teach them the recipe, either at their places after school or on holiday with their families in luxury hotel suites with private kitchens at Disneyland.

That's what happened in my head.

What actually happened was that all the kids ignored me except Megan O'Donnell, who sits next to me in class.

Megan came over chewing her hair and peered at the plate. 'What's that?' she asked.

I showed her. I'd known someone would ask, so I'd written what they were on the plate.

Megan stared at the words for ages, her lips moving silently.

Then she looked up at me.

'Apple fritters,' she said.

I smiled and nodded and wished Megan spoke sign language so I could help her improve her reading. It must be really tough being a slow reader. Plus, I admit, I had a quick vision of Megan winning the Nobel Prize for Reading and being my devoted friend for ever.

'I hate apple fritters,' said Megan. 'I don't like anything with apples in. My dad works at the abattoir and he reckons apples give you cancer. He's seen it in pigs.'

I decided it probably wasn't a good idea having a best friend who would get Dad overexcited, and that Ms Dunning probably had Megan's reading under control with the extra lessons each afternoon.

I smiled at Megan and turned to look for someone else with a better appreciation of apples, and nearly bumped into someone standing right behind me.

Darryn Peck.

'Frog fritters!' he yelled. 'Batts has got frog fritters!'

He started dancing round me, his mouth bigger and redder than an elephant's bum on a cold day.

'Frog fritters! Frog fritters! Frog fritters!' he chanted.

I tried to look bored, and waited for the more sensible kids to shut him up.

They must all have been away sick because the other kids in the playground started chanting too.

'Frog fritters! Frog fritters! Frog fritters!'

The only one who didn't chant was Amanda Cosgrove.

She stood over to one side, watching with a sad expression on her face, looking as if she wanted to carry me off to an international community service conference so that the major industrialised nations could rally round and help me.

I stood there, determined not to cry.

I didn't want to give Darryn Peck the satisfaction, and I didn't want to give Amanda Cosgrove the excuse.

I couldn't understand why a teacher hadn't come over to break it up.

Then I saw why. The teachers were all over on the oval helping a man unload the marquee for the parent and teacher barbie off the back of a truck.

The chanting continued.

Darryn Peck and three of his mates clomped around pretending to be sick.

I felt volcanoes building up between my ears and suddenly I had a strong urge to remove Darryn Peck's head with a pair of long-handled pruning shears and carry it into class on the plate and feed it to the frogs.

And I didn't care what the others thought, because I didn't want them as friends.

I didn't need them.

I could survive by myself.

That's when I decided that instead of killing Darryn Peck, I'd become a nun.

I'd take a vow of silence, which would be a walkover for me, and a vow of solitude, which wouldn't be much different from how things were now, and I'd spend the rest of my life watching telly.

I was just about to walk out of the school gates to make a start, when Amanda Cosgrove did something amazing.

She walked through the chanting kids and came up to me and pulled the Gladwrap off the plate and picked up a fritter and ate it.

She looked at the other kids and chewed it with big chews so everyone could see what she was doing.

The kids stopped chanting.

Darryn Peck screwed up his face.

'Yuk,' he yelled, 'Amanda Cosgrove's eating a frog fritter!'

Amanda ignored him.

She picked up another fritter and went over to Megan O'Donnell and held it out to her and gave her a steady look.

I put the plate down to tell Amanda about Megan's problem with apples, but before I could, Megan took the fritter and started eating it.

She didn't look as though she was enjoying it.

That didn't bother Amanda.

She picked up the plate and went round to each of the kids and held it out to them.

They each took a fritter.

And by the time six or seven of them were

chewing, and nodding, and smiling, the others crowded round and emptied the plate.

'Don't eat them,' shouted Darryn Peck. 'You'll get warts on your tongue eating frog.'

Everyone ignored him, except Amanda.

'You should know, Darryn,' she said, and even his mates couldn't help laughing.

Then the bell went.

Amanda held the empty plate out to me.

'Thanks,' I said.

I decided not to be a nun after all.

We went into class without saying anything else, but halfway through the morning, when Ms Dunning asked for volunteers to go out and help put up the marquee, I glanced over at Amanda and saw she had her hand up, so I put mine up too.

Inside the marquee, while we struggled with the thick ropes, Amanda looked at me.

'I'm sorry I took you being a community service project for granted,' she said. 'I promise I'll never think of you that away again.'

Her face looked so serious in the middle of all the curls that I could see she meant it.

I couldn't answer her because I was pulling on a rope, so I gave her a smile.

She smiled back.

But even as we grinned at each other, a tiny part of me wondered if she'd be able to keep her promise.

I tried to squash the thought, but it wouldn't go away.

It didn't stop me saying yes, though, when Amanda invited me to the milk bar for a milkshake later this arvo.

We're back in class now and Ms Dunning's telling us some really interesting stuff about the early explorers.

As they sailed new oceans and explored new continents, they had this nagging problem.

They weren't sure if they could trust their navigational instruments.

I know exactly how they felt.

There's a Carla Tamworth song called 'Drawers In My Heart' about a carpenter who can make a chest of drawers with silent runners and matching knobs, but he can't make a difficult decision.

I know how he feels, because I'm having trouble making one too.

Mine's even more difficult than his.

His is pretty hard—whether to tell his girlfriend he's backed his truck over her miniature poodle—but at least he decides what to do eventually.

He makes the poodle a coffin with separate drawers for its collar and lead, and leaves it where his girlfriend will find it.

I wish I could decide what to do.

I just want everything to work out fine like it does for the carpenter, who discovers he hasn't backed over the dog after all, just a bath mat that's blown off the clothesline.

Unfortunately, life isn't that simple.

For example, you'd think going for a milkshake

with someone after school'd be pretty straight-forward, right?

No way.

Amanda was a bit quiet walking into town so after we'd got the milkshakes, to make conversation, I asked her how long her parents have had the menswear shop.

We sat on the kerb and between slurps she told me they'd had it for seventeen years, and that her dad had been president of the Progress Association for six.

Then she started to cry.

It was awful.

She looked so unhappy, sitting there with big tears plopping into her chocolate malted.

I asked her what was the matter, but she couldn't see the question so I put my arm round her.

She took a deep breath and wiped her eyes on her sleeve and said she was fine.

I was just about to say she didn't look fine when a shadow fell across us. I thought it was a cloud, but when I looked up it was Darryn Peck.

He stood there with a smirky grin on his elephant's bum mouth and a mate on each side of him.

In his hand he had a bit torn out of a newspaper.

It was a photo.

The one of me and Amanda winning the race.

'I know how you feel, Cosgrove,' he smirked. 'I'd be bawling if I couldn't beat a spazzo.'

I amazed myself.

I just sat there without throwing a single container of milkshake in his face.

I must be getting old.

Instead I reached into my bag for my notepad and wrote 'She could beat you any day, cheese-brain'. While he was reading that I wrote him another. 'We both could.'

'Oh yeah?' he said, throwing the notes down.

I nodded.

Amanda read the notes and looked a bit alarmed.

'OK,' said Darryn, 'prove it. I'll race you both to the war memorial and back and if you lose, we get to give Curly Cosgrove a milkshake shampoo.'

Amanda looked more alarmed.

I stood up.

Dad always reckons I'm a blabber mouth and he's probably right.

'A proper race,' I wrote. 'On the oval. A hundred metres. Me and you.'

Darryn read the note.

'You're on,' he said.

I wrote some more.

'The loser has to eat a frog.'

Darryn read that note twice.

Then he gave his biggest smirk ever.

'You're on,' he said.

One of his mates, who'd been reading over his shoulder, tugged his sleeve.

'That big tent's up over the running track, Darryn.'

'OK,' said Darryn, not taking his eyes off me, 'Monday lunchtime, after they take the tent down.'

He screwed the notes up and bounced them off my chest.

'Don't have any breakfast,' he smirked as he swaggered off with his mates, 'cause you'll be having a big lunch.'

Amanda unscrewed the note and read it and looked up at me as if I was a complete and total loony, which I probably am.

Before she could say anything, a voice boomed out behind us.

'Amanda,' it roared, 'get out of the gutter.'

It was Mr Cosgrove, coming out of the menswear shop.

Amanda jumped up and her shoulders seemed to kind of sag and instead of looking at him she looked down at the ground.

I didn't blame her.

His grey-green checked jacket clashed horribly with his irritable pink face.

'You're a young lady,' he snapped at her, 'not a drunken derro.'

Amanda still didn't look up.

Then Mr Cosgrove saw me, and an amazing thing happened.

In front of my eyes he changed from a bad-tempered father into a smiling president of the Progress Association.

'Hello there,' he said.

I smiled weakly and gave him a little wave.

'We're very grateful to you,' said Mr Cosgrove, 'for giving up your time this evening.'

I looked at Amanda, confused, but she was still examining the footpath between her feet.

'It would have been a rum do,' continued Mr Cosgrove, 'if the president's daughter had been the only one at the community service evening without a community service project.'

I stared at him.

I fumbled for my notepad.

But before I could start writing, Amanda spoke.

'Dad,' she said in a tiny voice, 'you've got it wrong. Ro's not my community service project.'

Mr Cosgrove stared at her.

'But three days ago you told me she was,' he boomed. 'Who is?'

'I haven't got one,' she said in an even tinier voice, still looking at the ground.

Mr Cosgrove stood there until his face almost matched his shiny dark red shoes.

'That's just about what I would have expected from you, young lady,' he said finally. 'Come on, inside.'

Amanda didn't look at me, she just followed her father into the shop.

As I watched her go, I knew I'd have to make a decision.

Do I turn my back on a friend?

Or do I allow myself to be turned into a community service project?

A helpless case.

A spazzo.

Sympathetic smiles.

Well-meaning whispers.
For the rest of my life.
I still haven't decided.

I promised myself I'd make the decision while I was walking home and I'm almost there and I still haven't.

I wish I was the carpenter in the song.
Compared to this, it'd be a breeze.
Even if I had run over the poodle.

If you've got a tough decision to make, talk it over with an apple farmer, that's my advice.

They're really good at getting straight to the guts of a matter and ignoring all the distracting waffle. I think it comes from working with nature and the Department of Agriculture.

'It's simple, Tonto,' said Dad, after I'd explained it all to him. 'If you do it, it's good for her and bad for you. If you don't do it, it's bad for her and good for you. I care more about you than her, so I don't reckon you should do it.'

I thought about Amanda at home with her angry Dad.

I thought about how her face would light up when she opened the door and saw me standing there.

Then I thought about my first day at school and how people with a temper like mine aren't cut out to be community service projects because if we crack under the sympathy who knows what we might end up stuffing into someone's mouth.

Squishy soap.

Smelly socks.

A frill-necked lizard.

'You're right, Dad,' I said.

He nodded and reached into the fridge for a sarsaparilla.

'But,' I continued, 'I'm still gunna do it.'

Dad grinned.

'Good on you, Tonto,' he said. 'I knew you would.'

Like I said, apple farmers are really simple down-to-earth people.

'I've never been to a community service night,' continued Dad. 'Hang on while I chuck a clean shirt on.'

My stomach sagged.

I hope they're also the sort of people who keep promises about behaving themselves in public.

Amanda opened the door and when she saw me standing there, she just stared.

'Can I get a lift to the community service evening with you?' I asked. 'Dad's gone on ahead.'

Yes, I know, it was a bit theatrical. Runs in the family, I guess.

Amanda's face lit up.

Mr Cosgrove's did too.

Well, sort of.

He stopped scowling and by the time we arrived at the RSL club he'd even smiled at me and told me not to be nervous because everybody there would be very sympathetic.

They were.

Amanda took me around the crowded hall and introduced me to people.

'This is Rowena Batts,' she said. 'She's vocally disadvantaged but she's coping very well.'

And everyone nodded very sympathetically.

Just before the fifth introduction I stuck a cocktail sausage up my nose to make it look as though I wasn't coping very well, but the people still nodded sympathetically.

When Amanda saw the sausage she pulled it out and glanced anxiously over at her father, and when she saw he hadn't seen it, she relaxed.

'Ro,' she giggled, 'stop it.'

'I will if you do,' I said.

She frowned and thought about this, and then, because she's basically a sensitive and intelligent and great person, she realised what I meant.

At the next introduction she just said, 'This is Ro', and I said g'day with my hands and left it to the people to work out for themselves whether I'm vocally disadvantaged or an airport runway worker.

Then I realised we'd been there ten minutes and I hadn't even checked on Dad.

I looked anxiously around the hall for a ruckus, but Dad was over by the refreshments table yakking to an elderly lady. From his arm movements and the uncomfortable expression on her face I decided he was probably describing how codling moth caterpillars do their poos inside apples, but she might just have been finding his orange shirt a bit bright.

Amanda squeezed my arm and pointed to the stage.

Mr Cosgrove was at the microphone.

'Ladies and Gentlemen,' he said, 'welcome to the Progress Association's first Community Service Night.'

I smiled to myself because his normally gruff voice had gone squeaky with nerves.

'He's vocally disadvantaged,' I said to Amanda, 'but he's coping very well.'

Amanda didn't smile.

I don't think she understood all the signs.

Then I heard what Mr Cosgrove said next and suddenly I wasn't smiling either.

'Now,' he said, 'I'm going to ask each of our Helping Hands to bring their Community Service Projectee up onto the stage, and tell us a little about them, so that we, as a community as a whole, can help them to lead fuller and more rewarding lives. First I'd like to call on Miss Amanda Cosgrove.'

I stared at Amanda in horror.

She looked at me apologetically, then took my hand and led me up onto the stage.

Everyone applauded, except for one person who whistled. But then Dad never has grasped the concept of embarrassment.

I stood on the stage and a sea of faces looked up at me.

All sympathetic.

Except for Dad who was beaming with pride.

And except for the other Projects—a bloke with one arm, a young bloke in a wheelchair, an elderly lady with a humpy back, and a kid with callipers on her legs—who all looked as terrified as I felt.

Then a strange thing happened.

As Mr Cosgrove handed the microphone to Amanda and went down into the audience, my terror disappeared.

My guts relaxed and as I looked down at all

the sympathetic faces I suddenly knew what I had to do.

I knew I had to do it even if it meant Amanda never spoke to me again.

Amanda coughed and spoke into the microphone in a tiny voice.

'Ladies and gentlemen, this is Ro and I'd like to tell you a bit about her.'

I tapped her on the arm and she looked at me, startled.

'I want to do it,' I said.

I had to say it twice, but then she understood.

'Um, Ro wants to tell you about herself,' she said, looking worried.

I made my hand movements as big and slow as I could.

'We're not projects,' I said, 'we're people.'

I looked at Amanda and I could tell she'd understood.

She gripped the microphone nervously.

I looked at her, my heart thumping, and I knew if she was a real friend she'd say it.

'Ro says,' said Amanda, and her voice started getting louder, 'that she and the others aren't projects, they're people.'

There was absolute silence in the hall.

'I'm just like all of you,' I said. 'An ordinary person with problems.'

'Ro's just like all of us,' said Amanda. 'An ordinary person with ditches.'

She looked at me, puzzled.

'Problems,' I repeated.

'Problems,' she said.

'I've got problems making word sounds,' I said, 'perhaps you've got problems making a living, or a sponge cake, or number twos.'

Amanda said it all, even the bit about number twos.

The hall was still silent.

'You can feel sympathy for me if you want,' I continued, 'and I can feel sympathy for you if I want. And I do feel sympathy for any of you who haven't got a true friend.'

I looked over at Amanda.

As she repeated what I'd said, she looked at me, eyes shining.

We stood like that, grinning at each other, for what seemed like months.

Then everyone started clapping.

Well, almost everyone.

Two people were too busy to clap.

Too busy rolling on the floor, scattering the crowd, arms and legs tangled, brown suit and orange satin, rolling over and over, fists flying.

Dad and Mr Cosgrove.

I jumped down from the stage and pushed my way through the crowd.

People were shouting and screaming, and several of the men were pulling Dad and Mr Cosgrove away from each other.

By the time I got through, Dad was sitting on the edge of the refreshments table, gasping for breath, a red trickle running down his face.

I gasped myself when I saw it.

Then I saw the coleslaw in his hair and the piece of lettuce over one ear and I realised the trickle was beetroot juice.

Dad looked up and saw me and spat out what I hoped was a piece of coleslaw and not a tooth.

'That mongrel's not only a cheese-brain,' he said, 'he's a rude bludger.'

He scowled across at Mr Cosgrove, who was leaning against the wall on the other side of the room. Various RSL officials were scraping avocado dip off his face and suit.

Amanda and Mrs Cosgrove were there too.

I caught Amanda's eye. She lifted her hands and rolled her eyes.

Parents.

Exactly.

'He called you handicapped,' said Dad. 'I told him that was bull. I told him a person being handicapped means they can't do something. I told him when it comes to yakking on you're probably the biggest blabber mouth in Australia.'

'Thanks, Dad,' I said.

'Then he called you spoiled,' Dad went on, 'so I let him have it with the avocado dip.'

Part of me wanted to hug Dad and part of me wanted to let him have it with the avocado dip.

Except it was too late, his shirt was covered in it.

I made a mental note to tell Dad avocado suited him. At least it wasn't as bright as the orange.

I took one of my socks off and dipped it in the fruit punch and wiped some of the beetroot juice off his face.

'Are you OK?' I asked.

'I'll live,' he said, 'though I feel like I've been stabbed in the guts.'

I looked anxiously for knife wounds.

'Belt buckle,' explained Dad. 'I don't think it's pierced the skin.'

He was wearing the skeleton on the Harley.

'I'd better get cleaned up,' said Dad. He looked down at himself and shook his head wearily. 'I'll never get coleslaw out of these boots,' he said, and squelched off into the Gents.

I wrung my sock out and realised that about a hundred pairs of eyes were staring at me.

As I was one of the attractions of the evening I decided I should try and get things back to normal.

I picked up the bowl of avocado dip and a basket of Jatz and offered them around.

Nobody took any.

After a while I realised why.

In the avocado dip was the impression of Mr Cosgrove's face.

It wasn't a pretty sight.

Then I looked up and saw an even less pretty sight.

The real Mr Cosgrove's face, red and furious, coming towards me.

Mrs Cosgrove and Amanda were trying to restrain him, but he kept on coming.

He stopped with his face so close to mine I could see the veins in his eyeballs and the coleslaw in his ears.

'I don't want your family anywhere near my family,' he said through gritted teeth, 'and that includes you. Stay away from my daughter.'

He turned and grabbed Amanda and headed for the door.

Amanda gave me an anguished look as he pulled her away.

There's a horrible sick feeling in the guts you get when something awful's happening and you can't do anything about it.

I got it the day Erin died.

I got it tonight, watching Amanda being dragged away.

Then I decided that tonight was different, because I could do something about it.

Or at least try to.

I ran round in front of Mr Cosgrove and stood between him and the door.

'You're not being fair,' I said.

He stopped and glared at me.

I said it again.

Then I remembered he couldn't understand hands.

I looked frantically around for a pen.

You can never find one when you need one.

I'd just decided to go and grab the bowl and write it on the floor in avocado dip, when Amanda spoke up.

'You're not being fair,' she said.

Mr Cosgrove stopped glaring at me and glared at her.

'Just because you and Dad can't be friends,' I said, 'it doesn't mean me and Amanda can't be.'

Amanda was watching my hands closely.

'Just because you and Mr Batts can't be friends,' she said to her father, 'it doesn't mean me and Ro can't be.'

Mr Cosgrove opened his mouth to say something angry to Amanda, but before he could speak, Mr Ricards from the hardware store did.

'She's got a point, Doug,' he said. 'It's like Israel and Palestine and America and Russia.'

Mr Cosgrove glared at him.

The other people standing nearby looked at each other, confused.

Me and Amanda and Mrs Cosgrove weren't sure what he was on about either.

'It's like Steve and Rob and Gail and Terry,' said Mr Ricards. 'In "Neighbours".'

The other people nodded.

It was a good point.

Mr Cosgrove obviously didn't agree, because he glared at Mr Ricards again, and then at me.

'Stay away from her,' he ordered, and stormed out.

'Mum,' said Amanda, close to tears, 'it's not fair.'

'Don't worry love,' said Mrs Cosgrove, 'he'll probably calm down in a few days,'

She turned to me.

'I don't blame you love,' she said, 'but something has to be done about that father of yours.'

She steered Amanda towards the door.

'It's tragic,' Mrs Cosgrove said to the people around her as she went. 'That poor kid's got two afflictions and I don't know which is the worst.'

Me and Amanda waved an unhappy goodbye.

I tried to cheer myself up by thinking that at least I'd be able to see her at school. Unless Mr Cosgrove moved the whole family to Darwin. Or Norway. I didn't think that was likely, not after he'd spent so many years building up the menswear shop.

After a bit Dad came out of the Gents carrying his boots.

'Come on, Tonto,' he said, 'let's go. I need to get a hose into these.'

As we headed towards the door I saw how everyone was looking at Dad.

As if they agreed with Mrs Cosgrove.

That he is an affliction.

I felt terrible for him.

We didn't say anything in the truck on the way home because it was dark.

When we got here Dad made a cup of tea, but I wasn't really in the mood, so I came to bed.

Dad's just been in to say goodnight.

He looked pretty depressed.

I thanked him again for standing up for me and offered to buy him a new pair of boots for Christmas.

He still looked pretty depressed.

I don't blame him.

How's a bloke meant to have a decent social life when everybody thinks he's an affliction?

Amanda's Mum's right about one thing.

Something will have to be done.

For his sake as well as mine.

I woke up early and was just about to roll over and go back to sleep when I remembered I had some serious thinking to do.

So I did it.

How, I thought, can I get it across to Dad that he's his own worst enemy, including weeds, mites, fungi, mould and mildews?

I could just go up to him and say, 'Dad, you're making both our lives a misery, pull your head in'.

But parents don't listen to their kids.

Not really.

They try. They nod and go 'Fair dinkum?' and 'Jeez, is that right?' but you can see in their eyes that what they're really thinking is 'Has she cleaned her teeth?' or 'I wonder if I switched off the electric curlers in the tractor?'

Who, I thought, would Dad really listen to?

That's when I decided to write him a letter.

A letter from Carla Tamworth.

It's the obvious choice.

He worships every song she's ever written.

He's always sending her fan letters and pretending he doesn't mind that she never replies.

He'll be ecstatic to finally get one.

He'll frame it.

He'll read it a hundred times a day.

I grabbed my pen and notepad.

'Dear Kenny', I wrote. 'Thanks for all the fan letters. Sorry I haven't replied earlier but one of my backup singers has been having heaps of trouble with skin rashes and I've had to take him to the doctor a lot. The doctor's just discovered that the rashes were caused by brightly-coloured satin shirts, so if you've got any, I'd get rid of them. The whole band are wearing white cotton and polyester ones with ties now and they look very nice. By the way, it's come to my attention that both you and your daughter are having problems because of your loud behaviour. In the words of my song "Tears In Your Carwash", pull your head in. Yours sincerely, Carla Tamworth. PS. Sorry I couldn't send a photo, the dog chewed them all up.'

It's a pretty good letter even though I say it myself.

I'll have to type it though, or he'll recognise my writing.

Amanda's got a typewriter.

And it's Saturday morning so her Dad'll be in the shop.

And when we've typed it I'll copy Carla's signature off one of her record covers and post it to Dad and make sure I collect the mail next week so I can smudge the postmark.

I've never forged anything before.

I feel strange.

But it's OK if there's an important reason for doing it, eh?

I hope so.

I wonder if fate'll punish me?

For a minute I thought fate was punishing me straightaway.

I went out to the kitchen with the letter under my T-shirt to tell Dad I was just popping over to Amanda's for a bit, but he wasn't there.

Then I heard his voice out on the verandah.

And someone else's voice.

Ms Dunning's.

I panicked and stuffed the letter in a cupboard behind some old bottles.

Ms Dunning's got X-ray vision when it comes to things under T-shirts. Darryn Peck had Mr Fowler's front numberplate under his on Thursday and she spotted it from the other side of the classroom.

Then I panicked for another reason.

It had suddenly occurred to me what she was doing here.

Word must have got around about the fight last night and Mr Fowler must have sent her over to tell us that the Parents and Teachers Committee had discussed the matter this morning while they were making kebabs for the barbie and I was banned from the school.

I felt sick.

I had a horrible vision of being sent away to another school and having to sneak out at night to try and see Amanda and hitchhiking in the rain and being run over by a truck.

Ms Dunning gave a loud laugh out on the verandah.

I almost rushed out and told her it wasn't funny.

Then I realised that if she was out there chuckling, she probably hadn't come with bad news.

I went out.

'G'day Ro,' said Ms Dunning with a friendly grin.

I relaxed.

'G'day Tonto,' said Dad. 'I invited Ms Dunning out to take a squiz at the orchard. She's gunna do a fruit-growing project with you kids.'

I was pleased to see Dad had remembered his manners and was speaking with his mouth.

'Your Dad's offered to come talk to the class about apple-growing,' said Ms Dunning.

Suddenly I wasn't relaxed anymore.

Dad in the classroom?

Horrible pictures filled my head.

Several of them involved Dad singing and Mr Fowler having to evacuate the school.

I pulled myself together.

Dad and Ms Dunning were heading down to the orchard. I ran after them to try and persuade them that the whole thing was a terrible idea.

As I got closer I heard Dad telling Ms Dunning about the fight last night.

Admitting the whole thing.

In detail.

I couldn't believe it.

I wondered if a person could get concussion from coleslaw.

And Ms Dunning was laughing.

She was finding it hilarious.

I wondered if chalk dust could give you brain damage.

I grabbed Dad's arm to try and shake him out of it.

He turned and gave me a look and when I saw what sort of a look it was, half irritable and half pleading, and when I heard what Ms Dunning said next, about her breaking up with her boyfriend a month ago and giving him a faceful of apricot trifle, I realised what was going on.

I can be so dumb sometimes.

Dad hadn't invited her over for educational purposes at all.

He'd invited her over for romantic purposes.

And judging by all the laughing she was doing, she wasn't feeling deeply nauseated by the idea.

I gave them both a sheepish sort of grin and walked back to the house.

Correction, floated back to the house.

Everything's falling into place.

First there'll be a whirlwind romance, with Ms Dunning captivated by Dad's kindness—he never sprays if the wind's blowing towards the old people's home—and Dad bowled over by Ms Dunning's strength of character and incredibly neat handwriting.

Then a fairy-tale wedding at apple harvest time so Dad can use one of his casual pickers as best man.

And then a happy family life for ever and ever, with Ms Dunning, who'll probably let me call her Mum by then, making sure Dad behaves himself and doesn't upset people, particularly my friends' fathers, and keeps his singing for the shower.

Keeping Dad in line'll be a walkover for a woman who can make Darryn Peck spit his bubblegum into the bin.

Suddenly life is completely and totally great.

As long as Dad doesn't stuff it up before it happens.

The first fortnight is the dodgy time, that's when his girlfriends usually leave him.

He seems to be doing OK so far, but.

When they got back to the house, Ms Dunning was still laughing, and Dad said, 'Me and Ro usually have tea at the Copper Saddle on Saturdays, care to join us?'

I struggled to keep a straight face.

The Copper Saddle is the most expensive restaurant for miles, and the closest we've ever been to it is driving through the car park blowing raspberries at the rich mongrels.

Ms Dunning said she'd love to and we arranged to pick her up at seven-thirty.

That's still two hours away and I'm exhausted.

I spent ages helping Dad choose his clothes.

I managed to talk him out of the cowgirl shirt. For a sec I thought of trying to persuade him to get a white polyester and cotton one, but then I remembered he'd have to go to Mr Cosgrove for it.

We agreed on the pale green one.

It's almost advocado.

Since then, as casually as I can, I've been trying to remind him to be on his best behaviour.

'Ms Dunning doesn't like too much chatter,' I said just now. 'She always telling us that in class.'

Dad grinned.

'Teachers are always a bit crabby in class,' he said.

Then he messed my hair.

'I know how you feel, Tonto,' he said. 'Bit of a drag, having tea with a teacher, eh? Don't fret, you'll be fine with Claire, she's a human being.'

I know I'll be fine, Dad.

What about you?

It started off fine.

When we picked Ms Dunning up she said she liked my dress and Dad's dolphin belt buckle and I'm pretty sure she meant it about both of them.

When we got here the waiter sat us at the table and Dad didn't get into an embarrassing conversation with him about shirts even though the waiter's shirt has got a big purple ruffle down the front and Dad's got a theory that shirt ruffles fluff up better if you wash them in toothpaste.

Then the menus arrived, and even though they were as big as the engine flaps on the tractor, Dad didn't make any embarrassing jokes about recycled farm equipment or taking the menus home for spare parts or any of the other embarrassing things I thought at the time he could have said.

When we ordered, he even said 'steak' instead of what he usually says, which is 'dead cow'.

I started to relax.

At least I thought I did, but when I glanced down

at my knees they were bright pink, so I was obviously still very tense.

Ms Dunning asked Dad if he was going to the parents and teachers barbie tomorrow and he said he was looking forward to it.

He asked her what would be happening there, and she went into great detail about the chicken kebabs and the raffle and the fund-raising auction and the display of skywriting by Darryn Peck's brother and the sack race and the jam stall and the wool-carding demonstration by Mr Fowler's nephew.

I was totally and completely bored, but I didn't care because I could see they were having a good time.

Then the meals arrived.

They were huge.

The pepper grinder was as big as a baseball bat, and the meals were bigger.

We started eating.

Ms Dunning asked me about my old school and I told her, but I didn't mention Erin in case my eyes went red. I didn't want Ms Dunning thinking she was marrying into an emotionally unstable family.

Dad, who was repeating to her what I was saying, was great. He didn't mention Erin either, even though he's a real fanatic about me telling the truth. He reckons if I tell lies I'll get white spots on my fingernails.

Why couldn't he have stayed considerate and quiet and normal for the whole evening?

The disaster started when Ms Dunning said she couldn't eat any more.

She'd only had about a third of her roast lamb.

Dad looked sadly at all that food going to waste and I knew we were in trouble.

At first I thought he was going to call for a doggy bag, which would have been embarrassing enough in the Copper Saddle, but he didn't.

He did something much worse.

He told Ms Dunning how he'd read in a magazine somewhere that if you stand on your head when you feel full, you open up other areas of your stomach and you can carry on eating.

Then he did it.

Stood on his head.

The waiter walked out of the kitchen and saw him there next to the table and nearly dropped a roast duck.

All the people at the other tables stared.

I wanted to hide under the tablecloth.

I waited desperately for Ms Dunning to swing into action. If Darryn Peck stood on his head in class, she'd be giving him a good talking to before you could say 'dingle'.

But she didn't give Dad even a medium talking to.

She just watched him and laughed and said that she'd read in a magazine somewhere that if you stand on your head when you're full up you choke and die.

Dad sat back down and they both laughed some more.

I can't believe it.

OK, I know that inside she's deeply embarrassed, and that after tonight she'll never want to be seen dead in the same room as Dad again.

But why doesn't she say something?

Too nice, I suppose.

That's how she can sit through all those extra reading lessons with Megan O'Donnell without strangling her.

It's tragic.

Here's Dad, pouring her some more wine and chatting away happily about why he gave up drinking, and he doesn't have a clue that he's just totally and completely stuffed up his best romantic opportunity of the decade.

Because he's his own worst enemy.

And he doesn't have a clue.

And he won't till someone tells him.

Ms Dunning won't.

So it'll have to be me.

Me and Darryn Peck's brother.

While I was creeping out of the house this morning Dad gave a shout and I thought I'd been sprung.

'Jenny,' he called out, and I froze.

I took several deep breaths to try and slow my heart down and in my head I frantically rehearsed my cover story about going for an early morning run to train for the big race with Darryn Peck.

Then I checked my nails for white spots.

Then I remembered my name isn't Jenny.

Jenny was Mum's name.

I crept along the verandah and peeked through Dad's bedroom window.

He was still asleep, tangled up in the sheet, his Elvis pyjamas scrunched up under his arms. Dad's a pretty tense sleeper and I've heard him shout in his sleep a few times. Usually it's Mum's name, though once it was 'The hat's in the fridge'.

I stood there for a few secs watching him. There was something about the way he had his arms up against his chest that made him look very lonely, and seeing him like that made me feel even more that I'm doing the right thing.

I ran into town.

Along the road the insects were waking up, and judging by the racket they were making they thought I was doing the right thing too.

'Go for it,' a couple of million screeched, and another couple of million yelled, 'He'll thank you for it later.'

One said 'You'll be sorry', but I decided to ignore that.

I went to the bank and put my card in the machine and took out my life's savings.

Then I went across to the phone box and looked up Peck in the book. There were two, but I didn't think Peck's Hair Removal sounded right, so I went to the other one.

It was quite a big fibro place with a mailbox nailed to a rusty statue of a flamingo by the gate, and two motorbikes in the front yard.

I had to ring the bell four times before the front door half opened and a bloke with a sheet wrapped round his waist and a red beard peered out.

'Are you the skywriter?' I asked him.

He stared at my note, yawning and rubbing his eyes.

'You want Andy,' he said.

He looked at me for a bit, then turned and yelled into the house.

After he'd yelled 'Andy' the third time, a bloke with red hair and a tracksuit appeared, also rubbing his eyes.

'She wants Andy,' said the sheet bloke.

The tracksuit bloke stared at me.

'Andy!' he yelled.

Another head appeared round the door.

It wasn't Andy.

It was the one I'd been dreading.

Darryn.

He stared at me in amazement, then his eyes narrowed.

'What do you want?' he demanded.

'Get lost, Dumbo,' the sheet bloke said to him.

I was glad Darryn's family knew how to handle him.

'Vanish, pest,' the tracksuit guy growled at him.

They didn't have to be so nasty about it though.

Darryn looked really hurt, and for a moment he reminded me of Dad at the sports carnival after Mr Cosgrove had called him badly dressed.

Then Darryn scowled at me and vanished.

The door opened wider and a thin bloke in a singlet and shorts stepped in front of the other two.

I guessed he was Andy because on the front of his singlet was written *Crop Dusters Don't Say It, They Spray It.*

'What is it?' he said, looking at me.

'I think she's that girl from Darryn's class,' the tracksuit guy muttered to him. 'The one he's always on about. You know, the one that can't speak cause she was shot in the throat by Malaysian pirates.'

The three of them stared at me.

Andy was looking doubtful, and I knew I had

to grab his attention before Darryn came back and started telling him more stories about me.

I decided the note I'd written explaining everything might be a bit complicated to kick off with, so I showed Andy the money instead.

He looked down at the two hundred and ninety dollars in my hand.

'Tell me more,' he said.

Where is he?

It's twenty-three minutes past four and he was meant to do it at four.

Come on Andy, please.

Perhaps he's lost the bit of paper and he's forgotten what he's supposed to write. No, that can't be it, because after he finished laughing, and agreed to do it, he wrote it on his wrist.

If he doesn't get here soon it'll be too late.

Dad'll have upset and embarrassed every parent and every teacher at this barbie and they'll form a vigilante group and we'll have to move to another town.

He's already upset the lady on the jam stall by asking if he could taste all the jams before he bought one. She laughed but I knew that inside she was ropable.

And he's embarrassed Megan O'Donnell's dad by buying twenty raffle tickets from him just because the third prize is a Carla Tamworth CD.

Mr O'Donnell shook Dad's hand and slapped him

on the back, but I could tell that inside he knows we haven't got a CD player and he thinks Dad's a loony.

And at least six people have commented how Dad's purple and yellow shirt looks as though it's made from the same material as the big purple and yellow Parents and Teachers Association banner over the marquee. They pretended they were joking, but inside I bet they were nauseous.

At least the Cosgroves aren't here.

It means I won't see Amanda today, but I'm prepared to pay that price if it means Dad and Mr Cosgrove won't be stabbing each other with chicken kebabs.

Four twenty-four.

Come on, Andy.

Perhaps he's got mechanical trouble. No, that can't be it, everyone knows crop-dusters keep their planes in A-1 mechanical condition. Farmers won't hire you if you keep crashing into their sheds.

I've got a knot in my guts the size of Antarctica.

Relax, guts, it'll be fine.

That's the great thing about talking in your head. It takes your mind off stress and you don't get ulcers. If I wasn't having this conversation now I'd be a nervous wreck.

Oh no.

I can't believe what Dad's just done.

He's donated a song to the fund-raising auction.

He actually expects people to bid money for him to sing them a song.

This is so embarrassing.

I'd go and hide in the marquee if I didn't have to keep an eye out for Andy in case he's having trouble with his navigational equipment and I have to set fire to some chicken kebabs to guide him in.

Dad'll be so hurt when nobody bids.

I can picture his face now.

Good grief, someone's just bid.

Two dollars, that's an insult.

Haven't these people got any feelings?

And now four dollars from Doug Walsh's parents.

What are you trying to do, destroy my father's self-respect?

Dad's grinning, but inside he must be feeling awful.

Stack me, Ms Dunning's just bid ten dollars.

Why's everyone laughing? At least she's doing her best to make him feel better.

Oh.

The ten dollars is for him not to sing.

Mr Fowler has banged his auctioneer's hammer and declared her the successful bidder.

Everyone's laughing and clapping, including Dad, but inside he must be bleeding.

Four twenty-seven.

Andy, this is getting desperate.

I know skywriting is just a hobby for you, but it's a matter of life and death down here.

Now Ms Dunning's trying to persuade Dad to go in the sack race.

That woman is incredible.

Even though he's taken the sack off his feet and put it on his head and she must be burning up inside with embarrassment, she's still pretending she's enjoying herself so she doesn't hurt his feelings.

Definitely a saint.

Four twenty-eight.

Where is he?

If Andy Peck has flown to Western Australia with my two hundred and ninety dollars I'll track him down even if it takes me the rest of my life because it took me hundreds of hours helping Dad in the orchard to earn that money.

There's Amanda.

She must have just arrived.

Oh well, at least now I've got someone to moan to about the Peck family.

Oh no, if she's here, that means . . .

Mr Cosgrove.

There he is.

He's seen Dad.

Don't do it, Dad, don't take the sack off your head.

He's taken it off.

He's seen Mr Cosgrove.

They're staring at each other.

Oh no.

Wait a sec, what's that noise?

Is it . . ?

Yes.

It's a plane.

Andy Peck turned out to be a really good skywriter for an amateur.

Though as I'd paid him two hundred and ninety dollars I suppose that made him a professional.

Anyway, he did a great job and I'm really happy.

Fairly happy.

I think.

His letters were big and clear, huge swoops of white smoke against the blue sky.

As the plane started buzzing overhead, Mr Fowler stopped the charity auction. 'We'll take a breather,' he said, 'and enjoy the spectacle.'

Most people were already looking up.

'What's he writing?' asked a woman near me.

The Parents and Teachers Committee asked him to write the school motto,' said a man.

'I didn't think the school motto began with "Pull",' said the woman.

'Nor did I,' said the man, frowning as he looked up at the huge PULL hanging in the sky.

'It doesn't,' Amanda said in my ear. 'The school motto's "Forward Not Back".'

'He's not doing the school motto,' I said. 'He's helping me save my dad's social life.'

Amanda stared at me.

I looked over at Dad.

He wasn't even looking up. He was walking towards Mr Cosgrove.

That's when I got mad.

I wanted to yell at him.

'Listen, you cheese-brain,' I wanted to roar, 'I'm trying to tell you something.'

But you can't yell with your hands across a crowded school oval.

I was nearly exploding.

It was an emergency.

I put my fingers in my mouth and gave three of my loudest whistles.

Dad stopped and looked around and saw me.

I glared at him and pointed up.

He looked up.

Andy had almost finished the YOUR.

Dad stared.

So did Mr Cosgrove.

So did Amanda.

So did everyone.

Nobody spoke until Andy had finished HEAD, then a buzz of voices started.

Amanda gripped my arm. 'You didn't?' she gasped.

I was still glaring at Dad.

He was still peering up, puzzled.

Andy finished the IN.

' "Pull Your Head In," ' someone read. 'That's not the school motto.'

'It is now,' someone else said, 'so pull your head in.'

Everyone laughed.

I wanted to scream at them. Couldn't they see this was serious?

Andy finished the DAD.

Everyone went quiet again.

Dad was staring up, not moving a muscle.

Then he turned and looked at me.

I looked back at him as calmly as I could, even though my heart was thumping like a ten-million-watt compressor.

It was so loud I could only just hear the plane flying off into the distance.

Then everyone started talking in puzzled tones and Amanda grabbed my arm again.

'How did you do that?' she said.

The people around us stared.

'I wish I could get my Dad to pay attention like that,' said Amanda wistfully. 'Gee, you're clever.'

I looked at her wide-eyed face and hoped she was right.

Because when I looked back over at Dad, he'd gone.

I knew that would probably happen. I knew he'd need a few moments to think about it. Before we talk.

The other parents were whispering and pointing

at me and frowning, but I could tell that inside they knew it had to be done.

After a few moments I went looking for Dad.

He wasn't in the marquee.

He wasn't in any of the classrooms.

He wasn't in the Gents.

I went back to the oval thinking perhaps he'd decided to buy a book called *How To Win Friends And Influence People* which had been the next item in the auction, but when I got there the auction was over and people were starting to leave.

Amanda came running up.

'I just saw him driving out of the car park,' she said breathlessly.

I knew that might happen. I knew he might need a bit longer to think about it. Before we talk.

Amanda was looking at me in a very concerned way, so I explained to her that everything was under control.

Ms Dunning saw me and started to come over, but then Darryn Peck, who'd got overexcited at his big brother being the centre of attention, managed to set fire to one of the marquee flaps and Ms Dunning had to attend to that.

Mr and Mrs Cosgrove came over.

Mr Cosgrove was beaming.

'Well, young lady,' he said, 'for someone who can't speak, you certainly put that loud-mouthed father of yours in his place.'

Amanda squeezed my hand, which helped me not to do anything ugly.

They've just given me a lift home.

I made Mr Cosgrove drop me at the bottom of the orchard road because I don't think Dad'll want to see him at the moment.

I'm not even sure he'll want to see me.

Searching the orchard was a waste of time because after I'd searched the house and the shed I realised the truck'd gone so it stands to reason he has too but I searched the orchard anyway because a tiny part of me was hoping he was playing the game we used to play when I was a little kid where he'd hide in our old orchard and I'd have to try and find him and as I got closer and closer he'd make little raspberry noises with his mouth to give me a clue and when I found him he'd let me walk back to the house in his boots even though they came over my knees and I did a pee in one of them once.

He wasn't.

He's gone.

If I say it in my head enough times I'll get used to it and stop feeling so numb and then I can think what to do.

He's gone.

He's gone.

He's gone.

I'm still numb.

I can't even stand up.

I've been sitting here since I came back from the orchard and saw the letters on the kitchen table.

One was my letter to him from Carla Tamworth.

The other was in his writing on a piece of Rice Bubbles packet.

'Dear Ro,' it said, 'I feel pretty crook about all this and I don't want to think about it right now so I'm taking a hike. Go and stay with Amanda. Dad.'

He never calls me Ro.

On the table under the letters was eighty dollars.

Then I saw the cupboard where I'd stuffed the Carla Tamworth letter.

The door was open and the old bottle of rum that Dad hadn't chucked away in case a visitor wanted a drink was lying on the floor.

Empty.

That's when I knew I'd lost him.

Amanda and her family were pretty surprised when I arrived on the tractor.

They came out onto their front verandah and stared.

I explained what had happened, and how I'd needed the tractor because I'd brought all my clothes with me and I'd never have got the suitcase to their place by hand.

Mr and Mrs Cosgrove made me explain it all again.

Isn't it amazing how you can still do complicated explanations even when you're completely and totally numb inside your head?

Amanda was great.

She rushed over and dragged the suitcase off the tractor and said I could stay with them for the rest of my life if I wanted to.

Mr and Mrs Cosgrove were good too.

After I'd parked the tractor in their driveway next to their car and the colour had come back into their cheeks, they took me into the house and gave me a glass of pineapple juice and some chocolate biscuits and a toasted ham and cheese sandwich.

Even Amanda's little brother Wayne was fairly good.

When he'd finished telling everyone I couldn't have his room and I wasn't allowed to use his cricket gear or his bug-catcher or his video games, he disappeared and came back with a toothbrush which he said I could share with him as he only used it to clean the points on his train set about once a week.

I thanked him and explained I'd brought my own.

Amanda and me went and made up the camp bed in her room.

Then we sat on it and Amanda asked how I felt.

'Numb,' I said.

Even saying that one word wasn't easy because suddenly my hands were shaking so much.

She looked at me, concerned and puzzled.

'I don't understand,' she said. 'You feel like a dentist?'

I was just about to tell her again when suddenly I didn't feel numb any more, I felt completely and totally sick and I had to run to the toilet.

I wasn't sick but I had to lean against the wall while I shivered and cold sweat dripped off me.

Amanda's anxious voice came through the door.

'Are you OK?' she asked.

I opened the door and told her I'd be fine and that I'd see her back in her room.

I didn't want her skinning her knuckles trying to open the door with a knife.

After a bit I felt less shaky, so I came out.

On my way back I stopped in the hallway because I could hear Mr and Mrs Cosgrove talking about me in the living room.

'Sergeant Vinelli said there's not much they can do tonight,' said Mr Cosgrove. 'They'll put out a search call for him in the morning. Oh, and Child Welfare will have to be informed.'

'I'll see Mr Fowler at school tomorrow,' said Mrs Cosgrove. 'He's probably the best person to handle it. Poor kid. We should get the Community Service Committee to start a fund to help tragic cases like hers.'

'I hope they catch that hoon,' said Mr Cosgrove, 'and throw him in jail.'

I almost went in there and asked him how he'd feel if he'd just been humiliated in front of half the town.

But I didn't because, let's face it, you probably can't change people.

Mr Cosgrove'll probably always hate Dad and Dad'll probably always love eye-damaging shirts and there's probably nothing me or the Prime Minister or anyone can do about it.

Anyway, I didn't have the energy for another run-in with Mr Cosgrove because what with reading Dad's letter, and having the shakes in the bathroom, and standing there in the hallway realising I was back to being a project, I was feeling pretty depressed.

I went back to Amanda's room and went to bed.

'Ro,' said Amanda, 'I'm sorry about your dad, but I'm really glad you're here.'

'Thanks,' I said.

Mr and Mrs Cosgrove came in and said goodnight, and Mrs Cosgrove squeezed my hand and said she was sure everything would turn out fine.

I think it was them kissing Amanda that did it.

Suddenly I missed everyone so much.

Mum.

Erin.

Dad.

I managed to hang on till Mr and Mrs Cosgrove had switched the light out and closed the door, then I felt something rushing up from deep in my guts and the tears just poured out of me.

I didn't want them to, not in someone else's house, but I couldn't help it.

I pushed my face into the pillow and sobbed so hard I thought I'd never stop.

Then I felt someone get into the bed behind me.

It was Amanda.

She put her arms round me and stroked my hair while I cried and suddenly I didn't feel like a project at all, just a friend.

It's amazing how much better you feel after a cry and a sleep.

I reckon if people had more cries and sleeps, they woudn't need half the aspirin and ulcer medicine and rum in the world.

I don't feel numb this morning, or sick.

Just sad.

But life must go on.

That's what my teacher at my old school said after Erin died. The human organism, she said, can survive any amount of sadness if it keeps busy. She was a doctor, so she knew.

I'm keeping busy now.

I'm having this conversation in my head.

Plus I'm making apple fritters for Mr and Mrs Cosgrove and Amanda and Wayne's breakfasts.

Plus I'm putting a lot of effort into not making too much noise because it's only five-thirty and I don't want them to wake up till the fritters are done.

Plus I'm thinking.

I'm thinking how even though I feel very, very sad, I feel kind of relieved too.

All my life I've had this worry, deep down, that Dad would leave.

Now I don't have to worry about it any more, because he has.

I don't blame him, not really.

He's got his life too.

Who knows, he might finally meet a woman who doesn't embarrass easily and they might have a baby and he might finally get to have a daughter who can speak.

I wish I hadn't thought that, because now I'm crying again.

This morning would have been a disaster without Amanda.

First, while I was sitting in the kitchen making the drying-up cloth all soggy with tears, she smelt the smoke from the fritters and ran in and pulled them off the stove before the kitchen burnt down.

Then, when Mr Cosgrove came rushing out of his bedroom with a fire extinguisher, she explained to him that I always make fritters when I'm depressed, plus they were for his breakfast.

He shouted quite a bit, but she stood up to him.

I was proud of her.

Then, after Mrs Cosgrove had driven us to school and had gone off to see Mr Fowler, Amanda took my arm and we walked in through the gate together.

It's amazing how quickly word gets around in a small country town.

Every kid in that playground just stood and stared.

'What's the matter with you lot?' said Amanda. 'Haven't you ever seen an abandoned kid before?'

It wasn't the best line I'd ever heard, but it was better than I could have done at the time, and I was really grateful.

Everyone carried on staring.

Except Darryn Peck.

He swaggered over and I saw he was carrying a jar with a frog in it.

The biggest frog I'd ever seen.

Then I remembered.

The race.

'S'pose you'll want to chicken out now,' Darryn said to me with a smirk.

Amanda took a step towards him.

'She's not chickening out,' she said, 'she's just not feeling well. I'll race you.'

'Loser eats this, 'said Darryn, holding up the frog.

'I know,' said Amanda.

I felt like hugging her, but I didn't because emotionally deprived kids like Darryn Peck don't understand real friendship and they use it to get cheap laughs.

'Thanks,' I said to her, 'but I want to do it.'

I think she understood what my hands were saying.

Anyway, she understood what my face was saying.

I turned to Darryn and poked myself in the chest, and then poked him in the chest.

He understood what I was saying.

'Lunch time,' he said.

I nodded.

The frog gurgled.

All morning in class Ms Dunning behaved very strangely.

She hardly looked at me, and didn't ask me a single question.

To show her I needed to be kept busy, one time when she asked Megan O'Donnell a question I just walked out the front and wrote the answer on the board.

It didn't make any difference. I still spent the rest of the morning with my hand in the air, being ignored.

I couldn't understand it.

I looked at Amanda and I saw she couldn't understand it either.

Then things became clearer.

The lunch bell went, and Ms Dunning said, 'Ro, could I see you in the staff room please?'

The staff room was deserted because the other teachers were out on the oval taking down the marquee.

Usually when a teacher and a kid have a conversation in the staff room, the teacher stands still and the kid does a lot of nervous shuffling about.

Today with me and Ms Dunning it was the opposite.

I stood there while she did a lot of nervous shuffling about.

'Ro,' she said, 'before your dad disappeared, did he say anything about me?'

I shook my head.

Ms Dunning shuffled some more.

She looked pretty worried.

I wrote her a note.

'What's the matter?' I asked.

She read it and took a deep breath, but didn't say anything.

'It's OK,' I said, 'I won't blab to anyone else.'

She read that and gave a worried little smile.

'Ro,' she said after what seemed like a couple of months, 'your dad wants me to be his girlfriend, but I don't.'

I nodded. I knew that.

'And,' continued Ms Dunning, 'I told him that yesterday, just before your message in the sky, just before he disappeared.'

I didn't know that.

'And,' Ms Dunning went on, 'I'm worried that's why he's gone missing.'

I wrote her a long note telling her not to be silly, that my message was the reason he'd gone. Writing it made me feel incredibly sad. To cheer us both up, I asked her to be the line judge for my race with Darryn Peck.

She smiled and said yes.

Most of the school was out on the oval, lining both sides of the running track.

As Ms Dunning took her position, she saw the frog in the jar on the other side of the finish line.

'What's that?' she asked.

The whole school held its breath.

I did too.

If the race was banned now, Darryn'd be crowing for months about how he'd have won.

'It's what they're racing for,' said Amanda.

That girl's a future Prime Minister.

Ms Dunning gave a tired smile and said, 'I can think of more attractive prizes'.

As I walked to the start line, Amanda ran up and squeezed my arm. 'Don't slow down at the end like you did with me,' she said. 'Keep going.'

I didn't know she'd noticed.

But I was too tense to say anything.

I nodded and crouched down next to Darryn on the start line.

'They're good with cheese sauce, frogs,' he smirked, but before I could answer, Ms Dunning blew her whistle and I flung myself forward.

It wasn't a good start and I was off-balance for the first few steps.

Out of the corner of my eye I could see Darryn moving ahead.

I pounded my legs harder, but I couldn't get past him.

Sweat was running into my eyes.

We got closer and closer to the finish line.

Then I saw it. Next to Ms Dunning. A blur of bright purple and yellow. And I knew it was Dad.

I could see him waving his arms in the air, just like he did in the race with Amanda.

Suddenly my legs felt light as whips and I knew I was going to win.

I didn't care if Dad got so excited he kissed all

the teachers and made them all drop their lunches and stuck his hand into all their armholes.

That was his problem.

I was level with Darryn.

The finish line was rushing towards me.

I stretched my arms out and hurled myself at the excited purple and yellow blur and crossed the line with Darryn's feet thundering at my heels.

There was shouting and cheering and Amanda threw her arms round me and squeezed me so hard I couldn't suck air.

I barely noticed.

All I was really aware of was the purple and yellow blur, which now I was up close wasn't a blur at all.

It was the Parents and Teachers Association banner, rolled up in the arms of a teacher, a loose end flapping in the breeze.

Dazed, I turned away.

I felt sick, but that might have just been the run.

Keep busy, I thought, keep busy.

Darryn was sprawled on the ground, looking as sick as I felt.

His eyes flicked up at me, and then at the frog, and then at the ground again.

Just for a sec, while he was looking at me, he had the same expression he had yesterday after his brothers had been mean to him.

Suddenly I wanted to tell him to go home and tell his brothers to pull their heads in.

It wasn't the time to do that, so I found my bag and pulled out my lunch box and pulled out the apple fritter I'd been planning to pick the burnt bits off and have for lunch.

I held it out to Darryn.

He looked at it, then at me, puzzled.

I found my pad and pen but before I could write anything, Amanda spoke up.

'Frog fritter,' she said to Darryn.

What a team.

Darryn took the fritter, and just for a fleeting second I thought he looked grateful.

Hard to tell, on a face that spends so much of its time smirking.

I picked up the frog in the bottle and turned to ask Ms Dunning if she thought it would eat the other frogs in our classroom.

While I was writing there was a shout.

Mr Fowler, pink and agitated, was hurrying towards Ms Dunning.

'That blessed girl's locked herself in the stationery cupboard again,' he said.

Then he stopped and stared at me.

'Well someone has,' he said.

Everyone stood there for a bit.

Then I remembered and my heart tried to get out through my mouth.

Even though my lungs were still sore I made it into the school in about three seconds.

In the staff-room corridor I stopped in front of the stationery cupboard door and took the biggest breath I could and started to whistle 'Heart Like A Fairground' by Carla Tamworth.

I can whistle loud, but I'm a bit crook on tunes.

Mr Fowler and Ms Dunning and a crowd of kids arrived and they all stared at me as if I was loony.

I didn't care.

There was a rattle at the keyhole and the cupboard door swung open and there was Dad.

'About time,' he said. 'I forgot the peg and the pong in here'd strip paint.'

It was my turn to stare.

He was wearing a grey suit and a white shirt and a brown bow tie.

The suit was too short in the arms and the legs.

The shirt was so big that the bow tie was sticking up over his chin.

I didn't know whether to collapse into giggles like Ms Dunning was doing or forget that half the class were there and burst into tears.

'Dad,' I said, 'you look ridiculous.'

He gave me a nervous grin.

'That's what happens when you buy your clothes from a cheese-brain,' he said. 'Bludger doesn't have anything in your size.'

We gave each other a huge hug, though it wasn't easy for him because he couldn't move his arms that much.

Even though I was so happy I could hardly think, I made a mental note that brightly-coloured satin shirts are much more generously cut than suits, and therefore much better for cuddles.

Then, after he went and had a chat to Mr Fowler and Sergeant Vinelli and persuaded them that any man in a suit must be a responsible father, he took me and Amanda back to our place and we built a big bonfire and had sausages and marshmallows for tea.

After Dad got changed I was tempted to chuck the suit onto the fire.

I didn't.

I decided it might be useful to have it around, in case Dad gets out of hand again.

I might be totally and completely happy, but I'm not dumb.

Sticky Beak

For Chris, Sophie and Ben

I reckon there's something wrong with me.

There must be.

Normal people don't do what I've just done—spoil a wonderful evening and upset half the town and ruin a perfectly good Jelly Custard Surprise.

Perhaps the heat's affected my brain.

Perhaps I've caught some mysterious disease that makes things slip out of my hands.

Perhaps I'm in the power of creatures from another planet who own a lot of dry-cleaning shops.

All I know is ten minutes ago my life was totally and completely happy.

Now here I am, standing in the principal's office, covered in raspberry jelly and lemon custard, waiting to be yelled at and probably expelled and maybe even arrested.

I reckon it was the heat.

It was incredibly hot in that school hall with so many people dancing and talking in loud voices and reaching across each other for the party pies.

And I was running around nonstop, keeping an

eye on the ice supply and mopping up spilt drinks and helping Amanda put out the desserts and reminding Dad to play a few waltz records in between the country stuff.

I had to sprint up onto the stage several times to stop the 'Farewell Ms Dunning' banner from drooping.

Plus, whenever I saw kids gazing at Ms Dunning and starting to look sad, I'd dash over and stick an apple fritter in their hands to cheer them up.

Every few minutes I went and stood in front of the big fan that Vic from the hardware store had lent for the night, but I still felt like the Murray–Darling river system had decided to give South Australia a miss and run down my back instead.

Amanda was great.

How a person with hair that thick and curly can stay cool on a night like this beats me.

Every time she saw me in front of the fan she gave me a grin.

Don't worry, the grin said, everything's under control and Ms Dunning's having a top time.

That's the great thing about a best friend, half the time you don't even need words.

I'd just given fresh party pies to the principal and the mayor and was heading over to the food table with the bowl of Jelly Custard Surprise when the formalities started. The music stopped and we were all deafened by the screech of a microphone being switched on and the rumble of Amanda's dad clearing his throat.

Amanda's grin vanished.

I gave her a look. Don't panic, it said, once you get up to the microphone you'll be fine.

I didn't know if it was true, but I could see it made her feel better.

'Ladies and gentlemen,' said Mr Cosgrove, 'on behalf of the Parents and Teachers Association Social Committee, it's time for the presentation to our guest of honour.'

There was a silence while everyone looked around for Ms Dunning.

She was at the food table, looking startled, gripping Darryn Peck's wrist.

I felt really proud of her at that moment.

There she was, eight and a half months pregnant, hot and weary after spending the whole afternoon making the Jelly Custard Surprise, and she was still taking the trouble to stop Darryn Peck using my apple fritters as frisbees.

No wonder we all think she's the best teacher we've ever had.

Ms Dunning let go of Darryn Peck and went over and stood next to Mr Cosgrove while he made a long speech about how dedicated she is and how sad we all are that she's leaving the school but how we all understand that babies are the future of Australia.

Then Mr Cosgrove called Amanda to the microphone.

She was so nervous she almost slipped over in a drink puddle, but once she was there she did a great job. She read the speech we'd written in her loudest voice without a single mistake, not even during the difficult bit about Ms Dunning being an angel who shone with such radiance in the classroom we hardly ever needed the fluoros on.

After Amanda finished reading she presented Ms Dunning with a carved wooden salad bowl and matching carved wooden fork and spoon which the Social Committee had bought after ignoring my suggestion of a tractor.

Everyone clapped except me because I had my hands full, but I wobbled the Jelly Custard Surprise to show that I would have if I could.

Ms Dunning grinned and blushed and made a speech about how much fun she'd had teaching us and how nobody should feel sad because she'd see everyone most days when she dropped me off at school.

Even though it was a short speech, she was looking pretty exhausted by the time she'd finished.

'I'm pooped,' she grinned. 'Where's that husband of mine?'

Dad stepped forward and kissed her and she leant on his shoulder and there was more applause.

Dad gave such a big grin I thought his ears were going to flip his cowboy hat off.

I was grinning myself.

Dad's had a hard life, what with Mum dying and stuff, and a top person like him deserves a top person like Ms Dunning.

I reckon marrying Ms Dunning is the best thing

he ever did, and that includes buying the apple-polishing machine.

Seeing them standing there, smiling at each other, Ms Dunning smoothing down the fringe on Dad's shirt, I felt happier than I have all year, and I've felt pretty happy for most of it.

Which is why what happened next was so weird.

Dad cleared his throat and went down on one knee so his eyes were level with Ms Dunning's bulging tummy.

I wasn't surprised at that because he does it all the time at home. The mayor, though, was staring at Dad with his mouth open. Mayors get around a fair bit, but they probably don't often come across apple farmers who wear goanna-skin cowboy boots and sing to their wives' tummies.

As usual Dad sang a song by Carla Tamworth, his favourite country and western singer.

It was the one about the long-distance truck driver who listens to tapes of his two-month-old baby crying to keep himself awake while he's driving.

As usual Dad had a bit of trouble with a few of the notes, but nobody seemed to mind. Ms Dunning was gazing at him lovingly and everyone else was smiling and some people were tapping their feet, including the mayor.

I was enjoying it too, until Dad got to the chorus.

'Your tears are music to my ears,' sang Dad to Ms Dunning's midriff, and that's when my brain must have become heat-affected.

Suddenly my heart was pounding and I had a strange sick feeling in my guts.

I turned away.

And suddenly my feet were sliding and suddenly the Jelly Custard Surprise wasn't in my hands anymore.

The bowl still was, but the Jelly Custard Surprise was flying through the air.

It hit the grille of the big hardware store fan, and then everyone in the hall disappeared into a sort of sticky mist. It was just like when Dad sprays the orchard, except his mist isn't pink and it hasn't got bits of custard in it.

I stood there, stunned, while people shrieked and tried to crawl under the food table.

The mayor still had his mouth open, but now it was full of jelly.

Mr Cosgrove was staring down at his suit in horror, looking like a statue that had just been dive-bombed by a large flock of pink and yellow pigeons.

Darryn Peck was sitting in a Greek salad. I only knew it was him because of the tufts of ginger hair poking up through the sticky pink stuff that covered his face.

I blew the jelly out of my nose and ran out of the hall and thought about hiding in the stationery cupboard but came in here instead.

I'd have ended up here anyway because the principal's office is always where people are taken to be yelled at and expelled and arrested.

There's someone at the door now.

They seem to be having trouble opening it.

It's pretty hard getting a grip on a door handle when you've got Jelly Custard Surprise running out of your sleeves.

I'd help them if I wasn't shaking so much.

The door opened and Mr Fowler came in and it was worse than I'd imagined.

It wasn't just his sleeves that were dripping with jelly and custard, it was most of his shirt and all of his shorts and both knees.

On top of his head, in the middle of his bald patch, were several pieces of pineapple. Ms Dunning always puts crushed pineapple at the bottom of her Jelly Custard Surprise. It's delicious, but it's not really a surprise, not to us. I think it was to Mr Fowler though.

He saw me and just sort of glared at me for a bit.

I tried to stop shaking so I wouldn't drip on his carpet so much.

It was no good. I looked down and saw I was standing in a puddle of passion-fruit topping.

I made a mental note to write to the Department of Education and explain that it had dripped out of my hair and not out of Mr Fowler's lunch box.

Mr Fowler didn't seem to have noticed.

He strode over to his desk and wiped his hands on his blotter.

I waited for him to ring the District Schools Inspector and say, 'I've got a girl here who's been mute since birth and she came to us from a special school fourteen months ago and I thought she was fitting in OK but she's just sprayed two hundred people with Jelly Custard Surprise and so obviously she's not and she'll have to go back to a special school first thing in the morning'.

He didn't.

He just glared at me some more.

'I've seen some clumsy acts in this school,' he said, 'but I think you, Rowena Batts, have just topped the lot.'

I didn't reply because my hands were shaking too much to write and Mr Fowler doesn't understand sign language.

'I knew it was a mistake having food,' he continued, starting to rummage through the top drawer of his filing cabinet. 'That floor was awash with coleslaw from the word go. I nearly slipped over just before you did.'

My legs felt like they had jelly on the inside as well as the outside.

'You OK, Tonto?' said a voice from the door.

It was Dad.

His face was creased with concern and splattered with custard, and for a sec I thought he'd changed his shirt. Then I saw it was the blue satin one he'd been wearing all along, but the red jelly had turned it purple.

'I'm fine,' I said, trying to keep my hand movements small so I wouldn't flick drips onto Mr Fowler's files.

Ms Dunning came in behind Dad, just as splattered and just as concerned.

She gave me a hug.

'When you have bad luck, Ro, you really have bad luck,' she said. 'And after all the hard work you put into tonight.'

She wiped something off my left elbow, then turned to Mr Fowler.

'We want to get home and cleaned up, Frank,' she said. 'Can we talk about paying for the damage tomorrow?'

Mr Fowler looked up from the filing cabinet.

'No need,' he said, holding up a piece of paper. 'The insurance covers accidental food spillage.'

Ms Dunning gave such a big sigh of relief that a lump of pineapple slid off the top of her tummy. I caught it before it hit the carpet.

I could tell from Dad's face he wanted to get me out of there before Mr Fowler discovered a clause in the insurance policy excluding jelly.

To get to the truck we had to go through the school hall. It was full of people wiping each other with serviettes and hankies and bits torn off the 'Farewell Ms Dunning' banner.

I held my breath and hoped they wouldn't notice me.

They did.

People started glowering at me from under sticky

eyebrows and muttering things that fortunately I couldn't hear because I still had a fair bit of jelly in my ears.

Amanda came over, her hair rubbed into sticky spikes. 'If Mr Fowler tries to murder you,' she said with her hands, 'tell him to speak to me. I saw you slip.'

I felt really proud of her. Not only is she kind and loyal, but I only taught her the sign for 'murder' last week.

'Don't feel bad, Ro,' called out Megan O'Donnell's mum, scraping custard off her T-shirt with a knife. 'I'm on a diet so I'd rather have it on the outside than on the inside.'

There are some really nice people in this town.

But I do feel bad.

I felt bad all the way home in the truck, even though Dad made me and Ms Dunning laugh by threatening to drive us round the orchard on the tractor so all the codling moths would stick to us.

I feel bad now, even though I'm standing under a cool shower.

Because I didn't slip on some coleslaw and accidentally lose control of the Jelly Custard Surprise.

I threw it on purpose.

The great thing about talking in your head is you can say anything you want.

Even things you're scared to say in real life.

Even to your own Dad.

He's just been in to say goodnight.

The moment he stepped into the room I could tell he wanted to have a serious talk because he'd changed into his black shirt, the one with the yellow horseshoes on the front. Dad always wears that when he's planning a serious conversation.

'Feeling better?' he asked with his mouth.

Dad doesn't seem to talk so much with his hands these days.

'A bit better,' I said. 'How are the boots?'

'Gave them a rinse and they're good as new,' he said.

'Belt buckle?' I asked.

'Pretty yukky,' he said, grinning. 'Jelly in the eyeholes. Had to scrub it with my toothbrush.'

For about the millionth time in my life I thought how lucky I am to have a dad like him. I bet there aren't many dads who stay calm when they've got jelly in the eyeholes of their cow-skull belt buckle.

Dad cleared his throat, which meant he was either about to get musical or serious.

'Tonto,' he said, 'Amanda told me how that pud got airborne tonight. She said it was cause you turned away real quick while I was singing. I didn't think you got embarrassed any more at me having a warble in public.'

'I don't,' I said.

It's true. I did when we first came here, before people got to know Dad, because I was worried they'd think he was mental. But then one day I realised I didn't mind any more. It was at the wedding. The wedding was the happiest day of my life, and even Dad singing 'Chalk Up My Love In The Classroom Of Your Heart' to Ms Dunning at the altar didn't change that.

'So,' Dad went on, 'tonight's little mishap wasn't on account of me singing?'

I shook my head.

I know it wasn't, because Dad's sung heaps of other times since the wedding—at Ms Dunning's birthday party and at the school fund-raising bingo night and at the dawn service on Anzac Day—and no food's ended up in any electrical appliances on any of those occasions.

Dad looked relieved. Then he frowned, like he does when we're playing Trivial Pursuit and he gets a question about astronomy.

'Do you reckon there's a possibility,' he said,

'that tonight's mishap was the result of stress?'

'What stress?' I asked.

'The stress,' he said, 'of you having a teacher who's also your mum.'

'Definitely not,' I said, almost poking his eye out with my elbow. My hand movements get a bit wild when I'm being emphatic.

There's no way that could be it. I love having Ms Dunning living with us and she was tops in class. The number of times she must have been tempted to tell me to pay attention or I wouldn't get any tea, and she didn't do it once.

'The only stress I've suffered this year,' I said to Dad, 'was when that committee in Sydney ignored my nomination of her as Australian Of The Year.'

I was ropeable. How many nominations do they get that have been signed by thirty people? Even Darryn Peck signed after I gave him two dollars.

Dad looked relieved again. 'Just checking,' he said. 'By the way, Tonto, now she's not your teacher any more, it'd be real good if you could call her Claire.'

'OK,' I said, 'I'll try to remember.'

Dad frowned again, but this time really hard, like when the Trivial Pursuit question's about the digestive system of the West Australian bog leech.

I waited for him to speak.

I could see there was something else he wanted to ask me, but he was having trouble getting it out.

I decided to step in before he risked his health by standing on his head or doing any of the other things he does when there's a bit of tension in the air.

'Dad,' I said, 'I'm really happy you married Ms Dunning. I mean Claire. I think she's great and I wouldn't swap her for a prawn sandwich, not even with the crusts cut off.'

Dad grinned and gave me a big hug.

His hair smelt faintly of raspberry jelly.

'We'll have to get you some new shoes,' he said. 'Something with decent soles that'll grip coleslaw.'

I didn't say anything, I just tried to look as sleepy as I could.

Ms Dunning came in and gave me a kiss on the cheek and when I peeked she and Dad were creeping out of the room with their arms round each other.

They stopped in the hallway and kissed.

I bet there aren't many couples who still do that after a year of marriage.

It gave me a warm feeling inside.

But that was ages ago, and now I don't feel warm inside or sleepy.

I may never sleep again.

It's pretty hard to nod off when you've just chucked a dessert across a school hall and you haven't got a clue why.

Dad always reckons if you've got a problem, don't just mope around, do something about it.

When I woke up this morning I decided to do something about mine.

I grabbed my pen and tore a page off my drawing pad.

At the top in big letters I wrote, 'TO WHOM IT MAY CONCERN'.

Under it I wrote, 'SORRY'.

Then I had a think.

I wanted to choose my words carefully because you don't just scribble any old stuff when you're apologising to two hundred people.

It wasn't easy to concentrate, what with Dad revving the tractor outside and Ms Dunning whistling really loudly to herself in the kitchen, but after a bit I decided on the right words.

'If the school insurance doesn't cough up enough,' I wrote, 'send the extra dry-cleaning bills to me and I'll fix you up. It might take a while cause I only get $2.50 pocket money, but I earn extra helping

Dad in the orchard. Sorry for the inconvenience, yours faithfully, Rowena Batts. PS If there's anything that won't come out, bring the clothes round to our place. Dad knows how to shift problem stains using liquid fertiliser.'

When I'd finished I went into the kitchen to ask Ms Dunning to check the spelling.

She was standing at the stove reading the paper.

'Look at this,' she said excitedly. 'Carla Tamworth's singing at the showground, next Saturday.'

'I know,' I said.

'Dad'll be over the moon,' she said.

'That's right,' I said.

I didn't remind her that Dad and me had already been over the moon two weeks ago when the ad first appeared in the paper.

People who are having a baby in eight days go a bit vague, it's a known fact. No point making her feel embarrassed.

I made Ms Dunning take the weight off her feet while she checked my spelling and I did the eggs.

I've told her a million times that when you're having eggs with apple fritters the eggs should be runny, but she just can't seem to grasp the idea. She probably will when she's had the baby and her head clears, but.

Ms Dunning finished reading my public notice and got up and came over and put her hand on my shoulder.

'Inconvenience doesn't have an "s",' she said quietly. 'Ro, it's a good notice, but you don't have to do this, you know.'

I turned the heat down under the eggs and explained to her that in small country towns if you spray jelly onto people's clothes, bitter feuds can erupt and fester for generations.

She thought about that.

Even brilliant teachers don't know everything, specially when they're originally from the city like Ms Dunning.

'If I don't make amends now,' I told her, 'in fifty years time you could find someone's parked you in at the supermarket just on the day you're rushing to get over to the bank to pick up your pension.'

Ms Dunning thought about that too, frowning.

For a sec I thought she hadn't understood all my hand movements, but then she grinned and I could see she had. She's very good at reading sign now, just not so good at speaking it.

'OK, Ro,' she said, 'go for it.'

She gave my shoulder a squeeze and hurried off to have a wee, which is something else that happens a lot when you're having a baby in just over a week.

I'll be going for it as soon as I've finished breakfast.

Actually I'm not feeling very hungry, even though the eggs are perfect.

Every time I swallow there's a knot in my guts the size of Ayers Rock.

I think I'm a bit nervous about facing everyone after last night.

I'll be OK, though, as long as I can get the notice photocopied and stuck up everywhere before an angry mob grabs me and strings me up by my feet from the Tidy Town sign.

As I left our place I saw something that made me feel better.

A rainbow sparkling from one side of the orchard to the other.

We get them sometimes when Dad's spraying the trees with the big blower and the sunlight slants through the clouds of spray.

Today's was a beauty and I decided it was a good sign.

It wasn't.

It didn't even have a pot of gold at the end of it.

Just Darryn Peck.

Halfway into town I turned a corner and there he was, coming towards me with two of his mates.

He was carrying something in a cage. At first it looked like a white feather duster with a blob of custard on it, but I knew that couldn't be right. Even Darryn Peck wouldn't carry a feather duster around in a cage.

As he got closer I saw it was a cockatoo with

a row of yellow feathers sticking out the top of its head.

Then Darryn stopped kicking dust at his mates and saw me.

His red lips stretched into a smirk.

'Oh no, it's Batts!' he shrieked, backing away pretending to be scared. 'Don't go too close, she might be carrying a trifle and slip over.'

His mates thought this was so hilarious I looked away in case they split their daks.

Then Darryn did a strange thing.

He came over to me and spoke in a quiet, serious voice, just like a normal person. 'Was that an accident last night,' he asked, 'or did you chuck that trifle on purpose?'

I was so stunned, partly by the question and partly because I'd never heard Darryn say anything in a serious voice before, that my hands stayed where they were, gripped around my rolled-up notice.

We looked at each other for a moment, then Darryn nodded slowly. 'Good one,' he said, and winked.

People generally don't like being winked at by Darryn Peck. I've seen teachers fly into a rage and send him out to stand on the oval. But as I turned away and walked on, heart thumping, Darryn and his mates chortling behind me about how funny Mr Fowler had looked with pineapple on his head, I realised I was feeling better than I had all morning.

I almost went back and told Darryn about Mr Fowler wiping his hands on his blotter, but I resisted the temptation and hurried on into town.

It was just as well I did, because when I arrived at the newsagents my name was already mud.

Two elderly women I didn't even know glared at me across the top of their wedding magazines and muttered things to each other.

When I'd finished the photocopying, I gave them a notice each and hurried out.

The main street's always busy on a Saturday morning, but today there were even more people than usual. I crept along sticking notices on power poles and rubbish bins and hoped they hadn't come to get their hands on me.

A lot of them seemed to be staring at me. I kept my eyes on the ground except when I had to reach up with the sticky tape.

Which is why I didn't see the queue until I almost walked into it.

The queue that stretched out of the dry-cleaners and along the front of the cake shop next door.

I looked down again and hoped desperately that Mr Shapiro the dry-cleaner had started selling concert tickets to make ends meet, and that the people were queueing to buy tickets for next weekend's Carla Tamworth concert.

Then I remembered that the concert is part of the Agricultural Show, so it's free.

I looked up and saw that every person in the queue was holding a dress or a suit or a skirt and blouse, each one streaked and spotted with jelly and custard stains.

I hoped Mr Shapiro's dry-cleaning machines were in good running order.

People in the queue were starting to look at me and mutter to each other.

I could feel my face going red and the knot in my guts growing back to the size of Ayers Rock including the car park and the kiosk.

I'd have given anything at that moment to be able to speak with my mouth.

Money.

Jewels.

My softball bat and the blue satin dress Dad bought me to wear at the wedding.

Anything.

Just for two minutes so I could read my apology out in a loud clear voice and everyone could see that I meant it.

I squeezed the thought out of my head and took a deep breath and walked along the queue to where I am now, in front of Mr Shapiro's window, sticking up a notice.

It's taking me ages because my heart is pounding so hard I can hardly get the sticky tape off the roll.

I'm trying to ignore everyone behind me.

I'm having this talk in my head to try and take my mind off them.

It's no good, I can feel their stares boring into the back of my neck like enraged codling moths.

People in our town hate queueing at the best of times.

I'm terrified someone'll start shouting or jostling.

I reckon that's all it'll take to turn that queue into a furious, surging mob that'll grab me and rub my

nose in all those stains and cover me with custard
and chook feathers and parade me round town in the
back of a ute.

Oh no.

Someone's started shouting.

I braced myself against Mr Shapiro's window, hoping desperately that there were lots of officers on duty in the police station, and that they weren't watching the cricket with the sound turned up.

Then I realised it was Amanda doing the shouting.

She was calling to me from the doorway of her dad's menswear shop across the street.

'Ro,' she yelled, 'over here.'

I sprinted across the road and into the shop and crouched trembling behind a rack of trousers, hoping the people in the queue wouldn't follow. Or that if they did, they'd see all the neat piles of shirts and socks in Mr Cosgrove's shop and decide that having a riot would mean too much tidying up afterwards.

'Sorry to yell like that,' said Amanda. 'I'm serving, so I can't leave the shop.'

Then she noticed I was shaking like the mudguard on a tractor.

'What's wrong?' she asked, concerned. My hands were trembling too much to say anything so I just gave her one of the notices.

While she read it I glanced around the shop. There was only one customer and he seemed to be too busy looking at jackets to form a mob.

Mr Cosgrove was busy too, straightening each jacket on the rack after the customer had touched it.

I took some deep breaths and tried to calm down.

Mr Cosgrove turned with a smile.

'Can I help you?' he asked.

Then he saw it was me and his smile vanished.

He hurried over and steered me away from the rack of trousers.

I tried to show him that it was OK, I wasn't carrying any desserts, trifles or squishy cakes, but he wasn't paying attention.

He was glaring at Amanda.

'Outside,' he muttered to her, gesturing at me.

'Dad,' said Amanda indignantly, 'Ro's my friend.'

Amanda's getting really good at standing up to her father.

I was still feeling wobbly, so I leant against a colonial table with some polished horseshoes and a pile of neatly-folded shirts on it.

Mr Cosgrove snatched the shirts away.

'Dad,' said Amanda, even more indignant, 'last night was an accident. D'you think Ro threw that jelly on purpose?'

She gave me an apologetic grin.

I didn't want to say anything, but my hands wouldn't stay still. They've always told Amanda the truth and they weren't going to stop today.

'I did throw it on purpose,' I said.

Amanda stared at my hands, so I said it again.

She looked stunned.

But only for a moment.

She probably didn't mean to do it, but she glanced around the shop at all the neat new clothes. Then she grabbed my arm and dragged me out of the shop and into the milk bar next door.

I didn't blame her.

Even best friends can't put their dad's stock at risk in a recession.

She ordered us both milkshakes, and by the time she'd asked why I'd done it and I'd told her I didn't know and she'd screwed up her face and thought about that, they were ready.

The tables were all full, but as we went over everyone stared nervously at the double strawberry malted in my hand and suddenly there was a clatter of chairs and an empty table in front of us.

We sat down.

The people at the next table shifted too.

I gave them one of my notices as they went.

The people at the other tables watched me out of the corner of their eyes and muttered to each other.

We slurped for a while and I wondered gloomily if it'll take me as long to get used to the sound of muttering as it takes people who live near the railway to get used to the sound of trains.

Then Amanda's face lit up.

'The dribble,' she said with her hands.

I stared at her blankly.

'Last night,' she continued. 'You were upset about the dribble.'

I didn't want to hurt her feelings, so I chose my words carefully. I told her it was really thoughtful of her to use her hands so the other people in the milkbar couldn't eavesdrop, but that unfortunately I didn't know what she was talking about either.

She shook her curls, cross with herself, and tried again.

'The speech,' she said. 'You were upset about the speech.'

Even before her hands stopped moving I knew that was it.

Last night, before the party, the Social Committee changed their minds about me reading our speech to Ms Dunning. They reckoned if I read it with my hands and Amanda repeated it by mouth it'd take too long.

I was really hurt and disappointed, but I had an apple fritter and got over it.

As least, I thought I did.

Obviously deep inside I didn't.

Deep inside I must have wanted to push the whole Social Committee into an apple-polishing machine, but because an apple-polishing machine was too heavy to take to the party, I chucked the Jelly Custard Surprise into the fan instead.

It's scary, but at least now I know, which is a big relief.

'You're right,' I said to Amanda. 'That's it. Thanks.'

'It must be pretty frustrating sometimes, having bits missing from your throat,' said Amanda.

I nodded.

I wanted to hug her, but she was still slurping and I knew that if I made another mess my name would be mud in this town for centuries.

I should have guessed Amanda would come up with the answer. She's an expert at working out why people do things. When I'd nominated Ms Dunning as Australian Of The Year, Amanda had twigged straight off. 'It's to put her at her ease, isn't it,' she'd said. 'Show her you don't mind her marrying your dad.' Amazing. I hadn't even given her a hint.

And now, even more amazingly, she'd worked out something I didn't even know myself.

I gave her a grateful grin and we sat there slurping. Until an awful thought hit me.

'I've been frustrated heaps of times,' I said to Amanda, 'but I've never chucked a dessert before.'

We looked at each other and I could tell from her face that she was thinking what I was thinking.

What if something's snapped in my brain?

What if I could chuck something at any time?

Without knowing in advance?

I'll never dare do the eggs again.

Or carry out a chemistry experiment in class.

Or handle nonwashable paint.

My life will be a disaster.

I could be sent back to a special school.

Suddenly I knew what I had to do.

Amanda agreed.

We said oo-roo and I hit the road.

I've never walked home from town so fast, but you can't hang about when you're in desperate need of help and there's only one person who can give it to you.

The person who was told last year that if he didn't start controlling himself and staying out of fights he'd be in deep poo and who's managed it so well this year that he hasn't had a single major outburst apart from putting peanut butter in Trent Webster's ears which doesn't count because Trent provoked him.

I can hardly believe I'm doing this.

Asking Darryn Peck for help.

I knew exactly where to find him.

In the creek at the back of our orchard.

He always goes there with his mates and I knew that's where he was heading when I bumped into him this morning.

On the way I rehearsed what I'd say.

'Darryn,' I imagined writing on my notepad, 'you're a pretty unstable person but you've stayed out of trouble pretty well this year. Any tips?'

I imagined his sneer.

'Why don't you ask your old man,' I imagined him saying. 'He's more unstable than me and he hasn't been in a single fight or embarrassing incident for ages. Earbash him.'

'Don't be a thicko,' I imagined myself writing with a patient smile, 'Dad's stable cause he married Ms Dunning. I'm too young to marry a teacher. I need to know how you do it. Come on, Darryn. You can borrow my softball bat.'

As I got to the creek I decided that last bit sounded too desperate so I mentally rubbed it out.

Darryn wasn't there.

I hunted all through the bush on both sides of the creek in case he was being a comedian and hiding, but he wasn't.

Then it hit me.

He must have gone home while I was in town.

I needed a drink before I set off on the long walk to Darryn's place, and there was no way I was drinking from the creek, not after it had been touching Darryn Peck's rude bits, so I took the track that runs round the edge of the orchard and ends up at our place.

Just as well I did, because halfway along it I heard Darryn's voice, shouting something angry that I couldn't make out.

I turned a corner and there were Darryn and his two mates, standing at the base of a big tree, chucking apples up at one of the top branches.

'Don't just sit there, dummy,' Darryn yelled at something on the branch, and hurled another apple. His face was almost as red as his lips, and his voice had gone squeaky.

'Dork-brain,' one of his mates yelled up at the tree.

Then they just grunted for a bit while they concentrated on throwing apples.

I went closer to see what they were aiming at.

It was the cockatoo.

It was just sitting on the branch, not moving, with apples crashing into the leaves around it.

I couldn't understand why it didn't dive down

and rip a beakful of hair out of Darryn Peck's head. That's what I'd have done. Or at least fly away to safety.

Then I realised the poor thing must be in shock.

Little wonder.

One minute you're out for a Saturday morning walk with your owner, next minute he's having a major outburst, his first of the year, and he's chucking apples at you.

So much for Darryn Peck the self-control expert.

The cockatoo looked terrified.

I wanted to scream at Darryn and his mates to pack it in, but of course I can only do that sort of thing in my head, so I ran over to Darryn and knocked the apple he was about to throw out of his hand.

He spun round, startled.

I glared at him.

His red lips went into smirk position.

'Batts,' he said. 'Oooh, I'm scared. Don't hit me with a jelly, Batts.'

I thought for a sec of hitting him with a large rock, but then I remembered the terrified bird.

I gave Darryn a look which told him to go and boil his head in a pressure cooker full of root weevils.

He didn't seem to get the message.

'Mind your own business,' he sneered. 'That cocky's my property and I'll do what I like with it.'

'He's had it for six years,' said one of his mates.

'That's right,' said Darryn and threw another apple at the cockatoo.

I pointed to the broken apples all around us on the ground.

'Those are my property,' I said, speaking on behalf of the Batts family.

Darryn stared at me blankly.

I remembered he didn't understand sign.

I pulled out my notepad.

I've learned that notes work best when they're short.

'Apple theft,' I wrote. 'Five years jail.'

It's not true, of course, but I could see it got him worried.

We stared at each other for a while.

His elephant's-bum mouth started quivering at one corner, just a bit.

Then he turned and stalked off down the road.

His mates hurried after him.

'You leaving the cocky with her?' one of them asked.

'She can keep it,' Darryn said, looking back at me. 'They should get on well together. They're both spazzos.'

I ignored that.

I had more important things to think about.

I started climbing the tree.

It took me ages to get up there, partly because Dad's taught me never to rush at a tree, and partly because I'm scared of heights.

As I edged along the branch, my heart was pounding so loudly I was worried the cockatoo would take fright and do something silly.

It didn't look as though it was up to much flying. It looked as though the most it could 'probably manage would be a plummet to the ground.

I tried to calm it by explaining with gentle hand movements that not all humans are like Darryn Peck, only the ones who got too close to Mrs Peck's vacuum cleaner when they were babies and had their brains sucked out through their ears.

OK, it wasn't true, and the cocky probably couldn't understand sign language anyway, but it still seemed to make it perk up a bit.

Its crest feathers, which had been lying flat on its head in a sort of cowlick, suddenly sprang up like a bright yellow mohawk hairdo.

When I'd stopped being startled and almost falling out of the tree, I leant forward and unhooked its claws from the bark as gently as I could and lifted it towards me.

Its feathers felt stiff, which I assumed was nervous tension, and I could see its dark little tongue darting around inside its beak, probably because its mouth was dry with worry.

It seemed pretty dazed, probably from seeing all those apples being wasted, and it didn't flap its wings, which was just as well for both of us.

I put it inside my shirt and climbed down, praying that it was feeling too crook to sink its beak into my flesh.

It must have been.

As I hurried towards the house, I racked my brains for anything I'd ever read or heard about helping cockatoos recover from a traumatic experience.

Nothing sprang to mind.

I could feel the cocky quivering inside my shirt.

I didn't blame it.

Living with Darryn Peck for six years would be enough to give anyone a nervous condition.

When people are in shock they're given a cup of tea, so when we got home I gave the cocky one.

It wasn't interested, so I gave it a glass of water.

It drank some of that, then tried to eat the glass.

Obviously it was hungry.

There was a note on the kitchen table saying that Dad and Ms Dunning had gone shopping, so I had to take a punt myself as to what cockies like to eat.

It wasn't a very good punt.

The cocky ignored the corned beef, sniffed the cheese, spat out the Coco-Pops and did a poo on the apple fritter.

Then it closed its eyes.

I realised the poor thing must be exhausted.

I grabbed an apple box and made a bed in it with some towels from the bathroom and carefully laid the cocky inside.

That wasn't such a good move either.

I could tell the cocky wasn't comfortable by the way it scrabbled its claws and looked at me unhappily with its dark eyes and did a wee on my towel.

I remembered that some birds like to sleep on a perch.

It was worth a try.

I took all the clothes on hangers out of my wardrobe and pulled the top shelf out to make some headroom and lifted the cocky onto the hanging rail.

No sooner had it gripped the wood with its claws than its eyes closed and its head dropped and I was sure I could hear faint snoring.

It's been like that for hours.

I've been sitting here on my bed watching it in case it has a nightmare about apples.

I've also been working out how I'm going to break it to Dad and Ms Dunning that we've got a new addition to the family.

Sometimes good luck comes along exactly when you need it.

Like this arvo.

Dad and Ms Dunning came back with heaps of shopping, not just supermarket stuff but loads of parcels and boxes too.

While I was helping them carry it all in from the truck, I saw them looking at each other sort of sheepishly.

'Um, Tonto old mate,' said Dad, 'we haven't actually got anything for you.'

It was perfect.

There's nothing like parents feeling a bit sheepish to help things along when you're asking if you can have a cockatoo.

Dad and Ms Dunning were a bit alarmed at first, probably because they thought I was talking about buying a new one and they'd just spent all their money.

But when I showed them the one dozing in my wardrobe, and explained it was an abused bird that

I'd rescued from a dangerously unstable kid, they relaxed.

I told them that if the cocky could live with us I'd feed it and care for it and teach it to use the bathroom.

'Please, please, please, please, please,' I said until my hands ached.

I saw from Dad's face that he wanted to have a serious talk. Not with me, with Ms Dunning. I almost went and got his black shirt with the horse-shoes but decided not to.

I stayed in here on my bed while Dad and Ms Dunning went into the kitchen.

I crossed my fingers so tightly they went numb.

After what seemed like ages, Dad and Ms Dunning came back in. They had their arms round each other, which I knew was a good sign.

'Well Tonto,' said Dad, 'if you promise to feed it and clean it, you can keep it. I'll build it a cage in the packing shed.'

I gave them both a huge hug.

'There's one more condition,' added Dad. 'Darryn Peck's got to agree you can have it.'

I told them I was sure Darryn would agree because it's doing him a favour too.

This way he won't ever get into trouble with the law for mistreating a bird and possibly end up in a bloody shoot-out with officers from the RSPCA.

Ms Dunning held out a big shiny red apple.

'It'll probably be hungry when it wakes up,' she said.

I was really moved because it was exactly the same as the one I gave her the day she moved in with us.

Watching the cocky happily snoozing away I can see it's already feeling like one of the family.

Judging by the snores, though, I don't think it'll be waking up till the morning.

A big sleep's probably just what the poor thing needs.

In the morning I'll cut its apple up and we can have breakfast together on the verandah.

I'm feeling really attached to it already.

Almost like a parent.

Which is fine with me because in my experience parents hardly ever snap and even when they do they hardly ever chuck desserts, eggs, chemicals or nonwashable paint.

I knew something was wrong as soon as I woke up.

Dad was shouting.

Ms Dunning was yelling.

I could smell fish frying and nobody at our place likes fried fish.

I jumped out of bed and hurried towards the kitchen.

Something stabbed me in the feet.

I looked down and saw that my carpet was covered with lumps of apple and splinters of wood.

My floor looked like Tasmania, the bit that's been woodchipped.

The kitchen looked worse.

Apart from the woodchips all over the floor and the table and the sink, it was full of smoke.

Dad and Ms Dunning were standing on chairs holding brooms. Dad was shouting at Ms Dunning to get down because she shouldn't be climbing on chairs in her condition, and Ms Dunning was ignoring him and poking her broom up the chimney.

A cloud of soot floated down into her face, followed by a white feather.

My heart was thumping.

'Get down here, dork-brain,' Ms Dunning yelled up the chimney, 'or you're dead meat.'

I was shocked.

That's no way to talk to a cockatoo with a nervous condition.

I reminded myself that it wasn't Ms Dunning's fault, she's just been spending too much time with Darryn Peck and his mates.

Then I squeezed myself into the fireplace and climbed up onto the big log we keep there in summer and lifted both my hands up into the blackness.

I touched feathers.

I wondered if a cockatoo can recognise friendly hands in pitch darkness when it's got other things on its mind, like being called a dork-brain.

My fingers all stayed connected to my hands, so obviously it can.

Gently I lifted the cocky down.

In the darkness I could see a gleaming eye watching me.

As I wriggled out of the fireplace with the cocky clasped to my chest, Dad and Ms Dunning advanced towards me.

Their eyes were gleaming too.

'That bird's a flaming menace,' said Dad. He said it with his mouth, partly because he always speaks with his mouth when he's angry, and partly because his hands were full of bits of splintered wood.

160

'Look what it did to Claire's hand-carved salad bowl.'

I glanced down at the cocky's curved black beak. It looked strong, but not that strong.

'And the vicious cheese-brain had a go at my buckle,' continued Dad.

I looked at his belt and suddenly I felt the cocky's head feathers tickling me under the chin. I wasn't sure if that was because it had just gone mohawk or because my mouth had just fallen open.

The metal buckle looked as if it had been attacked with pliers. The Harley Davidson had a bent wheel and the skeleton riding it was completely missing a ribcage.

I looked at the cocky's beak again. Perhaps its mother had swallowed a lump of tungsten steel thinking it was a gumnut.

'And,' said Ms Dunning, 'it had a go at the kitchen table and the dresser and snatched the washing-up sponge out of my hand and nearly caused a fire.'

She pointed to the sink, where a charred sponge was floating in the frying pan.

It hadn't been fish after all.

'Just give me a few moments alone with it,' I said.

Dad and Ms Dunning looked confused. Perhaps they thought I meant the sponge. It's not easy expressing yourself clearly when you've got your hands full of sooty cockatoo.

I retreated into my room and put the cocky onto what was left of the hanging rail.

We both looked at the large jagged hole in the side of my wardrobe.

'It's OK,' I said, moving my hands slowly. 'Don't feel bad. You just panicked. That's normal, waking up in a strange place.'

I could tell from its blank expression and the big poo it did on my best shoes that it didn't have a clue what I was saying.

I wrote it a note.

It was worth a try. Cockies are very smart. I've seen them on telly pedalling little bikes and drawing raffles.

It ate the note.

There are times when it's a real pain not being able to speak. You want to scream with frustration, except of course you can't. So you make do with what you've got.

I put my face close to the cocky's and gave it a look.

'Don't be scared, you poor little thing,' the look said. 'I want to help you.'

'Rack off,' said the cocky.

I couldn't believe it.

Then I realised I must have misheard.

I was making the cocky feel nervous by being too close, that was all, and it had asked me to back off.

I moved my face back a bit.

'Get lost, dork-brain,' said the cocky. 'You smell. Go and fall off a rock.'

I was shocked.

But I tried to be understanding.

I gave the cockatoo another look.

'Don't be cross,' my look said, 'everything's going to be fine.'

'Get stuffed,' said the cocky.

I changed the look to 'I'm your friend'.

'Go kiss a chook,' said the cocky.

My face was aching, but I had one more go.

I gave it my best 'I'm going to look after you' expression.

'Suck a turnip,' said the cocky, and bit me on the nose.

After Dad had bathed the wound and put some antiseptic cream and a band-aid on it and the pain had died down, we got a metal bucket and put the cocky inside and fixed some strong chook-wire over the top.

Dad offered to drive it to Darryn Peck's, but I said I'd take it by foot. I could tell Dad was itching to get at Ms Dunning's salad bowl with the glue.

We're almost there, which is a relief.

It's not much fun walking with a bird in a bucket who keeps telling you to bite your bum.

It's a real shame because if it had a different personality we could have been really close.

As it is I'll be pleased to see the back of it.

The last thing I want in my life at the moment is an angry cockatoo.

There's a Carla Tamworth song called 'Compost Heap In My Heart' about a keen gardener whose sweetheart leaves her for a stock and station agent. Totally and completely grief-stricken, she goes out into the back yard and starts pulling his old cabbage stalks out of the compost heap. It's all she's got left of him. Then, deep in the compost, she finds a hose nozzle and remembers she hasn't washed the car for weeks.

That happened to me today.

I don't mean I found a hose nozzle in a compost heap.

I mean I started out doing one thing and ended up doing something else.

I started out taking a cocky with crook manners back to Darryn Peck and ended up nearly committing murder.

And now I feel sick in the guts.

Perhaps I'll feel better if I stop thinking about it.

That's what the keen gardener does. She stops

thinking about her sweetheart and concentrates on cleaning the car and feels much better. Specially when her sweetheart comes round to get his hose nozzle and slips on the wet driveway and breaks his pelvis.

Darryn Peck deserves to break his pelvis.

Well, get a cramp in it anyway.

The way he's treated this cocky is a disgrace.

Six years they've been together and when I arrived at his place he wouldn't even say hello to it.

'I don't want it,' he said. 'It's yours. It was a fair swap. I don't care if the apples weren't ripe.'

I could tell the cocky was hurt. When Darryn opened the front door it had put its crest feathers into the mohawk position so they stuck up through the mesh over the bucket. Now it slowly slid them back into the cowlick position.

I got out my notebook and pointed out to Darryn that a cockatoo is a living creature with feelings, even if it does have a violent nature and a mouth like a sewer pipe.

Darryn stared at the note, confused.

'What,' he said, 'you mean it's got bad breath?'

I wrote Darryn another note mentioning some of the things the cocky had been doing and saying.

He read it and I could tell he was genuinely surprised because his eyes went big and round, and Darryn's one of those people who thinks it's cooler to keep your eyes half closed all the time.

'Don't lie,' he said. 'Sticky Beak can't talk.

Sticky's never said a word, not even when I ran the electric current from the front door bell through his feet. He's a brainless dummy.'

The cocky looked up at him with moist eyes.

I took a deep breath and scribbled furiously on my pad.

'Perhaps if you weren't so cruel,' I wrote, 'he'd want to talk to you.'

'Bull,' said Darryn. 'Sticky's a dummy and a no-hoper. I've got a much better pet now. That's why I was setting feather-brain here free yesterday. Till you stuck your nose in.'

Darryn was lucky there wasn't a Jelly Custard Surprise nearby.

I stared at him in disgust.

No wonder Sticky Beak was so upset this morning.

This loyal loving pet had been dumped in the bush just because his fickle selfish owner had got some flashy buzzard or eagle or something.

Darryn must have seen my disgust because he started making excuses.

'I was returning him to his natural whatdyacallit,' said Darryn, 'habitat. Giving him his freedom. And if you think you can dump him back on me you can go fall off a rock.'

I wondered what sort of a jail sentence I'd get for giving a heartless monster a whack round the head with a metal bucket. Then I remembered the bucket had a cockatoo in it who'd already suffered more than enough.

I made do with a note.

'I'm not dumping him back on you,' I wrote.

I meant it. There was no way I was going to leave Sticky Beak at the mercy of heartless Darryn The Torturer Peck.

'I just came to find out what he eats,' I wrote. Lying doesn't count when it's to an inhuman fiend.

'Stay here,' said Darryn and went into the house.

There was an explosion of high-pitched barking and for a horrible moment I thought I was stuck with a cockatoo that ate dogs.

Then Darryn came back with a pinky-brown poodle yapping round his feet and handed me a plastic bucket full of striped seeds.

'Normally I'd charge you ten bucks for this,' he said, 'but you can have it for free if you rack off and never come back.'

I took the bucket.

Darryn picked up the poodle and I picked up Sticky Beak's bucket and walked away.

I could hear Darryn talking to the poodle, and the poodle replying in a sort of high-pitched growl.

'If you want a pet that can really talk,' Darryn shouted after me, 'get a poodle.'

That's when I started feeling sick in the guts.

I only just managed to stop myself from going back and making Darryn swallow all the birdseed. While it was still in the bucket.

I've been boiling inside ever since, and I'm nearly home.

I think that's just about the worst thing in the

whole world that one living creature can do to another.

Give it the flick just cause a replacement comes along that can talk better.

As I walked up our orchard road I tried to ignore the pain from the two buckets nearly dragging my arms off.

I had to think what to do.

I thought about telling Dad and Ms Dunning what sort of a life Sticky had had with Darryn Peck in the hope that they'd understand.

'We understand,' said Dad in my head, ruffling Sticky's crest feathers understandingly.

'We'd probably chew up salad bowls too,' said Ms Dunning in my head, 'if someone connected our feet to a front door bell.'

But what if they didn't say that?

What if they said, 'Get that vicious cheese-brain out of this house immediately'?

A bird could be killed stone dead by the shock and hurt of being rejected and abandoned twice in one weekend.

And even if Sticky survived, what if Dad took him over to the RSPCA depot with a note saying 'never to be released' and the poor thing ended up in some institution?

I knew what that'd be like.

I was in an institution for five years, and even though mine was a pretty good special school, I still spent a lot of nights crying.

I couldn't risk it.

So I didn't take Sticky Beak to see Dad and Ms Dunning, I took him to the old shed.

I reckoned it was a pretty safe alternative because Dad never uses the old shed. He reckons it's too far from the house.

Which it is if you've got to walk back from it after a hard day in the orchard, but it's not if you're looking for somewhere to hide a cockatoo with a loud voice and a sour view of the world.

The walls of the old shed are thicker than the walls of my wardrobe, but I couldn't afford to take any risks.

I had to think beak-proof.

I crept to the packing shed where Dad keeps his tools and junk and peeked inside.

Dad wasn't there.

As quietly as I could I borrowed his wire cutters and a roll of tying wire.

Behind the cool room were some sheets of metal from when the cool room was built and some rolls of thick chook wire from when the previous people kept chooks.

I had to be quiet dragging them over, but once I got them into the old shed I could make as much noise as I liked.

I've never built a cage before.

There must be some method of getting all the sides to stand exactly upright, but I couldn't crack it.

Still, I reckon what I've done'll do the trick.

I used the metal stakes Dad ties young trees to for the corners, and about a kilometre of tying wire, so it's pretty sturdy, and it's big enough for Sticky to fly around in as long as he doesn't try to get up too much speed.

And from the outside of the old shed you wouldn't even know it's there.

Sticky likes it.

Once I'd wired a branch across a corner for a perch he was onto it quicker than a little kid onto monkey bars.

I found some old metal dishes for his water and seed, and then gave him several meaningful looks.

In order they said:

'Don't be frightened.'

'We can go on outings.'

'This is just until Dad and Ms Dunning calm down about the wood chips.'

'Be good.'

Sticky went from mohawk to cowlick, so I could tell he understood.

I wired the last piece of chook wire into place and gave Sticky Beak a 'see you later' wave.

'Jump off a rock,' said Sticky, which I'm beginning to think is just his way of saying thanks.

I shut the door of the old shed and came over here to the packing shed to put the wire cutters back.

I've been standing here ever since having this conversation in my head.

I hated leaving Sticky there so I guess I'm trying to convince myself that I'm doing the right thing.

Well it's a bit late now cause I've done it.

What's that noise?

It's someone coming over from the house.

It's Dad.

Oh no, I'm still holding the wire cutters.

Too late.

He's seen me.

I'm lying here listening to a Carla Tamworth tape on my Walkman trying not to think about what's just happened.

It's not working.

The songs keep reminding me.

First there was the one about the heart that's aching so much that even two aspirin and a eucalyptus menthol oil rub can't take away the pain.

I spooled through that one.

Then there was the one about the woman who wants to cry but can't, not even when she goes to work in a sandwich bar making salad rolls with lots of onion.

I spooled through that one too.

And now, the final straw, I'm listening to one about a bloke who can't see things even when they're staring him in the face.

Not his clean socks or the crack in his bathroom mirror or his dentist who's secretly in love with him.

Me and Dad are like that bloke.

I don't mean because our dentist is secretly in love with us. The only thing our dentist Mr Webster loves is collecting rocks and that's no secret because he has the magazines in his waiting room.

I mean because me and Dad can't see things when they're staring us in the face either.

With Dad it's little things like not noticing I was holding the wire cutters when he walked into the packing shed this arvo.

'G'day Tonto,' he said, 'we've been wondering where you'd got to. There's something we'd like you to take a squiz at.'

For a horrible moment I was sure they'd found Sticky.

Ayers Rock dropped with a thud into my lower gut.

Then Dad grinned and said, 'Come on, race you back to the house', and I knew they hadn't.

He turned and started sprinting and I put the wire cutters back before starting off after him.

As I caught up to him I noticed he had blue paint in his hair.

Inside the house he made me close my eyes and then led me into the junk room.

Or what used to be the junk room.

When I opened my eyes Dad and Ms Dunning were standing there grinning like game-show hosts.

Ms Dunning had pink paint in her hair.

I could see why.

The entire room was pink.

Except for a blue ceiling and a blue light switch.

And it was full of stuff.

Not the old wellies and tractor parts and fishing rods and eskies and record players and camping gear and apple boxes that used to be there.

New stuff.

A cot decorated with sleepy bunnies and a change table with bashful koalas on it and a quilt covered with playful dolphins and curtains crawling with very friendly possums and a light shade infested with happy-go-lucky goannas.

'What do you reckon?' grinned Dad.

'We hope you approve of your new brother or sister's accommodation,' grinned Ms Dunning.

I tried to grin too, but I guess it wasn't very convincing.

Ms Dunning came over and put her arm round me.

'Ro,' she said quietly, 'we know you're disappointed about your pet, but we've got to be realistic.'

'That's right, Tonto,' said Dad gently. 'We can't have a kamikaze cocky in the same house as a bub, eh?'

'That's not what I'm disappointed about,' I replied. 'I thought the baby was going to sleep in my room.'

That had been the plan. We'd talked about it, me and Dad. It had been my idea, so that if the baby woke up in the night between feeds I could rock it back to sleep or keep it amused with hand-shadows on the wall. I can do a great shark.

'It was a really kind offer, love,' said Ms Dunning, 'but we've decided it'll be better off in the room next to us.'

'Claire's right,' said Dad. 'Better to have it where we can hear it yelling its little lungs out, eh?'

That's when it hit me.

The real reason I threw the Jelly Custard Surprise.

How come I didn't see it before?

It's been staring me in the face for months.

Well, hours, anyway, since I left Darryn Peck's.

The shock of finally seeing it made my heart go like a spray pump, and the smell of the paint started to make me feel like throwing up, so I came in here for a lie-down.

Usually if I want to blot something out of my mind the Walkman works really well.

Not tonight.

Even when I turn it up really loud and close my eyes really tight I can still see Darryn standing on his verandah holding the poodle, grinning like a loon because it can talk.

And Dad standing next to him doing exactly the same.

Except Dad isn't holding a poodle, he's holding a baby.

Dad always reckons if something's making me unhappy I should tell him about it.

He reckons it's better for a person to lay it out on the table than bottle it up and end up hiring a skywriter or something.

So first thing this morning I went out to the orchard and told him.

I was really glad I did.

At first.

'G'day Tonto,' Dad said, 'you come for a yak?'

I nodded.

I like yakking to Dad when he's on the tractor because he has to speak with his hands. Dad's got a pretty loud voice but it isn't a match for a 120-horsepower diesel.

I jumped up onto the front of the tractor so Dad could keep on slashing weeds while we talked.

'About last night,' Dad said. 'Don't worry, love, you'll get to spend heaps of time with the bub.'

'I know I will,' I said.

I took a deep breath.

My hands were shaking.

I hoped Dad would think it was the vibrations from the motor.

'I'm just worried,' I said, 'that when you've got a kid that can speak with its mouth, you won't want to spend heaps of time flapping your hands about with me.'

I tried to keep my hands relaxed while I said it. If you're not careful, when you're very tense you can get cramp in the middle of a sentence.

Dad stared at me for a long time.

The tractor started to shudder.

'Dad,' I said, 'you're slashing a tree trunk.'

He turned the tractor off, leant forward, grabbed me under the arms and swung me onto his lap.

It felt good, even though his belt buckle was stabbing me in the kidney.

'Ro,' he said quietly, 'that's dopey.'

Then he slid me onto the seat next to him and jumped up onto the engine cover and took his hat off and put one hand over his heart and tilted his head back and yelled up at the trees.

'I swear on my Grannies and Jonathans,' he shouted, 'that no kid will ever come between me and my precious Tonto, cross my heart and hope to get root weevil.'

I glowed inside.

I would have glowed even more if he'd looked at me and said it quietly, but with Dad you have to take him the way he is.

He jumped down from the engine and I slid down

from the seat and he picked me up and hugged me so tight that his belt buckle left an imprint on my tummy.

I glowed even more and Ayers Rock suddenly melted away and all that was left was a wonderful feeling that everything was going to be OK for ever and ever.

It lasted for about ten seconds.

Less time than the red back-to-front rodeo rider above my bellybutton.

Because I ruined it.

I've never known when to keep my hands quiet.

'For a moment there,' I said to Dad, 'I thought you were going to sing.'

Dad grinned.

'Almost did,' he said, 'but I couldn't think of a song that said exactly what I wanted to say.'

'Never mind,' I said, 'perhaps Carla Tamworth'll sing one at the concert on Saturday.'

Dad's face clouded.

'I've been meaning to tell you,' he said, 'I can't go to the concert on Saturday.'

I stared at him.

'Sorry Tonto,' he said. 'Not with the baby due on Sunday. Too much to do. You do understand, eh?'

I nodded.

I couldn't move my face, only my neck.

'Good on you,' said Dad. 'You can go with Amanda, eh?'

I nodded again.

'Run off and have your breakfast then, love,' he said, and fired up the tractor.

I walked away.

At that moment I couldn't have forced food down myself with a crowbar, but I knew Sticky Beak would be hungry.

When I got over here to the old shed and opened the door, Sticky blinked at me from inside his cage.

He looked as stunned as I felt.

Perhaps cockies have got super-sensitive hearing and he couldn't believe what he'd just heard.

A man who once drove six hours to get to a Carla Tamworth concert saying he can't be bothered taking his daughter to one six minutes away.

I wonder if cockies know about child neglect?

I shouldn't be talking like this, not even in my head.

Dad's just doing what any normal person would do in his position. Concentrating on the birth of his new baby. All fathers get a bit sidetracked when they've got a new kid on the way. Specially when it's one that doesn't have anything wrong with it.

What's so bad about that?

Nothing, and I shouldn't be blubbing like this, it's stupid.

I can see Sticky thinks so too.

I'm making his seed all wet.

He's just told me to fall off a rock.

I think he's trying to cheer me up.

Poor Sticky, he's the one who should be crying, not me. Stuck in here all by himself trying to recover from a nervous condition brought on by six years of inhuman treatment by a monster.

Darryn The Heartless Peck's the one who should be punished, not Dad.

I'm so excited.

All Sticky's problems are solved.

Well, they will be soon.

Once Amanda gets written permission to use her parents' video camera.

What's more, if my plan works, no Australian cockatoo or budgie or dog or cat or hampster or mouse need ever suffer again what Sticky has suffered.

Going to school this morning I didn't have a clue that this was going to be such an important day in the history of pet care.

For starters, I'd completely forgotten we've got a new teacher. I only remembered when Ms Dunning stopped the truck in front of the school gates and handed me a jar of home-made apple sauce.

'For your new teacher,' she said.

I groaned inside.

'Come on, Ro,' said Ms Dunning, 'a prezzie means a lot to us teachers on our first day.'

I couldn't believe it.

She's only been semi-retired for two days and

she's already forgotten that only crawlers and bad spellers give new teachers presents. That's why I wasn't carrying a plate of apple fritters.

I was about to remind her, but then I realised she must just be having a vague spell and I decided not to hurt her feelings. It can't be much fun, carrying a baby round inside you that uses up so much oxygen there's not enough left for your brain.

When I got out of the truck, all the kids that had crowded round to wave at Ms Dunning backed away, all nervously eyeing the jar of apple sauce in my hand.

I walked through them, hoping they'd notice the jar had a lid on and that there wasn't a single hardware store fan in the playground.

They didn't.

I could only see one kid who looked relaxed.

Darryn Peck.

He was standing just inside the school gate, smirking at me.

'Careful Battsy,' he said, 'don't trip over.'

I walked past.

He started walking behind me.

I ignored him.

I knew he was going to try and trip me, and I knew I could handle it.

I was wrong.

What threw me was that he used his brain.

He waited till I was almost across the playground, then gave a screeching cry, like a cockatoo.

For a sec I thought it was Sticky, that he'd escaped

and was looking for me.

I glanced up and that's when Darryn stuck his foot out.

I felt myself falling forward and my only thought was not to let go of the jar.

Then I realised I already had.

Me and the jar flew through the air.

I slammed into the ground.

The jar smashed through Mr Fowler's office window.

After a while, when I'd worked out which sounds were glass breaking and which were my ears ringing, someone lifted me to my feet.

It was Amanda.

She was white with fury and screaming at Darryn Peck.

'You're dead meat, Peck,' she yelled. 'My uncle's a solicitor.'

Darryn Peck was looking pretty pale too, but that was because he could see Mr Fowler storming towards us.

Mr Fowler was angrier than any of us had ever seen him.

He was so angry that not one person laughed at the apple sauce on his head.

'What happened?' he thundered.

There was chaos as everyone tried to tell him something different.

I kept out of it because my knees had started to hurt a lot and I wanted to see if there was any blood coming through my jeans.

After a few seconds Mr Fowler sent everyone to their classrooms.

Amanda hovered, still furious, still shouting, until Mr Fowler threatened to expel her.

Then he took me into his office.

The next few minutes were pretty hard on my nerves, partly because Mr Fowler wouldn't let me speak, and partly because he kept pacing up and down on his glass-covered carpet and I was worried he'd cut himself.

It was dumb. There I was, the victim of a tele-movie-sized injustice, and I was more worried about whether one of the people responsible would slash a major artery in his foot and I'd have to knot his whistle cord round his leg to stop the blood flow.

'I don't know what happened out there,' said Mr Fowler, 'and I probably never will. So I'll be charitable and assume it was an accident. That's two, Batts, in four days. One accident is unlucky. Two is careless. If there's a third . . .'

He stopped and put his face close to mine.

Apple sauce dripped onto my shoe.

' . . if there's a third, watch out.'

He turned away and I pulled my notebook out to scribble a note asking for a lawyer and a broom to sweep up the broken glass.

Before I could start writing, there was a knock on the door and a bloke stepped into the office. He was wearing jeans and a multicoloured shirt and he had a ponytail.

Great, I thought, here am I in the middle of

a travesty of justice and some high-school kid who's off sick with brain damage wanders into the wrong school.

'This is Mr Segal,' said Mr Fowler, 'your new teacher. Take her away, Mr Segal, before I forget I'm a Rotarian.'

On the way to class Mr Segal made conversation.

I wasn't really in the mood because my knees were hurting and I wanted some time to myself to plan Darryn Peck's death, but I could see Mr Segal was trying hard so I joined in.

'So,' said Mr Segal, 'you're Rowena Batts.'

I nodded.

'Mr Fowler's told me all about you,' said Mr Segal.

I nodded again.

'Never feel inferior,' said Mr Segal.

I shook my head. I could see he meant well.

'Pictures,' said Mr Segal, 'are more important than words.'

He smiled.

I smiled.

I didn't have a clue what he was on about.

Then I realised he must have been talking about his shirt, which had pictures of fish all over it.

It wasn't till much later, in class, that I realised he was talking about television.

By that time Mr Segal had talked about television a lot. He told us he believes television isn't studied enough in schools. We clapped and whistled, partly because we agreed with him and partly because you have to see how far you can go with a new teacher.

When we'd finished he told us we were going to spend the last three weeks of the school year studying television.

We clapped and whistled some more.

'Starting with a project,' he said when the noise had died down. 'Tomorrow you start making your own TV programmes.'

We stared at him in stunned silence.

For a fleeting moment I thought that perhaps he was a brain-damaged high-school kid after all.

'Hands up,' said Mr Segal, 'whose parents have got a video camera.'

Then we understood.

About half the class put their hands up.

I didn't. We can't afford a video camera. Not with an apple-polishing machine and a luxury nursery to pay for. But I was relieved to see Amanda with her hand up.

Mr Segal explained the project.

We've got to split into groups and we've got one week to make any TV programme we like as long as it's not rude or offensive to minority groups.

After the bell went, me and Amanda agreed to keep our group small.

Just her and me.

Then I saw Megan O'Donnell wandering around not in a group. I hate seeing kids left out of things just cause they're slow readers so I looked at Amanda and Amanda nodded and opened her mouth to ask Megan to join our group. Before she could, though,

Megan was grabbed by Lucy and Raylene Shapiro who asked her to help them make a documentary about the human side of dry-cleaning.

It was for the best. Megan's a nice person but she can get pretty nervous and she wouldn't have been comfortable doing what I've got in mind.

'Shall we do a comedy or a drama?' asked Amanda.

I told her I was thinking about something different and wrote it out so she'd get all the details first time.

'Let's do,' I said, 'a fearless in-depth current affairs report exposing to the world Darryn Peck's heartless and brutal treatment of poor old Sticky.'

Amanda grinned and nodded.

'Great,' she said, 'it's just what he deserves. Who's Sticky?'

Sticky's really excited too.

I've just told him about the project.

I didn't tell him last night because I didn't want him to suffer the crushing disappointment if Amanda's parents said no about the video camera.

I needn't have worried.

Amanda came running into school this morning with a bag over her shoulder and a big grin on her face.

'I've got it,' she yelled.

Darryn Peck looked up from Trent Webster's video camera which he was trying to focus on a pimple on Doug Walsh's bottom.

'Hope it's not catching,' he smirked.

He and his mates fell about.

Me and Amanda just smiled quietly to each other.

We resisted the temptation to tell him that soon he won't have much to laugh about because we didn't want him running off to South America and hiding.

As it turned out, it wouldn't have mattered, because for the whole day we didn't even get to take the lens cap off the camera.

For a bloke who wears fish shirts, Mr Segal's a real stickler for paperwork.

First he insisted on seeing written permission from the parents of everyone who'd brought a camera in.

Then he wasted hours ringing up Trent Webster's parents. He thought Trent's note was forged just because 'camera' was spelt without an 'e'. If he'd asked us we could have explained that Trent's mum had to leave school when she was eleven to look after the goats.

Then Raylene Shapiro put her hand up and said that her dad was wondering if the school insurance would cover damage to his camera.

Mr Segal called Mr Fowler in and asked him.

He said he'd check.

I was adjusting Amanda's camera strap at the time, and when Mr Fowler saw me with a camera in my hand he went visibly pale.

Then, just when me and Amanda thought we could start shooting our in-depth report, Mr Segal announced that first we all had to write scripts.

We did that for the rest of the day.

It was a bit tricky because we didn't want Darryn Peck to know we were writing about him, so we used a code name.

Poodle.

Mr Segal thinks we're doing an in-depth report about dogs who are mean to cockatoos.

At least writing the script gave me something

to show Sticky when I got home. I don't think he'd ever seen a current affairs script before because he tried to eat it.

'Sticky,' I said, 'stop that. Don't you want to be a star and an object of pity who's allowed to sleep in my room again?'

I don't think he understood the hand movements because he just looked at me with his beak open.

I wished I had Amanda there to explain it to him by mouth.

Then I remembered what Mr Segal had said about pictures being more important than words. I pulled out my notepad and drew Sticky a picture of me playing the in-depth report to Dad and Ms Dunning on our video and them tearfully inviting Sticky to live with us in the house.

He stared at it for ages and I could see his eyes getting moister.

I drew him another picture, of Darryn Peck being arrested by RSPCA officers and sentenced to ten years hard labour cleaning out the dog pound.

Sticky put his head under his wing and seemed a bit upset, so I reduced Darryn's sentence to five years.

It was the third picture that got Sticky really excited. I did it on two pages, and it showed our report being broadcast on telly, and people all over Australia who were about to abandon or neglect cockatoos thinking again.

I put in a few people who were about to abandon or neglect other things as well.

Dogs and cats.

Hampsters.

Kids.

Those people were all thinking again too.

Dad was one of them.

'Bottom plops,' said Sticky.

Poor old Sticky, he finds it really hard to express his emotions.

I know that inside he was just as excited and moved as I was.

I never realised making in-depth current affairs programmes was so hard.

For starters there's focusing the camera properly and waiting for planes to fly over so they don't mess up the sound.

Then there's asking the reporter if she'd mind changing her orange and purple striped T-shirt for a blue one and taking off the green eye shadow.

And on top of all that there's waiting for Ms Dunning to go into town for her check-up and Dad to go over to slash weeds at the other side of the orchard so you can do the introduction in the old shed without being sprung.

No wonder it costs millions when the networks do it.

We didn't get started till nearly lunchtime.

'OK,' I said when the mail plane had finally disappeared and all we could hear was Dad murdering weeds in the distance, 'camera going, take one.'

Amanda stepped forward onto the spot I'd

marked on the floor in front of Sticky's cage.

'This poor mistreated bird,' she said in a loud clear voice, 'has suffered some of the crookest treatment you could imagine.'

'Pig's bum,' said Sticky.

Amanda collapsed into giggles.

'It's just his way of agreeing with you,' I said.

Amanda collapsed into more giggles.

Some reporters have no respect for their director.

'Camera going, take two,' I said.

'This poor neglected bird . . .' said Amanda.

'Andy's been sick in the fridge,' said Sticky.

Amanda laughed so hard she had to bite her clipboard.

I could see it wasn't going to be easy.

I calmed myself down by telling myself that every TV current affairs show has a few of these sort of problems on the first day.

An hour later I wasn't so sure.

'Take thirty-two,' I said, my hand aching.

'This poor neglected . . .' said Amanda.

'Turnip,' said Sticky.

'I can't do it,' screamed Amanda. 'Not with him interrupting. That's it. I resign.'

I sat Amanda down and got her a drink and while she was having it I showed Sticky the pictures again to remind him how important it was that he keep his beak shut.

Then I held up four fingers to remind him that Ms Dunning's having a baby in four days so we can't afford to waste time.

He stared at my fingers, tongue darting about in his beak.

I knew how he felt. Thinking about it makes my mouth go dry too.

Amanda came over and had a look at the pictures.

She spent a long time staring at the people who had planned to abandon cockies and hampsters and kids but were changing their minds.

Then she looked at me and I could see her eyes getting moister.

'Sorry,' she said. 'Let's try it again.'

I didn't say 'Take thirty-three' because I didn't want to depress her. I just started the camera and waved.

'This poor mistreated bird,' said Amanda, 'has suffered some of the crookest treatment you could imagine.' She glanced down at her clipboard like a professional. 'In tonight's programme we talk to the boy who did it and doesn't care. A boy who . . .'

That's when the battery ran out.

I put the camera down so I'd have two hands to swear with, and Amanda explained that the camera had only come with one battery, and that it takes twelve hours to recharge.

We didn't waste the afternoon though.

We spent it teaching Sticky some nice things to say to Dad and Ms Dunning when they invite him to join the family.

It was hard work, but by the end of the afternoon he could say 'G'day' and 'Pig's bottom'.

The battery should be charged in another six hours.

It would be less, but Ms Dunning's using heaps of electricity in the kitchen. She's had the food processor going all evening, making a lemon and lime Jelly Custard Surprise for the Cake And Pudding section in the Agricultural Show on Saturday.

I hope she wins because then she and Dad will be in the right frame of mind to watch a moving and thought-provoking in-depth current affairs report.

OK, I admit it, filming Sticky up the tree was my idea, but if we hadn't tried it we'd never have seen Darryn Peck drowning his parents in the creek.

I had the idea this morning while I was doing the eggs.

Why not have Amanda do the introduction in front of the tree where Darryn abandoned Sticky?

It seemed like a good idea at the time.

When Amanda arrived at the old shed she agreed.

'Good thinking,' she said. 'Kill two birds with one stone.'

I put my hands over Sticky's ears and gave her a look.

'Sorry,' she said.

When we got to the tree I climbed it with Sticky on my shoulder, put him on the branch, showed him the pictures, climbed down, focused the camera on Amanda and gave her a wave.

'This poor mistreated bird . . .' she said.

Then she stopped.

Sticky had flown down and was standing on her head.

Six times I climbed the tree with Sticky and six times he flew down.

The sixth time Amanda lost her temper.

'Get up that tree, banana-head, and stay there,' she yelled at Sticky, who was trying to undo her shoelaces with his beak.

Even though I was feeling pretty tense myself on account of Ms Dunning having a baby in three days and us not even having done the introduction yet, I tried to calm her down.

'He's just feeling nervous,' I said. 'He's had a scary experience here. It's like us going to the dentist.'

It was no good.

Amanda was looking in the other direction.

'I said get up that tree!' she yelled at Sticky.

Sticky bit her on the ankle.

She screamed, then picked up an apple and threw it at him.

Luckily she missed, because Sticky wasn't in any condition to duck.

He was just standing there, rigid with shock.

Like me.

Amanda realised what she'd done and looked pretty shocked herself.

Before any of us could move, a voice came from behind us.

'Watch yourself, Cosgrove,' it said. 'You can get five years for chucking Batts' apples.'

We spun round.

Darryn Peck was standing there, smirking.

'Wish I could stay,' he said, 'but I can't hang around here all day watching you mistreat wildlife, I've got a miniseries to make.'

And he ran off down the track laughing to himself.

For a minute I felt as if I was going to explode with frustration and shrivel up with embarrassment at the same time.

Then I recovered the power of thought.

'Come on,' I said to Amanda. 'After him. This is our chance to talk to him about his crimes on camera.'

It took us a while because Sticky wouldn't get into his bucket before Amanda apologised.

'Sorry,' said Amanda at last, dabbing at her ankle with a hanky.

Then Amanda wouldn't go until Sticky apologised.

'Eat soap,' said Sticky.

'That's his way of saying sorry,' I explained to Amanda, pushing her down the track in the direction Darryn had gone.

As we got close to the creek we could hear Darryn shouting.

We crouched down and peered through the bushes and saw him and Trent Webster and Doug Walsh and a couple of kids on the other side of the creek.

Darryn was sitting on the bank with his head

in his hands while Trent filmed him with his camera.

'My parents,' sobbed Darryn loudly, 'both drowned. Swept off the bank by a freak wave in the middle of a picnic. I begged them to wear floaties.'

'Life jackets,' said Doug, holding up an exercise book. 'In the script it says life jackets.'

'Stop being a smartarse,' Darryn hissed at him, 'and try to arrest me.'

Doug stepped forward, and Trent swung the camera around till it was pointing at him.

'Police,' said Doug, reading from the exercise book. 'We've found your parents' bodies and they've both got lumps of concrete tied to their feet.'

Darryn jumped up and pulled a plastic sword from his belt.

'You'll never take me alive,' he shouted.

Doug stared at the sword.

'It says a gun in the script,' he said.

'Shut up and fall into the water when I kill you,' Darryn hissed at him.

Amanda nudged me.

'Start the camera,' she said and then she was on her feet yelling across the creek at Darryn.

'Darryn Peck,' she shouted, 'is it true that you had a cockatoo for six years?'

Darryn paused with the sword raised above his head and looked across at us. So did the others.

I switched on the camera and struggled to get Darryn and Amanda in focus at the same time.

'Pig's bum,' shouted Darryn.

'Is it also true,' yelled Amanda, 'that you ditched the cocky for a poodle?'

'Go suck a turnip,' yelled Darryn and went back to chopping Doug Walsh into tiny pieces.

Amanda and I discussed crossing the creek so he'd have to answer the questions, but it gets pretty deep in places and Amanda didn't want to risk it with the camera and I didn't want to risk it with Sticky.

'I've got a better idea,' I said. 'Let's go to his place and wait for him to get back. That's what they do on telly. They chase people through the house with the camera going and out into the back yard and finally corner them near the veggie garden where they break down and confess.'

I could see Amanda was having trouble with my hand movements.

I wrote it out.

Amanda read it and nodded.

'OK Ro,' she said in a loud voice so Darryn could hear, 'let's go back to your place and do a nature documentary about woolly aphids.'

Then we set off for Darryn's.

We didn't get there.

Darryn's place is on the other side of town, but in the main street we ran into a problem.

Dad and Ms Dunning.

Just as we were passing the dry-cleaners and Amanda was in the middle of pointing out Mr Shapiro's new van to me and I was wondering if old dry-cleaning vans feel as bad about being dumped as cockies and kids do, I saw Dad and Ms Dunning coming out of the hardware store carrying a baby car seat.

Normally I'd have been pleased to see them, but not today.

Not when I was carrying a bucket with a cocky in it that I was meant to have given back to Darryn Peck four days ago.

Dad and Ms Dunning hadn't seen me, so I grabbed Amanda and dragged her across the street and into her dad's shop.

Both Amanda and Sticky were looking at me as though I was mental, so I explained the situation to them.

'It's just for a couple of minutes,' I said, 'till Dad and Ms Dunning have gone.'

Sticky seemed happy with that, but Amanda looked nervously around.

The shop was empty apart from the usual rows and piles of neatly-folded clothes.

We could hear Mr Cosgrove in the changing cubicles, telling a customer that grey-green was definitely this year's colour.

I put my hand on Amanda's arm and gave her a look.

'Relax,' it said, 'I haven't chucked a dessert for nearly a week.'

But that's not what was worrying Amanda.

'Dad doesn't like animals in the shop,' she said quietly, 'not since Ray Hempel's cattle dog tried to round up all the suede jackets.'

I put Sticky's bucket down behind a rack of moleskin pants, partly so Mr Cosgrove wouldn't see Sticky if he came out of the cubicles, and partly so Sticky wouldn't have to listen to himself being compared to a dog.

Cockatoos mustn't like moleskin pants.

Either that or metal buckets.

Because just as Mr Cosgrove came out of the changing area and saw me and started looking nervous, there was the sound of fencing wire being ripped and suddenly Mr Cosgrove had something to be even more nervous about.

Sticky, flying screeching around the shop.

Amanda screamed, Mr Cosgrove yelled, and

the customer, who was coming out of the cubicles doing up his pants, grabbed his briefcase and held it in front of his privates.

Sticky swooped down, snatched up a pair of orange and brown checked shorts from a table display, flew twice round the shop with them in his beak, and dropped them onto a pile of pink shirts.

'Stop that,' yelled Mr Cosgrove.

I could understand why he was so upset, I've never liked orange and pink together either.

Then Mr Cosgrove noticed that Amanda was holding the video camera.

'Switch it on,' he shouted at her. 'The insurance'll never believe us otherwise.'

I grabbed a towelling bathrobe and waited for Sticky to land so I could gather him up in it.

Sticky didn't land for quite a while, mostly because Mr Cosgrove kept throwing shoes at him and swiping at him with belts.

I pleaded with Amanda to get her dad to stop, but every time she tried to say something to him he yelled at her to keep on filming.

Sticky swooped round and round the shop, snatching up socks and ties and thermal underwear and knocking over piles of cardigans and footy tops.

By the time he finally landed on a rack of safari suits and I was able to get him into the bathrobe and then into the bucket and wire the chook mesh down securely, the shop was pretty untidy and Mr Cosgrove was an even brighter purple than Dad's wedding shirt.

'Your parents are gunna hear about this,' he roared as Amanda bundled me out of the shop.

'Don't worry,' Amanda said to me outside, 'he'll calm down once we get everything back in the right piles.'

I tried to be angry with Sticky on the way home, but I couldn't.

I glared at him a few times, and each time he went from mohawk to cowlick and looked down at the bottom of the bucket.

'This poor mistreated bird,' he said, 'has suffered.'

I was pretty impressed. It was quite a mouthful, even if he had heard it thirty or forty times.

But it didn't change the fact that we'll have to finish the in-depth report without him. We can't creep up on Darryn Peck's place tomorrow with a deranged cocky swooping around flinging washing and dog food all over the place.

'Fraid you'll have to stay put tomorrow,' I told Sticky as I shut him in his cage with fresh seed and water. 'It'll just be for one day.'

'I can't do it,' screeched Sticky. 'I resign.'

I felt awful as I walked to the house.

I still do.

I should have been more honest with Sticky. I should have explained that if Mr Cosgrove rings Dad before tomorrow, we're both in deep cocky poo.

But then what's the point in us both having a knot in our guts the size of Ayers Rock including the car park, the kiosk, the motel, the air strip and all the rubbish bins?

It's eight-thirty and he hasn't rung yet.

Dad's just been in to say goodnight and if Mr Cosgrove had rung I know Dad would have said more than, 'By the way, how's the telly project going?'

'OK,' I said.

I put my hands under the sheet.

'Has to be finished tomorrow, doesn't it?' he asked.

I nodded.

'Think you'll make it?' he asked.

I nodded.

'Good on you,' he said. 'Sounds like a top show, endangered wildlife. As long as you don't include codling moths.'

I smiled.

'G'night, Tonto,' said Dad. 'I've got to get back to Claire. She's teaching me how to fold nappies her way.'

That was ten minutes ago.

My hands are still under the sheet, fingers crossed so tightly they feel like cocky claws.

I burnt the eggs this morning.

It's the first time I've ever done it, and I could see it made Ms Dunning suspicious.

'Are you OK, Ro?' she asked, but it wasn't the tone of voice your dad's wife uses, it was the tone of voice a teacher uses when you're daydreaming and burning the chemicals in science.

Or the eggs.

'Sorry,' I said, blowing at the smoke, 'I was miles away.'

That was a slight exaggeration.

In my head I'd only been three metres away, over by the phone, waiting for it to ring and Mr Cosgrove to say that he wasn't letting Amanda use his video camera anymore and that he had the address of a really good home for uncontrollable cockies and kids.

Ms Dunning and Dad went back to their conversation about babies' names.

'Caroline,' said Ms Dunning.

'Carla,' said Dad.

'Amelia,' said Ms Dunning.

'Leanne,' said Dad.

'Lachlan,' said Ms Dunning.

'Clarrie,' said Dad.

'Our neighbours had a turtle called Clarrie,' said Ms Dunning.

'My dad's name was Clarrie,' said Dad.

'I'm not really hungry,' I said. 'Bye.'

As I left the house the phone still hadn't rung.

I decided Mr Cosgrove must still have been tidying up the shop.

I could hardly breathe by the time I got to the end of Darryn Peck's street in case Amanda wasn't there or was there but didn't have the camera.

She was there.

She had the camera.

'I reminded Dad you're a disadvantaged person,' said Amanda. 'Sorry.'

I gave her a hug.

Normally I'd have been ropeable, but sometimes you have to be lenient when a clever and generous best friend's trying to stop your life from going down the dunny.

Even if later the same day it ends up down there anyway.

Getting into Darryn Peck's place was easier today than it would have been six months ago because six months ago his three big brothers were still living at home and there was always at least one of them lying in the front yard under a motorbike with a spanner at all hours of the day and night.

This morning the front yard was empty except for a few bushes near the front door.

Me and Amanda went and crouched in them, camera and clipboard at the ready.

'He's definitely still in the house,' said Amanda, using her hands. 'I've been at the end of the street since six-thirty.'

She's incredible. She'll be on national television by the time she's twenty-three.

After I finished telling her that, we headed for the front door.

Then I had a thought.

'If he sees us ringing the bell,' I said, dragging Amanda back into the bushes, 'he could lock himself in the bathroom. We've got to take him by surprise. Round the back.'

We crept along the side of the house, ducking under the windows, and peered round the corner into the back yard.

Darryn's mother was kneeling at a small table just outside the back door, making strange noises.

'Oochy, oochy, oochy,' she went. 'Goo, goo, goo, goo, goo.'

It sounded like she was feeding a baby. I knew she hadn't had a baby recently, but for a sec I thought maybe she was feeding someone else's as a part-time job.

Then she moved a bit and I saw it wasn't a baby but the poodle, which was standing on the table looking bored while she combed its curls with a tiny comb.

'Who's a beautiful girl then?' cooed Mrs Peck.

The dog didn't answer, but I could see it eyeing Mrs Peck's hairdo, which was very similar to its own, and wishing it had a tiny comb too.

Then Mr Peck came out of the house and started making baby noises as well.

'Ga, ga, ga, ga, ga, ga, ga, ga, ga, ga,' said Mr Peck.

You don't often hear a forklift-truck operator talking like that.

I could feel Amanda shaking with silent laughter and I put my hand over her mouth just in case.

Mr Peck tilted the poodle's head up and pushed its legs a bit further apart. 'First prize,' he said, speaking into his fist, 'goes to Amelia Peck Hyloader The Third.'

Then me and Amanda stiffened.

Darryn was coming out of the house.

He stood watching his parents, shoulders drooping.

Then he took a deep breath and spoke.

'Dad,' he said, 'why can't we go to the cricket tomorrow? You promised.'

Mr Peck answered without looking up from the poodle. 'You know why,' he said. 'We've got Amelia in the show.'

Darryn's shoulders drooped even further. 'You've got her in a show every Saturday,' he said bitterly.

'Don't raise your voice to your father,' said Mrs Peck, not looking up either, 'it's making the dog nervous.'

Darryn looked at his parents for a moment and then turned and walked towards us.

We flattened ourselves against the fibro but he came round the corner with his head down and walked straight past us.

Amanda nudged me and headed after him. I switched the camera on and by the time they were halfway across the front lawn I had them both in focus.

'Darryn Peck,' said Amanda in her best reporter voice, 'is it true that you ditched your faithful cockatoo for a poodle?'

Darryn swung round.

'I hate that poodle,' he shouted, 'I've always hated it.'

Then he realised who he was talking to and froze.

That's when I saw the tears in his eyes.

Darryn Peck was crying.

I turned the camera off.

'But you did abandon a cockatoo,' persisted Amanda, before she felt me gripping her arm and saw Darryn's tears and realised it was time to shut up.

'Yeah, what of it?' Darryn said, but his heart wasn't in it.

He looked so helpless and unhappy I wanted to put my arms round him.

Then he took a step forward and for a sec I thought he was going to grab the camera and hurl it over the neighbour's fence.

Instead he turned and ran into the house.

Amanda and me looked at each other.

'We could do an in-depth report on Darryn's parents,' she said quietly.

I shook my head.

It wouldn't change anything.

We walked into town without saying much and when we got to school I gave her the camera and she gave me a hug and I set off for home.

I'm almost there.

I'm hurrying so I can see as much of Dad as possible in the little bit of time left before the baby's born, because afterwards I'm going to be pretty busy with the club.

The club I'm going to start.

It's got four members already.

Me, Sticky, Darryn Peck and Mr Shapiro's old van.

I could tell something was wrong as soon as I walked into the house.

Ms Dunning's Jelly Custard Surprise, the one she'd made for the Show, was sitting on the kitchen table without a flyscreen over it.

I knew she'd never leave it like that on purpose because everyone knows you can't win a prize in the Cakes And Puddings section if you've got fly footprints in your whipped cream.

Then Dad and Ms Dunning came into the kitchen and I could tell from their furious faces they had something more important on their minds than dessert.

For a while they just stood there glaring at me, and I realised they were struggling to control themselves.

By the time Dad finally spoke in a tight angry voice my heart was thumping faster than the fridge motor.

'I'm very disappointed in you, Ro,' he said.

'We're both very disappointed in you,' said Ms Dunning.

My mind was racing.

Had Mr Segal rung up asking why I wasn't at school?

Had Darryn gone out into the back yard and strangled the poodle and his parents were blaming me?

'We agreed you'd take that cockatoo back,' shouted Dad, 'didn't we?'

Ayers Rock hit me in the guts.

They'd found Sticky.

I started to ask if he was OK but the words froze on my hands.

Because I saw what Dad had on his hands.

Blood.

I couldn't believe it.

I'd seen him shoot at birds in the old days, before we had nets in the orchard, but now he's a big supporter of all the wildlife on the protected list.

Obviously poor old Sticky wasn't on his list.

Suddenly Ayers Rock wasn't in my guts any more, it was in my head and it had gone volcanic and I couldn't stop myself.

I erupted.

I wanted to shout and yell and scream, but all I could do was fling my hands around faster than I ever have before.

Hand movements might be hard to understand sometimes, but when they're that big and that fast everyone knows you're shouting.

'It's not fair!' I yelled. 'You're having a baby, why can't I have a cocky?'

Dad opened his mouth to answer but I hadn't finished.

'Why do you need a baby anyway?' I shouted. 'You've got me. What's wrong with me?'

Through my tears I saw Dad close his mouth.

'That's why you're having one, isn't it?' I yelled, banging my elbow on the fireplace. 'It's because there's something wrong with me. Isn't it? Isn't it?'

Dad and Ms Dunning were staring at me, stunned, so I thumped my fist down on the table to jolt them out of it.

The Jelly Custard Surprise wobbled.

I grabbed it and lifted it above my head and braced my legs to hurl it against the kitchen dresser as hard as I could.

But I didn't.

Because as Dad and Ms Dunning raised their hands in front of their faces I saw two things.

The blood on Dad's hands was coming from several small cuts on his palms and fingers.

And gripped in Ms Dunning's hands were several splinters of wood with bits of sleepy bunny on them.

Even as I pushed past Dad and Ms Dunning I knew what I'd find in the nursery. When I got in there it was even worse than I'd imagined.

The floor was littered with splintered pieces of bashful koala.

Torn shreds of playful dolphin were strewn over what was left of the baby's cot.

Frayed ribbons of friendly possum hung from the curtain rail.

The light shade was a tattered wreck with barely a scrap of goanna left that you'd recognise as being happy-go-lucky.

'That vicious cheese-brain tore the place apart,' shouted Dad furiously behind me, 'I tried to grab the brute but it pecked my hands and flew off.'

'It was in a frenzy,' said Ms Dunning.

'You've had it cooped up somewhere around here, haven't you?' demanded Dad.

I thrust the Jelly Custard Surprise at Dad and ran out of the house.

Dad shouted at me but as I ran down the verandah steps I heard Ms Dunning telling him to let me go.

I didn't care.

All I wanted was to find Sticky.

I went to the old shed but the cage was empty and a panel of chook-wire fencing was hanging loose. I kicked it and said some rude things in my head about people who spend so much money on baby things that they haven't got enough left over to buy decent cocky-proof tying wire.

Then I went looking for Sticky.

That was hours ago.

I've been all through the orchard and all round the creek and up the tree where I first found him and halfway into town.

I couldn't call his name of course so I had to make do with rattling some seed in his tin.

Pretty hopeless, because anyone can rattle seed in a tin.

Darryn Peck or Dad or Mr Cosgrove, with an apple or a gun or a noose made from a tape measure behind their back.

No wonder I couldn't find him.

He's probably migrated to Indonesia or Sulawesi or somewhere.

So I've just been sitting here, in his cage, looking at the remains of the pictures I drew him.

I really loved that cocky, even though he chewed everything up.

I haven't felt this lonely since Erin died. She was my best friend at the special school I used to go to and she was crook a lot but it was still a terrible shock when she died.

I felt pretty bad then too, but at least then I had a dad who really loved me.

I thought I'd managed to sneak into bed without being spotted but Dad came in.

I kept my head under the pillow but I knew it was him because he flicks his belt buckle with his thumbnail when he's nervous.

Or angry.

He stood there for ages without saying anything.

I guessed he wasn't angry any more. When Dad's angry you always know about it. At least he and Sticky had one thing in common.

Dad still didn't say anything.

For a moment I thought he was pausing for effect like he usually does before announcing a big surprise, but he wasn't.

When he finally spoke it wasn't 'We're having the baby adopted', it was 'Tonto, are you awake?'

I didn't move.

He went out.

In the old days, before his head was full of new ways to fold nappies, he'd have asked at least twice.

Then Ms Dunning came in.

I knew it was her because when she sat down the bed springs sagged violently. They're fine with one person on them but not three.

I kept my head under the pillow.

She didn't ask if I was awake, but that was probably because she's a teacher. Teachers always assume you'll be awake once they start talking.

'Ro,' she said, 'I've got something to tell you. Dad wasn't sure if you should know this, but I think you should.'

She paused.

I held my breath.

Teachers must do training in how to grab your attention without using loud music or explosive devices.

'But first, Ro,' Ms Dunning said, 'we're not trying to replace you. We'd never do that.'

I stuck my hands out from under the sheet and made the sign me and Dad invented for a defective apple.

Ms Dunning put her hands over mine.

'You're not defective,' she said. 'You've got a speech problem you handle like a champ and if the baby's born with a similar speech problem I know it'll handle it like a champ too.'

That got me out from under the pillow.

I rolled over and stared at Ms Dunning.

A similar speech problem?

The baby?

For a sec I thought Ms Dunning was having another vague spell and had got her words mixed up, but then I saw from the expression on her face that she hadn't.

'It's possible,' she said. 'The doctors have never told you this, but they reckon they know why you were born mute.'

I stared at her even harder.

I'd asked the doctors that a million times and each time they'd said I was a Medical Mystery and given me a lolly.

'They reckon,' continued Ms Dunning, 'it's because of some genetic problem that's been in either your dad's family or your mum's family for generations. They don't know which.'

My brain was going like a GT Falcon with twin injectors.

If it was Dad's that would explain why he'd never told me.

If I was him I'd be too embarrassed to yak on about something like that as well.

'If it's a problem on Dad's side,' Ms Dunning went on, 'then the baby could be born mute too.'

We looked at each other for a while.

I didn't know what to say.

Ms Dunning looked pretty sad.

She leant over and kissed me on the cheek. 'We decided to tell you because we want you to feel better,' she murmured. Then she went out.

I've been lying here for a long time, staring into the darkness.

I've been thinking how, if the baby's born mute, I can help it.

Teach it sign language.

Show it how to write really fast so it can get its order in to the school tuck shop before all the devon and chutney sandwiches are gone.

Demonstrate what you have to do with your nose when you're cheering your best friend up with a look.

I've also been thinking what great parents I've got.

Well, good parents.

Well, their hearts are in the right place.

Even though I brandished a Jelly Custard Surprise at them in the kitchen and my pet cocky murdered all their sleepy bunnies, they still want me to feel better.

I know I should feel better, but I don't.

Because even dads with hearts in the right place are only human.

And if that baby talks, what chance have I got?

It's a funny thing, the human brain.

I don't mean to look at, though I saw one in a jar once in a museum and it did look a bit weird, like scrambled eggs when you don't wash the mushroom juice out of the pan first.

I mean the way it works.

When I woke up this morning I decided I'd spend the day helping Dad and Ms Dunning clean up the baby's room.

While I was getting dressed I had the thought that if we pulled the old shed apart and sanded the wood we could probably build some pretty good baby furniture out of it.

While I was tying my left shoe I remembered my softball bat. We could sell that and use the money to buy blue and pink paint.

Then, while I was tying my right shoe, I forgot about all those things totally and completely.

Because I started thinking about Darryn Peck.

I was sitting on the bed bending over, so perhaps the blood sloshing around in my head made my brain short-circuit or something.

Or perhaps I was just trying to take my mind off Sticky.

Anyway once I started thinking about him I couldn't stop.

I thought about how Darryn and me are in the same boat.

I thought about the poodle.

I thought about how much easier it'd be to compete with two kilos of curly fluff and a squeaky bark than with a kid who'll probably be singing opera by the age of three.

I thought about how I wished I could swap places with Darryn, and what I'd do if I was in his shoes, and how he'd probably never think of doing the same because he's not real bright.

Then I thought about him crying and my guts felt strange and I don't think it was because I hadn't had any dinner.

Dad and Ms Dunning were still asleep.

I wrote them a note, left it on the kitchen table, grabbed a couple of cold apple fritters from the fridge and slipped out of the house.

On my way into town I thought about how weird the human brain is.

There I was, on what was possibly my last morning ever as a single kid, walking away from possibly my last ever morning cuddle with Dad without some noisy brat yodelling in our ears and dribbling on his shirt.

Just to save Darryn Peck from a life of misery.

It was still early when I reached town and the main street was almost deserted. Just a couple of shopkeepers hosing the footpath and Mr Shapiro polishing his new van.

He called me over.

I hesitated, wondering if he was going to hand me a bill for burnt-out dry-cleaning machines, but he smiled and beckoned.

'Good on you, love,' he said, and gave me two dollars.

I spent it in the newsagents on a new notepad and pen because getting through to Darryn Peck can involve a lot of writing. Particularly when he's still ropeable about being ambushed with a camera and sprung with tears in his eyes.

When I got to Darryn's place I rang the bell and stood there holding up the first note.

'Don't do anything violent,' it said, 'until you've read this note. I'm here to help you avoid a life of misery. There will be no charge for this service.'

Darryn opened the door in his pyjamas.

He stared at me, ignoring the note completely, and took a menacing step towards me.

'You can't have him,' he said.

I took a step back, wondering what he was talking about.

Then I heard a distant voice and I knew.

'Go suck a turnip,' said the voice.

I pushed past Darryn and ran through the house, past a startled Mr and Mrs Peck who were at the kitchen table shampooing the poodle.

I burst out of the back door and there in the corner of the yard was a big cage and sitting on a branch in one corner calling me a big fat wobbly bottom was Sticky.

Darryn ran past me and into the cage and grabbed Sticky off his perch and held him tightly.

'He's mine,' said Darryn fiercely.

'You dumped him,' I scribbled on my pad, just as fiercely.

'Darryn,' shouted his father from the back door, 'if you're letting that bird out keep it away from Amelia.'

Darryn's face sagged.

'I only dumped him for them,' he said, nodding towards the kitchen. 'I reckoned things might be better if they thought I was shifting over to poodles.'

He looked bitterly towards the kitchen.

'Fat chance,' he said.

'Darryn,' shouted his father, 'Amelia's having a sleep on your bed. Don't disturb her.'

Darryn gave Sticky a hug.

'I should never have done it,' he said sadly. 'But Sticky's forgiven me, haven't you mate.'

'Drop off a log,' said Sticky.

'See,' said Darryn, beaming, 'he's talking to me now.'

He gave Sticky another hug and I had to admit it did look as though Sticky had forgiven him. He wasn't shredding Darryn's ears or anything.

For a sec I was tempted to grab Sticky and run for it and hide out for a couple of years, just him and me, on a deserted island off the Philippines, but I decided against it.

Sticky gave me a look. 'Thanks for everything,' it said, 'but I'm home now.'

Darryn let me have a couple of private minutes with Sticky to say goodbye.

We both got pretty moist in the eyes, Sticky and me, and while I was showing him a picture of me coming to visit him often, and he was telling me to bite my bum, I made a promise to myself that one day I'll have a cocky all of my own.

It occurred to me, as Darryn was putting Sticky back into the cage, that Ms Dunning had probably felt the same way about having a baby.

Then I took Darryn for a long walk and wrote him lots of notes and slowly he grasped my plan to save him from a life of misery.

He was a bit doubtful at first, but when we got here to the showground he realised what a great plan it is.

Everything's set up, Darryn's in position, people have started arriving, and we're just waiting now for the mayor to declare the Agricultural Show open.

The plan didn't work.

I still can't believe it.

Everything went as smoothly as a well-oiled apple-polishing machine and the plan still didn't work.

I waited till the judging had started in the Dog tent, then I wheeled the extra display stand in.

Mr and Mrs Peck were so busy fussing about with their poodle that they didn't notice me getting into position next to them at the end of the row of dogs.

I timed it spot on.

Just as the judges were inspecting Amelia Peck Hyloader The Third, I whipped the cover off my stand.

The judges moved on, peered over their clipboards, and the blood drained from their faces.

It was probably the first time they'd seen a boy on a dog display stand.

Darryn was brilliant.

He panted and got up on all fours and looked at his parents with mournful eyes and let his tongue loll out.

He looked exactly like a boy whose parents treat him worse than a dog.

That's when everything went wrong.

Mr and Mrs Peck didn't sweep him up in their arms and weep and say how sorry they were and promise never to boot him out of his room again when the poodle wanted a nap.

They didn't even look at each other and say, 'Let this be a lesson to us not to neglect Darryn in future'.

Mrs Peck just screamed.

And Mr Peck just shouted, 'Darryn, get off there this minute, you're upsetting the dogs'.

Darryn was very good about it all.

After we'd run for it and hidden behind the Jam And Preserves tent and seen that no one was following us, he thanked me.

'It was a good try,' he said sadly.

Then he went off to find his mates.

I felt awful.

I wrote a long note explaining that it was all my idea and that Darryn shouldn't be punished because he'd only agreed to do it because he was gullible, and I left it under the Pecks' windscreen wiper.

Walking back across the car park I was spotted by the one person I didn't want to be spotted by.

Mr Segal.

'Rowena,' he called out, 'about your TV project.'

It was too late to run.

Mr Segal sprinted over and blocked my way.

'Brilliant,' he said, breaking into a grin, 'I haven't laughed so much for ages.'

It took me a while to grasp what he was saying because I couldn't take my eyes off the dinosaurs on his shirt.

I stared at him and tried to smile back.

'You and Amanda have got a big future in TV comedy,' he said. 'Well done.'

I found Amanda over by the sheep and cattle enclosure.

She explained that because ten seconds of Darryn Peck crying wasn't really enough for an in-depth current affairs report, she'd handed in the tape of Sticky flying round the menswear shop and her dad throwing shoes at him.

'Mr Segal wants to show it at a video festival,' Amanda said excitedly. 'Pretty good eh?'

I said it wasn't bad, but that I wasn't really in the mood for celebrating.

Amanda, because she's a true friend, didn't pester me for details, she just squeezed my arm and we went over to the stand to find a good position for the Carla Tamworth concert.

As we passed the Cakes And Puddings tent I saw a familiar hat weaving towards us through the crowd and my heart started thumping like a Saint Bernard's tail.

It was Dad.

He'd come to see the concert with me after all.

We ran towards him, me waving like a loon, until I saw what he was carrying.

A Jelly Custard Surprise.

'Can't stop,' he said, 'it's melting,' and he hurried into the Cakes And Puddings tent.

I stared after him and blinked hard.

He was just dropping off Ms Dunning's entry.

Amanda took my arm and we found a good pozzie halfway up the stand.

There was a support band playing a song about a person whose heart had been run over by a steamroller, which was pretty right for the way I was feeling.

Then a ripple of alarm ran through the crowd.

People started craning to see.

There was some sort of commotion.

Up on the stage someone seemed to be having a heated discussion with the lead singer of the support band.

My guts froze.

I recognised the purple shirt and the white hat with the tractor exhaust stains.

It was Dad.

'It's your dad,' yelled Amanda, who'd obviously forgotten she was meant to be a true friend.

People turned round and stared at me and I wanted to hide under the seat, but it was just a bench and there wasn't room.

The lead singer of the support band stepped up to the microphone shaking his head.

'One of your local blokes wants to sing,' he said, 'and because he's a pushy so and so we've decided to let him.'

The support band filed off the stage leaving Dad standing at the mike by himself.

Dad cleared his throat.

'I'd like to sing a little number I wrote myself,' he said.

I couldn't believe it.

Dad didn't write songs.

Even as Dad was clearing his throat again, people started throwing things.

Chip cartons.

Cigarette packets.

Bottle tops.

A couple of people yelled out to give him a go, and the rest of us just sat there stunned that anyone would try and sing to a crowd of this size without a guitar.

Dad started singing and a lot more people started throwing things.

Beer cans.

Ice creams.

Bits of hot dog.

It was the worst I'd ever heard him sing.

He was off key and none of the lyrics rhymed.

But I didn't care.

Because Dad stood there ignoring the food and garbage raining down on him and the crowd yelling 'Jump off a cliff' and 'Take a hike' and 'Get stuffed', and sang to me.

He didn't take his eyes off me the whole time he sang, and I didn't take mine off him.

Part of me wanted to yell at the crowd to shut

up, but the other part of me was too busy glowing like a two-million-watt bulb.

The song was about a girl who's lived most of her life without a mother and so her father decides to give her the most precious gift he can think of.

A brother or sister.

When he'd finished, and the crowd had all booed, and I'd wiped my tears away, I wanted to jump up on my seat and cheer my lungs out.

I couldn't of course, and it took Amanda about a minute to stop looking dazed and do it, and during that time I found myself thinking how you never have a kid sister or brother with a good cheering voice around when you need one.

Then I ran down to the stage and Dad, who was splattered with beer and ice cream and bits of hot dog, hugged me so tight he left a red mark just above my bellybutton.

It wasn't his belt buckle, it was tomato sauce.

'I'd better ring home,' said Dad, 'see if the baby's coming.'

I couldn't have agreed more.

As we hurried to the pay phone we passed the Cake And Pudding tent.

I glanced inside, and across the heads of all the people, over in one corner, in front of the big hardware store fan, I was sure I saw Darryn Peck with Ms Dunning's Jelly Custard Surprise raised above his head.

We made it to the hospital just in time.

Dad sat me in the waiting room and gave me some money for the drink machine and hurried through the swing doors with Ms Dunning.

It was a long wait.

I had a drink every half hour and tried to ignore a little kid with blonde hair who kept pointing to me and saying to her dad, 'There's something wrong with her'.

I almost strangled her a couple of times, but spent the rest of the time straining to hear something.

Anything.

Then Dad appeared flushed and red-eyed and grinning and took me inside to a ward.

Ms Dunning was sitting up in bed.

She was flushed and red-eyed and grinning too.

Lying on her chest was a small wrinkled baby.

It wasn't making a sound.

Come on, I said inside, come on.

'This is your sister,' said Dad in a wobbly voice. 'Her name's Erin.'

Even when I heard that I didn't stop holding my breath, not until Erin opened her mouth and gave a howl that rattled the windows.

Then I realised I was bawling my eyes out, but it didn't matter because Dad and Ms Dunning were too.

After a while, when we'd pulled ourselves together, and I was holding Erin, I noticed that the little blonde kid had wondered in, probably attracted by the noise Erin was making.

'Look,' said the kid to a nurse, 'the girl that's got something wrong with her, she's picked up that baby.'

I turned and spoke to her.

I knew she was too young to understand hand movements, but I wanted to say it.

'This is my sister,' I said, 'and there's nothing wrong with either of us.'

Gift of the Gab

For my grandparents

It's not fair.

I don't reckon the police should lock people up without hearing their side of the story.

My side of the story's really simple.

I did it, but there was a reason.

I tried to explain to Sergeant Cleary why I did it. In the police car I wrote down in my notebook everything that happened today. Even the things that'll probably make Dad send me to bed early when he hears about them.

I showed my statement to Sergeant Cleary while he was locking me in this cell.

'Not now, Rowena,' he said.

I could see he wasn't interested, though that might have been because Dermot Figgis was trying to bite him.

Police officers in small country towns have it really tough. The police stations are always understaffed. The only other officer on duty here today is Constable Pola, but he has to stay at the front desk in case of emergency calls or exciting developments in the car racing on TV.

Once Sergeant Cleary got Dermot into a cell, I tried to explain again. I banged on a wall pipe with my pen, like they do in prison movies.

'Message from Rowena Batts,' I banged in Morse code. 'I only did it because of the dog poo.'

That was ten minutes ago.

Sergeant Cleary hasn't been back.

He probably doesn't know Morse code. Either that or I didn't send it properly because my hands are shaking so much from outrage at Dermot Figgis and from worry about what's going to happen to me.

Sergeant Cleary's probably ringing Dad now.

'Mr Batts?' he's probably saying. 'We've got Rowena in the lock-up. We'll be charging her and putting her on trial as a criminal.'

Just thinking about it gives me a lump in the guts bigger than Antarctica.

Poor Dad. I hate putting him through this. The shame. And the lawyer's fees. He's got enough on his plate with the root weevil in the back paddock.

If only the police would listen to me.

That's the worst thing about being born with bits missing from your throat and not being able to talk with your voice, some people just won't listen to you.

Which means they never hear your side of the story.

The police are hearing Dermot Figgis's side. They can't help hearing it, he's been yelling it from the next cell for the last fifteen minutes.

'Rowena Batts attacked my car,' he's yelling. 'She filled it up with stewed apples.'

He's right, I did, but as I said before, there was a reason.

It's all here in my notebook. Including diagrams so the jury at my trial can see exactly what happened.

Some of the diagrams are a bit wobbly. It's hard to do neat drawing while your hands are trembling with outrage and indignation. The dog-poo diagram for example. It looks more like two shrivelled sausages. I'd better label it so there's no misunderstanding.

And I'd better draw a diagram of the war memorial so the jury can see where the whole thing started.

This morning at the Anzac Day dawn ceremony.

Anzac Day's a very special day for me and Dad. It's our most important day of the year, including Christmas, birthdays and the release of a new Carla Tamworth CD.

It's the day Mum died.

So if anyone spoils it, I get pretty ropable.

I started getting ropable with Dermot Figgis at about 6.05 this morning.

As the first rays of the sun appeared over the supermarket, the crowd around the war memorial went quiet and Mr Shapiro played 'The Last Post' on his trumpet. Then we started the two-minute silence for the Aussie soldiers and other people who died in wars.

Dad reckons there were millions of them, including his grandfather who died in World War One, so even though it's not the most important part of the day for me, I try to concentrate.

This morning it was impossible.

Dermot Figgis and some of his hoon mates were doing the sausages. The footy club always does a sausage sizzle on Anzac Day so people who get emotionally drained by the ceremony can have a hot breakfast after.

As the two-minute silence began, Dermot started chopping onions really loudly.

Everyone glared at him, including me.

Then I glanced anxiously at old Mr Wetherby. He was actually in World War One and saw quite a few of his mates die. It can really stress you if you're trying to think about people who've died and other people are chopping onions noisily, specially if you're ninety-eight.

I could see Mr Wetherby trembling in his wheelchair. For a sec I thought he was so angry he was having a seizure. Then I realised he was just excited because he was being filmed by a TV crew as one of the oldest diggers in the state.

Dermot carried on chopping.

I decided if I go that selfish and dopey when I'm eighteen, I'll book myself in for a brain transplant.

I should have given Dermot a brain transplant there and then.

I would have done if I'd known what he was going to do half an hour later.

The two-minute silence ended and Dad stepped forward and cleared his throat.

Everyone stared. Some people looked cross and others rolled their eyes.

'Oh no,' someone muttered.

I couldn't believe it. What were they upset about? They all knew Dad was going to sing, he does every year.

It couldn't have been his clothes. Me and Dad got up extra early this morning and put a lot of effort into choosing him a respectful Anzac Day outfit. Black boots. Black jeans. Black shirt except for a tiny bit of yellow fringing. And he'd swapped his cow-skull belt buckle for one with an angel riding a really clean Harley.

The TV cameraman swung his camera away from Mr Wetherby and pointed it at Dad. I don't think he'd seen an apple farmer that well-dressed before.

Mr Cosgrove, the president of the Anzac Day committee, was glaring at Dad even harder than he'd been glaring at Dermot Figgis.

'Excuse me,' I said to Mr Cosgrove sternly. 'I think you're forgetting something. Anzac Day isn't just the day we remember the victims of war, it's also the day my mother died.'

Mr Cosgrove didn't understand all the words, of course, because he doesn't speak sign language, but I could tell he got the gist because he gave a big sigh.

Dad sang the song he always sings at the Anzac Day dawn ceremony. It's a beautiful Carla Tamworth country and western ballad about a truck driver whose wife dies and for the rest of his life he refuses to sell his truck because it's got the impression of her bottom in the passenger seat.

It makes me very sad, that song, because Mum died soon after I was born, so I haven't got those sorts of lasting memories of her.

It affected everyone else too, even though Dad's not that great a singer. Mr Wetherby dabbed away a tear and quite a few other people put their heads in their hands.

I could tell everyone was having strong feelings.

All except Dermot Figgis.

I heard giggling and turned and there was Dermot, dopey blond dreadlocks jiggling as he and his mates pointed at Dad and stuffed hot-dog buns in their mouths to stop themselves laughing.

They weren't doing a very good job.

World War One exploded in my head.

I stormed over to Dermot, determined to shut him up.

On the way I picked up a large plastic bottle of mustard.

The human brain's a weird thing.

When it's scared it stops working.

Mine did just now, when I heard Sergeant Cleary coming along the corridor towards the cells.

He's here to charge me, I thought, and transfer me to a remand centre for juvenile offenders.

Then my brain switched itself off.

I know why it did that. I spent five years in a special school once because of my throat problems and I never want to go back to an institution again. Not even if I end up a top surgeon or private detective. I won't charge kids from institutions who need treatment or a missing pet or parent found, but I won't be able to go to them, they'll have to come and see me on my yacht.

It's OK, but. Sergeant Cleary didn't charge me. Not yet. He just came down to tell Dermot Figgis to be quiet.

Dermot's brain went into hibernation too when he saw me storming towards him this morning holding a large bottle of mustard.

The whole town knows I stuffed a live frog into a kid's mouth once, a kid who wasn't respectful to Mum's memory, and Dermot must have thought I was planning to squeeze a bottleful of mustard into his.

I wasn't. I was just going to threaten him with it, that's all.

Dermot stepped away uncertainly, trod on a raw sausage, slipped, fell backwards and ended up sitting in a plastic bin full of ice and water and drink cans.

His mates cacked themselves.

Dermot's face went dark red.

That's when I did a dumb thing. I put my hand out to help him up.

When I think about it now, I feel faint. Dermot's years older than me and he could have crushed my hand like sausage meat in that big paw of his.

He didn't, but.

He let me pull him up. Then, as his mates went silent and embarrassed, he realised what he'd done and snatched his hand away.

He glared down at me with narrow eyes.

'You're history, kid,' he growled.

'Cheese-brain,' I replied. He doesn't speak sign, but I could tell he got the gist because his face went an even darker red.

Shaking, I went back over to Dad and concentrated on listening to the last few verses of the song.

When Dad finished, rather than let any more hoons spoil our sad mood further, we hopped onto the tractor and went over to the cemetery.

Or we would have done if the tractor hadn't broken down halfway there.

'Poop,' said Dad, using his mouth, which he always does when he's cross with himself.

I knew Dad was wishing we'd brought the truck. The only reason we brought the tractor was because it was hooked up to a trailer-load of mouldy apples Dad had promised Mr Lorenzini for his pigs.

It wasn't so bad. We had the tractor going in under an hour. It would have been less, but the apples attracted a lot of flies so we could only work one-handed.

The tractor broke down again halfway into the cemetery carpark.

'You go on ahead, Tonto,' said Dad. 'I'll fix this mongrel and catch you up.'

I was really pleased to hear him say that, partly because I really wanted to get to Mum's grave, and partly because I could tell he wasn't angry.

Tonto was a character in his favourite TV show when he was a kid, and he never calls me it when he's angry.

That's an example of why my dad's so special. A lot of dads, if the tractor was being a real mongrel, would get totally and completely ropable and spoil the most special day of the year.

Not my dad.

No, it's me who ended up doing that.

I knew there was something wrong with Mum's grave even before I got close to it.

It's in the top part of the cemetery with a really good view over the town. Because it's on a slope, you can see the flat grassy part of the grave as well as the headstone when you climb up to it.

I saw two small black things on the grassy part.

I knew they weren't lizards because they didn't scuttle off as I crunched towards them through the dry grass.

When I saw what they were, I felt a stab in the guts.

Dog poo.

Some mangy mongrel had done a poo on my most special place in the world.

Luckily, I always carry tissues on Anzac Day. I pulled a handful from my pocket, grabbed the two long hard shrivelled black objects and chucked them as hard as I could into the bush at the back of the graveyard.

'Sorry, Mum,' I whispered.

Then I heard Dad crunching towards me, so I stuffed the tissues back into my pocket.

He didn't have to know.

No point making him suffer too.

Funny, me thinking that. Given what's happened since. Dad wouldn't have suffered half as much from a bit of dog poo as he will when he finds out what I've done.

Oh well, at least we had our special time with Mum today.

'You OK, Tonto?' said Dad after we'd sat by the grave for about half an hour, alone with our feelings.

'I'm fine,' I replied. 'What about you?'

Dad's been a bit depressed lately. He always gets a bit depressed around Mum's anniversary. This year he's been more down than usual. I reckon it's the root weevil in the back paddock.

'I'm fine too,' said Dad. 'Now we've had our special time.'

That's the great thing about a dad who can speak with his hands. You can have a conversation even when both your throats are clogged up with tears.

We stood up and gave each other the hug Mum would have given us if she'd been around.

That's when I heard it.

A horrible, braying, jeering sound coming from the trees at the top of the cemetery.

Dermot Figgis and his hoon mates.

They swaggered out into the open, yelling and pointing to us and laughing.

I realised what the braying sound was.

Dermot was singing Mum's special song. The one Dad had sung at the war memorial. OK, Dermot could do the tune a bit better than Dad, but he was doing it in a mocking, sneering voice.

My guts knotted.

Then suddenly I knew.

The dog poo.

Suddenly I knew how it had got onto Mum's grave.

A dog didn't leave it there.

A mongrel did.

I stared at Dermot and World War One and World War Two both exploded in my head at the same time.

Dad put a hand on my arm.

'Ignore him,' he muttered. 'He'll get his.'

Dad was right about that.

A couple of lines into the song, Dermot forgot the words, which Dad would never do. Dermot gave us the finger and ran laughing into the trees with the other hoons.

I don't remember Dad leading me back to the carpark.

All I remember is what I saw there behind some bushes up the other end of the carpark from the tractor.

My heart started thumping so hard I thought my special black Anzac Day T-shirt was going to rip.

Dermot Figgis's car.

I knew it was his because he's the only person in town with a 1983 Falcon sprayed purple.

Dad hadn't seen it. He was too busy frowning at the tractor.

'I don't reckon she'll make it to Lorenzini's place hauling all these apples,' said Dad, unhooking the trailer. 'The distributor's gunna cark it any sec. How do you feel about staying here with the trailer while I go and ask Mr Lorenzini to come and fetch you and the apples?'

I found myself nodding really hard.

'If those hoons come back, just ignore 'em,' said Dad. 'They're all whistle and wind.'

I pretended not to hear him.

Dad gave me a squeeze and chugged off on the tractor.

As soon as he was out of sight, I dragged the trailer up to the other end of the carpark. It took ages and I nearly dislocated my shoulder, but I did it.

Then I grabbed the spade off the back of the trailer, opened Dermot's driver's door and started shovelling gunky apples into his car as fast as I could.

It was hot work, but I got them all in. When I'd finished, the cow-pattern seat covers were buried and you couldn't see much of the steering wheel.

Then I had an extra idea. I groped down into the squishy apples till I felt Dermot's keys in the ignition. I started the engine, groped some more till I found the heater knob, switched the heater on full and locked all the doors.

Revenge felt good.

But only for a sec.

Dermot's angry yell, ringing out across the carpark, put an end to that.

The human heart's almost as weird as the human brain.

It does exactly the same skip when you feel love as when you feel fear.

Mine did it just then, when I heard Sergeant Cleary coming back again with someone else. The other footsteps sounded like Dad. He's got metal tips on the heels of his cowboy boots and they click on lino.

The thought of seeing Dad made my heart skip with love.

The thought of him seeing me here in a cell made my heart skip with fear at exactly the same time.

Then, after all that, it wasn't Dad, it was Dermot's mum. She must have metal tips on her heels too.

When I saw her hair bobbing past the window in my cell door, my heart skipped again. It always does when I see people's mums. It's not love or fear, but. I think it might be jealousy.

My heart's been doing a lot of skipping today.

It did a huge one earlier when I saw Dermot and his mates running at me across the carpark, yelling furiously.

For a sec I stood, frozen.

I thought I could hear stewed apples bubbling away behind me in Dermot's car, but then I realised it was my tummy churning with fear.

My heart started pumping and I ran.

I thought I could get away because even though I'm much smaller than Dermot, I'm a good runner. Dermot and his mates play footy, but they also smoke and eat heaps of sausages.

Boy, was I wrong.

Dermot must have been doing extra training, or perhaps he was just extra furious, because I could hear his pounding feet getting closer behind me as I sprinted along the road back to town.

The road's called Memorial Drive. It's lined with trees and each tree's got a metal plaque on it in memory of a soldier who was killed in World War One. Their families planted the trees when that war ended, so the trees are over eighty years old and pretty big.

I was grateful for that today.

When I started hearing Dermot's angry breath behind me, wet and raspy, I knew my only chance was to be a better climber than him.

Dad's taught me a lot about climbing trees, including how you should never rush at one.

Except in emergencies.

I rushed at the nearest tree.

The trunk was big and smooth, but Dad once showed me some tricks for getting up big smooth trees. Luckily my hands weren't too sweaty and soon I was hauling myself up onto the first branch.

I clambered up into the high branches among the foliage.

Below I could hear Dermot swearing. I was in luck again. His mum didn't seem to have shown him any tree-climbing tricks.

My heart was skipping all over the place as I wrapped my arms round a branch and listened to the hoons trying to form a human pyramid. I could half-see them through the leaves. The pyramid kept collapsing and there was lots of swearing about people standing on other people's faces.

Then something ripped through the leaves close to my face.

And again.

'Aim for her head,' one of the hoons yelled.

They were chucking rocks at me.

I huddled against the branch, desperately hoping there were enough leaves to camouflage me. And wishing it was an apple tree so at least

I'd have something to chuck back at them.

More rocks crashed through the leaves.

I heard a car approaching. It slowed down, then drove on.

'That's illegal,' shouted one of the hoons at the car. 'Driving and using a mobile. I'm calling the cops.'

The driver must have beat him to it because about ten minutes later, just as I'd decided to climb down and offer to show the hoons how to throw straight in return for my freedom, I heard Sergeant Cleary's siren approaching.

'Run!' someone yelled.

'No,' shouted Dermot. 'I want the cops to see what she's done.'

Sergeant Cleary made the hoons stand on the other side of the road while I climbed down. As I slid down the trunk past the metal plaque I noticed the tree was in memory of Private Ern Wilson, killed 1917, aged nineteen.

'Thanks, Ern,' I said silently.

When Sergeant Cleary saw the apples cooking in Dermot's car, his mouth gave a little grin before he could stop it. The police in our town have had a lot of trouble with Dermot's car.

Dermot went mental.

'It's not funny,' he yelled and tried to grab me.

Sergeant Cleary pushed Dermot back. He wasn't smiling now.

'You're right, son,' he said. 'It's a serious crime, attempted assault. Do it again and I'll take you both in.'

Dermot tried to grab me again.

Sergeant Cleary took us both in.

Except that Dermot's being released now.

I can see him and his mum out in the corridor. She's got her arms round him in a big hug.

He's lucky, having a mum who's got a motel. Sergeant Cleary's got a lot of rellies who visit from interstate.

Why are my eyes going all hot and damp? Police perks are a fact of life, nothing to get upset about.

It's not that.

There's another reason my cheeks are wet.

Watching Mrs Figgis hug Dermot makes my heart give the most painful skip of all.

Because even if I sit in this cell for the rest of my life, my mum can never come here and hug me and set me free.

I still can't believe it.

There I was, mentally preparing myself for jail, feeling lucky I can have these conversations in my head so at least I wouldn't get too bored in the clink, not for the first couple of years at least, when suddenly I heard a rattling and Sergeant Cleary opened my cell door.

'OK,' he said, 'hop it.'

I stared at him.

'Off home,' he said, 'and don't upset any more eighteen-year-olds.'

'But,' I said, gobsmacked, 'aren't I under arrest?'

Sergeant Cleary watched my hands closely, frowning, but he didn't understand.

I wrote it in my notebook and showed him.

He gave a weary grin. 'No, Rowena,' he said. 'You're not under arrest. What you did was technically a crime, but under the circs, given that Dermot Figgis had it coming, and given the stress you must be under with that dopey dad of yours, I've decided not to charge you.'

As I followed Sergeant Cleary down the corridor to the front desk, I wrote indignantly in my notebook.

'What do you mean, dopey dad?'

Sergeant Cleary gave a sigh.

'I don't mean anything,' he said. 'I'm just saying it must be tough for you having a dad who's a bit of a ratbag.'

For a sec I couldn't speak. My hands were rigid with anger. I wondered how many years in jail I'd get for filling up a police car with rotting apples. We've got heaps more back at the orchard.

Constable Pola looked up from the TV.

'Don't get us wrong,' he said. 'Your old man's a nice bloke. It's just that he's a bit of a disaster area in the singing and clothing departments.'

It was an outrage. The police are meant to be tolerant and understanding. We did a project on it at school.

Sergeant Cleary offered me an oatmeal biscuit.

'We're not having a go at you,' he said gently. 'You do a top job, coping with him. We understand it's a tough call for a kid, having an embarrassing dad, that's all.'

I ignored the biscuit.

I didn't ignore the vicious insults about Dad.

I grabbed a sheet of paper off the desk and wrote on it in big letters so they'd understand.

'MY DAD IS THE BEST DAD IN THE WORLD. IF YOUR WIFE DIED, YOU'D PROBABLY TRY TO CHEER YOURSELF UP BY WEARING BRIGHT SHIRTS AND SINGING COUNTRY MUSIC TOO.'

Sergeant Cleary and Constable Pola looked up from the sheet of paper and exchanged a glance. I could see they'd never thought about it that way before.

Sergeant Cleary pushed about six biscuits into my hand and steered me out the door.

'I haven't told your dad about this,' he said. 'I didn't want him coming down here and singing at me.'

He went back into the police station. If I could, I would have shouted after him that Dad doesn't sing at just anyone, only when he's feeling really moved.

I thought about putting it in a note and leaving it under the windscreen wiper of the police car.

I didn't, because what Sergeant Cleary had said was starting to sink in.

He hadn't rung Dad.

Dad didn't have to know what had happened.

I was still standing there, weak with relief, when a woman got out of a van and came over to me.

'Rowena?' she said.

She was tall and blonde and wearing posh clothes and for a millionth of a sec I had a totally and completely dopey thought.

That Mum hadn't died after all, that she'd just lost her memory and wandered off and now she'd got it back and here she was.

Then I remembered that Mum wasn't tall and blonde. In the photos in Dad's album she was shorter than him, with dark hair. And she had smiling eyes.

This woman was smiling, but her eyes weren't.

'Hello,' she said. 'I'm Paige Parker.'

Of course. That's where I'd seen her before. On telly, on that current-affairs show.

I saw the van she'd just got out of had a TV logo on it.

'You been having a bit of a run-in with the police?' she asked.

I didn't know what to say. I was confused. If Paige Parker and her TV crew were filming a story on Mr Wetherby as one of the oldest surviving diggers in the state, why was she interested in me?

Then I twigged. Mr Wetherby isn't much of a talker, not since his teeth got a bit loose. Ms Parker must be looking for other local personalities to pad out her story. People with World War One relatives and quiet teeth. The police must have given her my name. Kids with bits missing always get heaps of viewer interest, specially if they're into crime.

Except I'm not into crime. Not really. I had to explain that to Ms Parker before I was branded a crim on national TV.

I handed her the police biscuits and pulled out my notebook.

'I was just getting Dermot Figgis to back off,' I wrote, 'like our soldiers did to the Germans in World War One.'

I handed her the page and waited for her to thank me for linking my explanation to her story about Mr Wetherby.

The cameraman was getting out of the car. Perhaps she was going to thank me on camera.

Then I realised what a total and complete idiot I was being. I snatched the page back from her and turned and sprinted down the laneway next to the police station.

'Rowena,' I heard her yelling. 'Wait.'

I didn't.

I ran across the supermarket carpark, round the back of the newsagent and hid in the fruit shop's big waste bin.

It was pretty revolting in there. Today's a public holiday so it hadn't been emptied since yesterday and the heat had made all the fruit and veg scraps go mushy.

It was like I was being punished for what I did to Dermot Figgis's car.

But I stayed in there till I was sure the TV people had gone.

If I'd appeared on TV, Dad would have seen it and then he'd have known about Dermot's car and me being hauled in by the cops.

Dad works very hard at being a good dad. He's not so hot on punishment and discipline, but he does it if he thinks he has to.

He'd really think he had to if he heard about the car and the cops. Which would totally and completely ruin what's left of Mum's special day.

I wish I didn't have so much cabbage slime in my shoes. It's hard to walk fast with soggy socks and I want to get home as quickly as I can so Dad and me can get back to being really close and I can forget about all the crook stuff that's happened today.

Oh no, I've just had an awful thought.

The TV people probably know where I live.

Dermot Figgis certainly does.

It's not over yet.

I hurried into our driveway and stopped dead.

The hairs on the back of my neck stood up. Or they would have done if they hadn't been sticky with peach juice and mushy cauliflower.

A strange car was leaving the house and coming towards me.

My brain twitched with fear but it didn't switch off.

Who was it?

One of the TV people?

Dermot Figgis in a hire car?

Luckily our driveway's really long because it goes right through the orchard, so I had time to duck behind a tree before the car got close.

As it bumped past I had a look inside. There was only one person, a bloke a bit older than Dad with black curly hair and a suit.

Dermot Figgis's lawyer?

A TV producer who'd been to see Dad about the screen rights to my life of crime?

I hurried up to the house, my chest tight and not just because the watermelon juice in my T-shirt was drying all stiff.

Claire was in the kitchen washing up and keeping baby Erin amused with the timer on the oven.

'G'day, Ro,' she said. 'What's that in your hair?'

I looked at my reflection in the oven door.

'Lettuce,' I said. 'Don't worry, I'm planning to hose it off.'

Claire grinned. She's got really good at understanding sign language since she married Dad. Less than a year and she knows 'planning'. Not bad.

Erin gave a big chortle and pointed to my head. Two-month-old babies think soggy lettuce on the scalp is the funniest thing they've ever seen.

'Who was that who just left?' I asked, trying to keep my hands steady.

Claire hesitated, but only for a sec.

'Bloke Dad used to know,' she said. 'He's passing through town. Dropped in for a cuppa.'

I concentrated on tickling Erin under the chin so Claire wouldn't see how relieved I felt.

'Dad's outside,' said Claire. 'Spraying the back paddock.'

I wasn't surprised to hear that. Dad always has a spray on Mum's anniversary. Spraying perks him up when he's feeling down. He sprays on the day his mum died, too, and every time a big bill arrives. When Erin peed on his Carla Tamworth records, he sprayed for about six hours.

I took a deep breath and hoped there hadn't been any other visitors before the one I'd seen. TV journalists, for example, or motor-vehicle insurance investigators.

I went out to the back paddock. Dad was on the tractor. He must have fixed it because it was hauling the big blower up and down the rows of trees as good as new.

Dad looked at me through the misty clouds of spray.

I looked back anxiously, trying to tell whether he was angry or upset. I couldn't see his face. When Dad sprays he pulls his cowboy hat down over his eyebrows and ties a scarf round his nose and mouth. He reckons it's just as good as a spray suit and doesn't make him feel like a Martian.

I could tell from the way he was sitting that everything was OK. Dad's one of those people who, when they've heard something that makes them angry or depressed, their shoulders sort of hunch up and they hardly ever steer a tractor with their feet like Dad was doing now.

I felt wobbly with relief.

Dad waved and told me to stand back while he finished spraying.

'OK,' I said. 'Then we'll get the album out and look at photos of Mum.'

That's another good thing about having a dad who can speak with his hands. You can have a conversation even when he's got a scarf over his mouth and you've got a two hundred horsepower blower roaring away next to your ear.

I stood back and watched Dad blasting the root weevil, plus any blue mould, codling moths and apple scab that happened to be in the area.

They wouldn't have known what hit them.

Just like I didn't know what hit me a few minutes later.

Dad finished the last row, switched everything off and strolled towards me, tipping his hat back and pulling his scarf down.

'G'day, Tonto,' he said. 'I was worried about you. Thought Dermot Figgis might have clogged up the car wash and flooded the town.'

My insides dropped, but only a little way because Dad was hugging me so tight.

How did he know about Dermot's car?

Then I saw the empty trailer, still caked with bits of rotten apple, sitting in the corner of the paddock.

Of course. Mr Lorenzini must have told him.

I looked anxiously up at Dad.

'Good one, Tonto,' he said proudly, grinning down at me.

I gaped at him. I almost asked him to say it again with his hands in case the blower had damaged my eardrums.

'That'll teach Dermot Figgis to mock the memory of a fine woman,' continued Dad. 'I've rung Mrs Figgis and told her that if Dermot's got a problem with what you did, he can come out here and I'll hose his car out myself. Then I'll do his mouth.'

I sagged against Dad's chest, dizzy with relief.

'And I rang Sergeant Cleary, too,' Dad went on, 'and told him that next time he decides to lock you up, I want to know pronto. I asked him why he hadn't rung me, but he wouldn't say. Just kept saying it didn't matter cause he'd already released you. I reckon he's a ratbag.'

I grinned into Dad's shirt.

'Here,' said Dad, stepping back and rummaging in his pocket, 'I want you to have this to help you pass the time if you find yourself in the slammer again.'

He pulled out his hanky and unwrapped something silver and shiny.

It was a mouth-organ.

Dad blew a few notes and handed it over.

'It was my grandfather's,' he said. 'His mates sent it home after he was killed in the war.'

Then Dad launched into a Carla Tamworth song about a bloke sitting in jail waiting for his sweetheart to turn up so he can prove he didn't murder her. She turns up eight years later because it's taken her that long to finish the tunnel she's dug to rescue him.

I tried to play bits of the tune, but I didn't do a very good job. It's not easy, playing a harmonica when your throat's all lumpy with happiness.

Has any kid in the history of the world had such a completely and totally top dad?

No way.

The rest of the day was perfect.

Well, almost.

Me and Dad and Claire cooked a fantastic dinner. Claire put chopped onion in the apple fritters and they tasted better than they ever have in my whole life.

Claire was great the whole evening. It's only her second anniversary of Mum, and these occasions can be pretty tough for a new wife.

She handled it brilliantly, even when Dad got a bit carried away and went on about what a great talker Mum was. He told the story about the time he invented an apple-polishing machine and his dad's pit bull terrier fell in and its face got polished so much it lost most of its fierce looks and Mum persuaded the local RSPCA officers not to prosecute Dad even though Grandad really wanted them to.

'She won 'em over just with words,' said Dad, misty-eyed. 'Didn't need to use beer or apple pies or anything, the Gab didn't.'

Mum's family name was Gable before she was married, and because she was so good at stringing words together, Dad used to call her 'the Gab'.

'That must be where Ro gets being such a great talker from,' said Claire, smiling at me. 'The gift of the Gab.'

That's the nicest thing anyone has ever said to me with their mouth. I'm making my pillow damp now, just thinking about it.

I reckon Mum would be glad that Dad's got a top person like Claire for a new wife. And a top baby like Erin for a new daughter. She'd reckon he deserves to be happy.

And I agree with her.

Which is why I'm so worried about the phone call this evening.

Dad answered it, and when he'd hung up he turned to us, his face alarmed and a bit disbelieving like he'd just heard someone had invented a tractor that could fly.

'That TV mob that was at the ceremony this morning,' he said, 'they want to film me tomorrow for their show.'

Claire hugged him. She looked concerned too.

'How do you feel about that?' she said.

Dad glanced at me. He must have noticed I was feeling anxious too.

'OK,' said Dad, 'I s'pose.' He frowned, then gave a sort of grin. 'Perhaps I'll get my own series.'

Normally if he said something like that, Claire would tickle him till he begged for mercy. This time she just chewed her lip.

I tried to look on the bright side.

Sergeant Cleary must have given the TV people Dad's name as a colourful local personality with a relative who died in World War One and good teeth.

Which is fine except for one thing.

Some people can feel really hurt if unkind things are said about them on national TV.

Things like 'one of the biggest ratbags in the district'.

It was worse than I'd feared.

I tried to keep them away.

I got up really early and stuck a big sign on our front gatepost. 'Danger,' it said. 'Root Weevil Plague. Keep Out.'

They ignored it. Their van just roared up the driveway. Perhaps TV people aren't very good at reading.

By the time I got up to the house, they were already talking with Dad in the lounge-room.

I pressed my ear to the door, trying to hear what they were saying. It was no good, I couldn't catch a word. Erin was crying in her room and she's loud enough to drown out tractors with holes in their mufflers.

Then Claire hurried into Erin's room and the crying stopped.

I pressed my ear to the door again.

'Cock-eyed,' I heard Dad say. 'Totally and completely cock-eyed.'

Claire appeared, jiggling Erin.

'Ro,' she said. 'Fair go. How's a bloke meant to be his sparkling best in an interview when he's being eavesdropped on?'

I lifted my hands to protest, but Claire just grinned.

'Anyway,' she continued, 'you won't miss anything. The minute they've gone he'll be dancing around telling us everything he said.'

I went outside and did some digging.

Digging's my best thing for stress. There's something about shoving a spade into dirt that really takes your mind off tension and worries.

I'm digging Erin a sandpit. It's a surprise for when she's old enough to hold a bucket. Up till today it hasn't been a very big sandpit because I haven't been stressed that much lately.

It's pretty big now, but.

And I still couldn't stop worrying.

What had Dad meant by 'cock-eyed'?

Was he saying he'd rather be described as cock-eyed than a ratbag?

Or had he just been telling his funny story about when he sang a country and western song at his uncle's funeral and the congregation just stared at him cock-eyed, mostly because he was at the wrong funeral?

The more I dug, the more I reckoned it was the funny story.

Finally I heard the TV people drive off in their van.

I raced indoors, grabbing my mouth-organ off the verandah in case Dad wanted some music played while he entertained us with the best bits of his interview.

He didn't.

I could tell from the way he was sitting slumped forward. And from the way Claire had her arms round him and her head against his neck.

My insides went splat like an over-ripe apple.

'What happened?' I asked.

Dad had his face in his hands and Claire was staring at the floor, so they didn't hear me.

I knelt down in front of them.

Claire jumped. She seemed alarmed to see me. She gave Dad an anxious nudge.

'Didn't the filming go well?' I asked.

'They didn't do any filming,' said Claire. 'They want to do it later in the week.'

'Eh?' I said, using the special sign me and Dad have worked out for a stunned pit bull terrier staggering out of an apple-polishing machine. 'Later in the week? But Anzac Day was yesterday. Why are they taking so long to do the segment?'

'Turns out,' said Dad quietly, 'the sneaky

mongrels didn't come to town to film an Anzac Day segment. They came to film me.'

I stared at Dad while I digested this.

For a sec I hoped his distraught expression was just from the stress of being a star and wondering which belt buckle to wear.

It wasn't.

'Or rather what I should say,' said Dad angrily, 'is that they came to film a heap of cock-eyed lies and nonsense.'

He stood up and stormed out of the room.

His bedroom door slammed.

I started to go after him. Claire grabbed me.

'Let me talk to him first,' she said. 'Please.'

I didn't take much persuading because I've got something even more important to do.

I'm on my way to do it now.

That's one of the great things about talking with your hands. You can run all the way into town and then yell at someone straight away without having to catch your breath.

How dare Paige Parker try and get a mean cruel comedy segment out of a great dad just cause he's a bit eccentric.

Anyway, why shouldn't an apple farmer sing country and western songs? Country and western singers are allowed to have apple trees.

Let's see what Paige Cheese-Brain Parker has to say about that.

I know where she's staying.

Posh TV people don't stay in cheap motels or caravan parks, and there's only one posh motel in town.

I just wish it wasn't Mrs Figgis's.

I thought I knew the worst thing that could happen at Mrs Figgis's motel.

I thought it was if Mrs Figgis caught me and made me hose out Dermot's car.

Boy, was I wrong.

What happened was much worse than that.

I was scared Mrs Figgis would be at reception, so I didn't go there to ask which unit Paige Parker was in. Motel owners have to spend long hours at the reception desk in case the guests try and steal the pens.

As it turned out I didn't need to ask. I guessed a TV star would be in the Honeymoon Suite cause it's got a spa and a microwave.

At least I was right about that.

I crept across the carpark towards the Honey-moon Suite, ducking down behind the cars so I couldn't be seen from the office.

Suddenly a car door opened and almost bashed me in the head.

A grown-up got out of the car.

It was Mrs Figgis.

'Rowena Batts,' she said loudly.

I froze, wishing there was a very deep sandpit nearby so I could bury myself.

There wasn't.

'Um . . .' I said. 'Er . . .'

My hands flapped helplessly.

It's really hard making excuses when the other person doesn't understand sign and you can't think of anything to say even if they did.

'You poor kid,' said Mrs Figgis. Except she didn't sound very sympathetic. 'I think what your father did to you is a disgrace.'

I stared at her.

What did she mean?

'No wonder you do crazy things,' said Mrs Figgis, glaring at me angrily. 'I'd want to kill him if I was you.'

I started to back away, wondering if the pressure of living alone with Dermot had made her go mental.

'It's OK,' she said, 'I know who you're here to see. Go on, she's in 23.'

I hurried over to the Honeymoon Suite before Mrs Figgis snapped and attacked me with her shopping bag.

Paige Parker opened the door while I was still bashing on it.

Her face relaxed and she put her hand on my shoulder. 'Rowena,' she said, 'what a nice surprise. Come in. Come in.'

I went in.

'Have a seat,' said Paige Parker.

I didn't. I went over to the big mirror on the wall, picked up a lipstick from the clutter of makeup on the bench, and wrote in big letters on the glass, 'LAY OFF MY DAD.'

'Rowena,' said Paige Parker, 'we have to talk.'

I glared at her. Nobody tells me to talk if I don't want to.

I tore a page out of my notebook and handed it to her. The writing wasn't great because I'd done it while I was running into town, but she could still read it.

'It's not fair,' it said. 'Dad had an unhappy childhood. Now he's a top dad. Don't make fun of him.'

Paige Parker gave a big sigh.

On the TV next to her a video was playing. On the screen white mice were running around in cages. They were pretty weird mice. Some had no tails. Others didn't have enough legs. She was probably planning to make fun of them next.

'Rowena,' said Paige Parker, 'there's something I have to tell you.'

She sat on the settee and patted the cushion next to her.

I stayed standing.

'This isn't going to be easy for you to hear,' said Paige Parker softly, 'but I sense you're a person who would rather know the truth.'

Suddenly the sound of her fake-friendly voice and the smell of her perfume was making me feel a bit queasy.

What was she going to tell me?

That Dad once got into a fight with Mr Cosgrove at a community service night and pushed his face into a bowl of avocado dip?

That Dad once jumped up on stage at a Carla Tamworth concert and sang a song to me even though the whole crowd was chucking stuff at him?

I knew that.

I knew everything she could tell me about Dad.

That's what I thought.

Boy, was I wrong.

'Rowena,' said Paige Parker in a soft voice, the sort of voice people use to speak to very little kids. 'I'm not doing a story about eccentric dads. I'm doing a story about the chemical sprays that farmers use on their crops.'

Suddenly I felt better. Dad's an expert on sprays. He uses heaps. He's always giving other farmers advice about them. He'd be perfect for a segment on sprays as long as he didn't try and talk with his scarf over his mouth.

That's what I thought.

'To be more exact,' continued Paige Parker, 'I'm doing a story on farmers who use sprays in a harmful way.'

She pointed to the TV screen. The poor mice with bits missing were still scampering around.

'These mice,' said Paige Parker, 'were all born with physical problems. All for the same reason. Before they were born their mothers were exposed to large amounts of chemical farm spray.'

I stared at the TV, my head spinning. It was the most outrageous accusation I'd ever heard.

'My dad's never hurt mice,' I said angrily. 'We haven't even got mice on our farm.'

I could tell she didn't understand me, but that didn't stop her. She picked up a fat wad of photocopied pages and looked straight at me.

'University tests,' she said, 'have shown that sprays can hurt people as well. If their mothers were exposed to lots of spraying, people can be born with physical problems too.'

Suddenly I was feeling very queasy.

'Your dad,' she said, 'does a lot of spraying.'

Suddenly I couldn't breathe.

Then I realised what's happened.

This is Mrs Figgis's revenge for what I did to Dermot's car. She's told the TV people a whole lot of made-up lies about Dad and sprays. She's forged university documents. She's found a video of mice who've been in car accidents. She's made it look like it was Dad's fault I was born with bits missing from my throat.

I tried to explain all this to Paige Parker. I tried to explain that the doctors have always said that my throat was probably a genetic problem I got from Mum or Dad. I tried to explain that me and Dad had our yearly medical check-up only two months ago and the doctors said we were as fit as fleas.

My hands were shaking so much with rage and indignation I could hardly write.

Paige Parker made me sit down.

She told me she's got some other evidence. 'Gold-plated' was how she described it.

I'm letting her show it to me.

We're driving there now in the TV van.

I'm not worried, but.

It'll be as ridiculous as all the other stuff.

But it's important I see it. It's important I see exactly what vicious hurtful lies Mrs Figgis and Paige Parker have cooked up between them so I can get Paige Parker sacked from her job and Mrs Figgis run out of town.

I don't want to think.

I don't want to remember what I've just seen.

I just want to lie here under this tree and look up at the leaves. If I keep staring at the leaves, I won't have to remember.

It's no good.

I can't get the pictures out of my mind.

I've seen some pretty bad paddock damage in my time. From drought. And bushfire. And truck mud-racing. Once at school I saw a photo of what a war can do to an orchard. But I've never seen anything like what Paige Parker showed me today.

When we got out of the TV van I just stared.

It was a big paddock and once it would have had fruit trees.

Now it's just got rows of withered tree skeletons standing in a wasteland of dead grass.

Not burnt.

Not drought-affected.

Not bombed.

Just dead.

'A few weeks ago,' said Paige Parker, suddenly using her TV voice, 'this was a normal healthy orchard. Then we had it sprayed.'

'What with?' I whispered.

My hand-movements were so small she couldn't have understood even if she'd known sign, but she must have seen in my face what I was asking.

'We used a lot of different sprays,' she said. 'Including, for purposes of scientific research, sprays now on the danger list. Sprays that farmers were still using in this district up until about ten years ago.'

I realised Paige Parker had paused, and was staring at me intently.

'Farmers,' she said, 'including your father.'

When I heard this, the tree skeletons started to wobble in front of my eyes and not just because I was standing in the sun.

Then I had a thought.

'How come,' I wrote shakily on my notepad, 'our orchard doesn't look like this?'

I held the notepad up so Paige Parker could read it.

'Because,' she said, 'we used more chemicals than even the most enthusiastic farmer would use. We wanted to show viewers just what this stuff can do. So they can make up their own minds. About whether these chemical cocktails have the power to tragically ruin the lives of young Australians like you, Rowena.'

I stared at the paddock. No fruit. No leaves. No birds. Not even any insects.

I've seen Paige Parker do heaps of segments on TV.

Her facts have always seemed pretty good to me. They've never looked to me like she's cooked them up with a revenge-crazed motel proprietor.

What if she hasn't now?

What if these ones are true?

Suddenly I felt weak and had to hold on to the fence.

Then I snatched my hands away in case they'd sprayed that too.

Paige Parker put her hand on my shoulder.

'I'm sorry we had to show you this, Rowena,' she said, not softly but loud as if she was speaking to several million people. 'We felt you deserved to know the truth.'

Even though my eyes were full of tears, I noticed the cameraman was filming me.

If I could, I would have screamed 'STOP!' But I couldn't, so I ran.

I dashed across the road and jumped into a gully and sprinted along a dry creek bed so they couldn't follow me in the van.

I heard them running after me for a bit. Then the cameraman tripped over something, went sprawling and swore.

'It's OK, Mike,' I heard Paige Parker say, 'we've got enough.'

I kept running for ages until I came to this tree.

It's a huge tree and it's very green, but even several million leaves aren't enough to distract me.

My chest's hurting.

It's hurting partly from the run and partly from the awful thought I'm having.

The thought that if Paige Parker is right, and Dad did use too much spray before I was born, then he could have caused a terrible, terrible thing to happen.

He could have caused Mum to die.

As I ran home, trying to keep tears out of my eyes so I didn't crash into trees, I knew exactly what I wanted Dad to do.

I wanted him to get a microscope and a bloodhound and a team of private detectives and come up with some evidence of his own.

Evidence to prove he didn't use too much spray when I was inside Mum.

Evidence to prove he didn't make my throat turn out crook.

Evidence to prove he didn't kill Mum.

'Dad,' I wanted to beg him after I burst into the house. 'Prove they're wrong. Prove you didn't do it. Please.'

But I couldn't.

He was sitting at the kitchen table, shoulders slumped, staring at a slice of toast. He'd probably been there since the TV people left this morning.

He looked so unhappy I couldn't make him feel worse.

How would he have felt, his own daughter demanding proof and not trusting him?

So I just clenched my guts into a small tight knot and said, 'I know you didn't do it, Dad.'

He hugged me so tight that the fringe on his shirt left little dents in my cheek.

'I'd never do anything to hurt you, Tonto,' he whispered.

He hugged me for so long that Claire got worried about dehydration and made us a cup of tea.

It was a kind thought, but I needed more than tea.

What about Mum? I wanted to ask, but I couldn't.

And then, when Dad had wiped his eyes and built up his strength with a cuppa and a mouthful of toast, he told me without being asked.

His evidence proved everything I wanted it to prove, everything I needed it to prove so our lives could go back to being the same.

Except that by the time Dad had finished, my life had changed totally and completely for ever and ever.

I'm lying here on my bed and my brain feels like someone's been bashing it with the wardrobe.

It's in shock.

It can't take everything in.

Perhaps if I start at the beginning and go through it all again slowly, it'll cope better.

First Dad opened his cardboard expanding file, the one he keeps all his Carla Tamworth fan-club newsletters and other important documents in. It was already on the kitchen table instead of under the bed where he usually keeps it.

'This,' he said, 'was my bible.'

He slid a crumpled piece of paper across the table to me. It was covered with numbers written in biro, dirty thumbprints and what looked like a couple of squashed flies.

'This was given to me fifteen years ago,' said Dad, 'by the top agricultural chemical bloke in the state.' He took the piece of paper back and smoothed it out carefully, eyes shining like it was a satin shirt he'd found in the two-dollar bin at the op-shop.

'Every squirt of spray I used in those days,' said Dad, 'I bought from Stan. And I stuck to his instructions like it was the holy book.' Dad pointed to the numbers on the paper. 'How much. How often. How much water to mix in. Look, he even wrote down how thick my rubber gloves should be.'

Claire was standing behind Dad, rubbing his shoulders.

'Those old-time salesmen really knew their

stuff,' she said. 'It was their whole life. My dad sold stationery. He could name eleven different types of paper clip.'

I was so relieved to see Dad's evidence I wanted to snatch the piece of paper and cover it with kisses.

I didn't, partly because of the squashed flies and partly because there was something really important I had to ask Dad.

I took a deep breath.

'Dad,' I said, 'how did Mum die?'

I first asked him that when I was seven and he held my face gently in his hands and said, 'Peacefully, soon after you were born.'

I didn't ask for more details because he was crying at the time and I didn't want to upset him more.

Also I had a terrible suspicion her dying might have had something to do with me being born, so I didn't want more details in case they upset me more.

Now, suddenly, this arvo, I did want more details.

Dad was looking pretty strong, staring at that piece of paper, and I felt he could probably cope.

Boy, was I wrong.

He shut his eyes and his shoulders slumped even lower.

'Jeez, Tonto,' he said with such tiny hand-movements it was like he was whispering,

'I've done a terrible thing.'

I stared at him in panic.

Oh no, I thought. Please don't say you were so besotted with love for Mum that you forgot to check your bible and you accidentally mixed up a lethal dose of spray and a cloud of it floated into the house while Mum was only wearing undies.

Please don't say that.

Dad took a very deep breath, then sighed and let his hands drop onto the table.

Claire hugged him and stroked his hair.

'Tell her,' she said quietly to Dad. 'You'll have to sooner or later.'

Dad nodded.

He looked at me and his face was scared.

Then he got up from the table and went out of the kitchen and I heard him go into his bedroom and open the wardrobe.

For a sec I thought he was going to hide in it. When a pet cockatoo I used to have ripped Erin's room to shreds before she was born, I felt like spending the rest of my life in my wardrobe. I would have done if the cocky hadn't ripped it to shreds too.

Dad came back into the kitchen.

He was still looking scared and he was carrying an old cowboy-boot box.

'Rowena,' he said, and took another deep breath.

I took one too.

He only calls me that when things are really serious.

'Rowena,' he went on, his voice wobbling, 'I haven't told you the truth about how Mum died.'

I tried to swallow but my mouth felt drier than an over-sprayed paddock.

Dad took the lid off the boot box and lifted out some old newspaper cuttings. He put them on the table. I studied them, desperately hoping I wouldn't see any words like 'lethal dose of spray' or 'only wearing undies'.

The cuttings were yellow and the print was faded. For a sec I thought that's why I couldn't read them. Then I realised they were in a foreign language.

'Rowena,' said Dad, 'Mum was knocked down by a car in France.'

I stared at him.

'France?' I said, once my hands had regained the power of speech. 'France the country?'

'We were on a trip,' said Dad quietly. 'Me, Mum and you. Two months after you were born. We were staying in an old town with narrow streets. A car was going too fast . . .'

He stopped.

I felt like I was trying to breathe under stewed apples.

'The car hit her,' he whispered. 'It hit her and didn't stop. She was killed.'

293

His hand was trembling as he touched a blurry photo of Mum in one of the cuttings.

Claire was biting her lip and stroking his hair.

I just sat there, stunned, my whole life changed.

How could he do it?

How could he lie to me all this time?

After a bit, another question forced its way into my thoughts.

'Did they catch him?' I asked.

Dad shook his head.

'Some people reckoned they knew who it was,' he said. 'A local. But there was no proof. And you know how overworked police are in country towns. And anyway, what did it matter, she was dead. I was just so grateful it wasn't worse.'

I didn't understand.

Wasn't worse?

'How could it have been worse?' I yelled so loudly I knocked over the tomato sauce.

His eyes suddenly filled with tears.

'She could have been holding you,' he said. 'I was holding you, but she could have been.'

He put his arms round me and I started crying too.

After a while I pulled away.

'Why didn't you tell me?' I asked.

Dad stared at his hands.

'You were a kid,' he said, 'and . . . and I

didn't want you brooding about it all. I just wanted you to be happy.'

Then Claire put her arms round us both and murmured something to Dad about a tape.

Dad took an old walkman cassette out of the boot box and handed it to me.

'I recorded this in France,' he said. 'The day before Mum was killed.'

I stared at the tape.

For a sec I thought it was going to be Dad singing.

Then Claire explained.

Which is how come I'm lying here on my bed holding a tape of my mother's voice.

A voice I've never heard.

All my life I've tried to imagine it. A warm, soft, gentle voice. A strong, cheeky, laughing voice.

A loving voice.

And now, when at last I'm able to hear it, I'm scared.

But I'm going to do it now.

I'm putting the tape into my walkman.

I'm switching it on.

Now I understand.

Now I know why Dad's nuts about Carla Tamworth.

One of Australia's top country and western singers sounds just like my mum.

Except my mum's got a better voice.

I can't stop saying it.

My mum.

Singing just for me. Well, that's what I'm pretending.

The tape's pretty confused at first. Just heaps of loud voices talking over each other in French. That must be why Dad's never given me the tape before. It would have been a total and complete giveaway about France.

There's loads of clinking. Sounds like they're in a pub. Either that or an apple-sauce bottling factory.

Dad drops the tape player at one point and

says 'poop' and spends ages fiddling with the microphone.

Then a man makes an announcement in French and people clap. Either that or the place has got a tin roof and it starts to rain.

Then Mum starts to sing and the place goes quiet.

I'm not surprised.

She's brilliant.

She sings a country and western song about a dingo trapper who breaks his leg in the desert. He can't walk so his faithful old dog drags him back to town. It takes a week because the dog is caught in a dingo trap and she's got to drag that too.

There's a bit the trapper says in the chorus that gets to me every time.

'I know you love me
I know you're doing your best,
That's why I'm not angry
You've got my head in an ants' nest.'

Each time I play it my chest goes all tight with love for her.

I've had to stop playing it, partly because my chest's hurting and partly because I don't want to wear the tape out. It's got to last me for the rest of my life.

Erin's just started crying in her room.

I reckon she's going to have a voice just like Mum's.

I wish it could have been me.

I wish I could have had Mum's voice.

Instead of just a mouth-organ.

But I'm not going to think about that because I've got something much more important to think about.

Somewhere in a village in France is the bloke who killed my mum.

Free and alive and unpunished.

I've got to think how I can change that.

I've got to think how I can get to France and find him and prove he did it and bring him and his car to justice.

It won't be easy.

I'm lying here thinking of all the practical parts of it and I feel like my head's in an ants' nest too.

But one thing's for sure.

I'm going to get the mongrel.

I lay awake for hours wondering how a person with ninety-seven dollars in her savings account can get to France.

A garage sale?

A raffle?

A bank loan?

Trouble is, I can't tell anyone why I need to go. People just don't buy raffle tickets or give bank loans for missions of revenge.

Plus Dad wouldn't let me go. He hates me missing school. And he obviously thinks bringing a murdering hit-and-run driver to justice is too dangerous or he'd have done it himself.

At 2 a.m. I still hadn't solved the problem of how to get to France so I got up for a dig. I have some of my best ideas while I'm digging.

Except this time I didn't get to do any.

I'd just collected the spade off the verandah when Dad appeared wide-eyed at the back door.

'Rowena,' he said. 'No.'

He lunged towards me and grabbed the spade.

'You don't have to do that,' he said. 'I admit it. Mum isn't buried in the town cemetery, she's buried in France.'

I stared at him in horror.

His body sagged inside his Carla Tamworth pyjamas.

'Mum's grave here is just a pretend one,' he said miserably. 'A kind of memorial. I'm sorry, love.'

I felt sick.

All these years I've been visiting the wrong grave.

Then I stared at the spade in Dad's hands and felt even sicker.

He thought I was going to dig up Mum's grave to see if it was real.

'Dad,' I said weakly, 'I was only going to dig a sandpit.'

I took him down the garden and showed him.

There was an awkward silence. I could tell Dad was embarrassed he'd thought I could do such a thing. But grown-ups never really know what kids are capable of. Specially when it comes to catching hit-and-run drivers who've killed their mums.

'Dad,' I said, 'I want to go to France to visit Mum's real grave.'

I was telling the truth. I do want to visit it. I want to cut the grass on it and put fresh flowers on it and kneel down on it and tell her I've dealt with the mongrel who killed her.

Dad crouched down in the moonlight and studied the hole.

'Good-sized sandpit,' he said.

'Dad,' I said, sticking my hands in front of his face. 'Please. Take me to France.'

'It'll need a fair whack of sand,' said Dad.

I grabbed him and shook him. He grasped my hands and held them tight.

'Not now,' he said. 'One day, but not now.'

I tore my hands free.

'Why not now?' I demanded.

Dad hugged himself even though it wasn't the slightest bit cold. Maybe polyester satin pyjamas aren't as warm as they look.

'I can't afford it,' he said, 'and you've got school and I've got to deal with these TV clowns and Erin's too young to travel and . . .'

I interrupted him.

'You took me to France when I was as young as Erin,' I said.

Sometimes parents dig holes for themselves that are even bigger than sandpits.

Dad sighed.

'That was different,' he said. 'Mum's mum was living in Canada. You were her first grandchild. She sent us plane tickets so we could take you over there to show her. Mum arranged for us to stop off in France on the way back cause I'd never seen my grandfather's war grave.'

'So,' I said, 'you know how it feels to really want to see a grave.'

'I didn't want to see it,' he said. 'Mum made me.'

I was very close to hitting him with the spade.

'Tonto,' he said, 'I do know how you feel, but it's just not possible now. We'll go in a year or two, cross my heart and hope to get blue mould.'

'It's not fair,' I said bitterly.

But actually I wasn't that bitter because Dad had just given me another idea.

I know how I can get to France.

It won't be easy and I'll have to wag school tomorrow, but if I can pull it off I'll be on the plane in a week.

Grandad was killing ants when I arrived.

'Mongrels,' he was yelling at them.

He stood on his front step whacking them with a broom that was almost taller than he was.

Then he saw me and glared, panting. His skin was bright red under the white bristles on his face and head.

I felt like a little kid again. It used to really scare me when I was younger and Grandad's face would suddenly go red, usually from yelling at Dad or ants.

Grandad took a step back. 'Who are you?' he said. 'What do you want?'

I stood there, dumb.

I hadn't expected that.

It wasn't much of a welcome from my only living grandparent. Specially after I'd travelled three towns down the highway and walked forty-five minutes from the bus-stop.

'What's the matter?' demanded Grandad. 'Cat got your tongue?'

He didn't recognise me. I was confused. He couldn't have lost his marbles, he's only eighty-one. Mr Wetherby's ninety-eight and he knows the names of all his great-grandchildren and their Telly Tubbies.

Then it hit me. I hadn't seen Grandad for three years. People can change a lot in three years. He hadn't, but I had. My hair was much lighter three years ago.

I hunted in my bag for a piece of cardboard and my texta. I could have booted myself up the bum. On the bus I'd written the things I needed to say to Grandad on bits of cardboard and I'd completely forgotten to do one introducing myself.

I did a quick one now and held it up to him. 'I'm Ro,' it said. 'Your granddaughter.'

He stared at it for a long time. I wondered if I should write another one saying 'Your son Kenny's girl'.

Then he grinned. 'Rowena,' he said. 'Jeez, you've grown. Still dumb, but.'

I nodded and gave him a rueful shrug to show him it's no big deal.

He thought of something and glared again.

'Did that no-hoper son of mine send you?' he growled.

I shook my head. I didn't bother going into

more detail on a piece of cardboard. Grandad knows Dad hates him and doesn't want to see him. From the scowl on Grandad's face I could tell he felt the same.

Instead I found the first message I wrote on the bus and held it up.

'G'day, Grandad,' it said. 'I've come to ask you a very big favour.'

Grandad read it and scowled again.

'I'm not seeing that bludger son of mine,' he said. 'Not till he apologises.'

I sighed. This was what I'd feared. I was hoping we wouldn't get sidetracked into Dad and Grandad's war, but Grandad obviously still feels as strongly about it as Dad does. The last time they saw each other, Christmas three years ago, Grandad had too much homemade alcoholic cider and yelled at Dad and Dad called him a booze bucket and a viper-mouthed old troll and a pathetic excuse for a father.

It's tragic. I've even heard Dad talking about Grandad in the past tense, i.e. 'my dad's name *was* Clarrie', as if he'd carked it.

I decided to write another card explaining to Grandad that my visit had nothing to do with Dad.

Before I could, Grandad grabbed my hand.

'Hungry?' he asked.

I shook my head. I'd had an apple fritter walking from the bus-stop.

'Bulldust,' said Grandad. 'Kids are always hungry.'

He dragged me into the house. It was gloomy inside and smelt of old blankets and bacon. As I followed him down the passage I tried not to think about what might be waiting for me in the kitchen. It's not Grandad's fault. When people live alone and have to get through whole loaves of bread by themselves, life must be a continual race against blue mould.

In fact the slices he cut me looked pretty fresh. And the butter was from the fridge. I started to relax.

'Do you like jam?' said Grandad.

I hesitated, wondering how long the average solo pensioner takes to get through a jar of jam. Particularly one who prefers homemade cider to spreads.

'Course you do,' said Grandad. 'All kids like jam.'

He opened a new jar of apricot and spread it on the bread really thickly. I realised I was pretty hungry after all.

Then Grandad went over to the stove, picked some pieces of cold bacon out of a fat-congealed pan, laid them carefully on the bread and jam, shook tomato sauce onto the bacon, put the top of the sandwich on and slid it towards me.

'My favourite,' he said.

My stomach tried to hide under my liver.

Don't get ill and offend him, I told myself. Remember why you're here.

I took a deep breath, silently asked Mum to wish me luck and held up the next piece of cardboard.

'Can you take me to France,' it said, 'to see my mum's real grave?'

Even before Grandad had finished reading it, his face twisted into a snarl.

'France?' he spat. 'I wouldn't go to that dung heap if you paid me a million dollars.'

I hoped he was just grumpy because I wasn't eating the sandwich.

I pressed on with the next card.

'I'll pay you back for the plane ticket when I'm older,' it said.

'If you go to that death-trap of a country you won't get to be older,' snapped Grandad. 'My father went there and was killed. Your mother went there and was k . . .'

His voice petered out. He obviously wasn't sure if Dad had told me the secret about Mum. Then his voice came back.

'If you think I'm setting foot in France,' yelled Grandad, 'your brain's as dud as your throat.'

It wasn't looking good, but I wasn't despairing. I still had one more card.

I held it up.

'You could visit your dad's war grave,' it said.

'Why would I want to do that?' growled Grandad.

I stared at him, shocked.

Poor bloke. His dad was killed before he was born. It's tragic when a kid doesn't even get to meet a parent. If only his dad had left a tape of himself singing a country and western song.

Then I remembered the mouth-organ.

I took it out of my bag.

'This was your dad's,' I wrote on a piece of cardboard. 'Would you like it?'

Grandad stared at the mouth-organ, face going bright red again. Then he grabbed it and threw it into my bag.

'Get out,' he said. 'How dare you come here upsetting an old bloke. You're worse than your ratbag father. Out!'

He grabbed me and pushed me down the passage and out of the house and slammed the door behind me.

I stood in the front yard, shaking and indignant.

He could have just said no thanks.

For a sec I wanted to yell at him that he was a viper-mouthed old troll, but the cardboard was probably too thick to push under his door so I didn't.

I turned sadly and headed back to the bus-stop.

About fifty metres down the road I heard his voice.

'Rowena,' he was shouting, 'wait on.'

I turned, my heart doing a skip, and saw him hurrying towards me.

Yes, I thought, he's changed his mind. He's remembered the life-insurance money he got when grandma died and he's decided to spend it on getting closer to the father he never knew.

I held out my hands to give Grandad a hug.

He held out his hands too.

In them was a soggy paper bag.

'You forgot your sandwich,' he said.

This bus ride home is taking forever. If it doesn't reach town soon I might have to eat the sandwich.

At least it's giving me time to think.

Poor Grandad, not being able to get revenge for his dad's death. That's the crook thing about wars. You can't bring people to justice because they're allowed to kill each other.

Poor Dad, growing up with such an angry father. I reckon Dad's done a pretty good job, turning out so different. I'd rather have a dad with a bright-red shirt than a bright-red face any day.

I just wish he'd told me the truth about Mum.

I sort of understand why he didn't, but. He knew the most important thing was for me to feel close to Mum. He knew how far away France would seem to a kid.

He was right, it does seem far away.

Every time I try and think of a way of getting there, it seems further.

But I've got to get there.

If I can't think of a legal way soon, I might have to do something really desperate.

And I don't mean eat the sandwich.

As I hurried along the road to our place, I was so busy worrying how I could get to France I didn't notice the purple thing standing by our gate till I almost bumped into it.

Dermot Figgis's car.

My guts went tight.

I ducked behind a tree and crouched in some undergrowth.

The car was standing with all its doors open. The cow-pattern seat covers were spread out on the roof. The Simpsons car mats were on the bonnet.

Heart thumping, I wondered if Dermot had come to take my hairdryer so he could dry out the car quicker.

Tough luck, I thought. I haven't got a hairdryer.

Then I heard voices.

I peered through some couch grass and saw

Dermot and another bloke squinting up our driveway.

'Doesn't look any different,' said the bloke doubtfully. 'Looks the same as any other orchard.'

'It's a chemical bombsite,' said Dermot. 'Makes the Iraqi oilfields look like a national park. That's what the TV crowd told my mum.'

'Ripper,' said the bloke, scribbling in a notebook. 'If I can get that clown Kenny Batts to talk I'll get a front page out of this.'

Suddenly I recognised the bloke. Stan Gooch, a reporter with the local paper. He plays footy in the same team as Dermot Figgis. And there was Dermot, dobbing Dad in to him. Spreading lies and hurtful gossip.

I very nearly let Dermot have it. The bloke on the farm next to ours keeps horses and I could have had Dermot's car full of horse manure if they'd kept talking for another hour or so.

I didn't, but.

It was more urgent to warn Dad. Having your name dragged through the mud on national TV is bad enough, but on telly there's always the hope that people will be watching a video or changing the oil in the tractor when it's on.

Everyone round here reads the local paper.

I crept back down the road, jumped the fence, ran through the orchard and burst in through the back door.

'Where's Dad?' I said to Claire, who was

doing some paperwork at the kitchen table. 'The local paper's after him.'

Claire took a moment to understand my hand-movements. Then she gave a groan. 'Not the local paper as well,' she said. 'You'd better warn him. He's in the big shed.'

Typical Dad, I thought as I hurried out to the shed. When things get tough he always likes to keep busy. Probably changing the gaskets in the apple-polishing machine.

At first I couldn't see him in the gloom of the shed.

I pulled out the mouth-organ and played a few notes. Hand-movements aren't much use attracting someone's attention if they've got their head up an apple-chute.

'Over here, Tonto,' he called out.

He wasn't changing the gaskets in the apple-polishing machine. He wasn't even picking dust out of the grease nipples. He was sitting in the corner of the shed behind a pile of apple boxes eating a bacon and jam sandwich.

'Those TV mongrels have been trying to get me on the blower all day,' he said. 'Thought I'd be safer out here in case they turn up in person.'

He didn't say the word but I knew what he was doing.

Hiding.

I was shocked. Dad never hides from trouble.

All my life he's faced up to it and usually sung it a song.

Now he looked so sad and stressed I didn't know what to say.

I told him I'd do the same thing in his position. It wasn't true, but he'd lied about Mum to save my feelings so I thought it was only fair.

I took a deep breath and wished I didn't have to tell him about the local paper.

As it turned out, I didn't.

Claire came into the shed carrying Erin and her bankcard. She held the card out to Dad.

'Take it, love,' she said. 'Go to France till this blows over. Please.'

My heart started thumping so loudly I thought for a minute the apple-polishing machine had switched itself on.

Say yes, I begged him silently. Even if you don't want to, say yes for Mum.

Dad stood up.

'Thanks, love,' he said, 'but I'm not blowing all our savings. I'm staying here to fight the mongrels.'

My guts felt like stewed apple sliding down the inside of a car windscreen.

Claire sighed. 'You're going to fight the local paper as well?' she said.

I could see this rocked Dad. He hesitated for a bit, and when he spoke his voice was much quieter than it usually is.

'I can't leave you here with the bub,' he said. 'It'd be different if we could afford tickets for all of us.'

Claire gave a grim smile.

'I'll be OK,' she said. 'I've handled worse than a few pesky journalists.'

She has too. She used to be a teacher and once she took Year Six on a camp.

Dad was still hesitating.

I was holding my breath.

Claire looked hard at Dad, flicked her eyes towards me and back to Dad. She didn't think I saw it, but I did.

'I think you should,' she said to Dad.

Dad put his arms round her and the baby and buried his face in her hair.

'OK,' he mumbled.

'Yes!' I wanted to shout, but of course I couldn't.

I gave Claire a hug too, and told her she's the best step-mum in the history of the world, including Hollywood.

We've been making travel plans all evening. There's heaps of arrangements to make. We're going to drive to the city tomorrow and make them there, where the local paper can't find out about them.

My guts are in a knot.

I've been lying here in bed for hours, playing Mum's tape and thinking about what I've got to do when I get to France.

I feel like my head's in an ants' nest again.

It's pretty normal though, eh, not being able to sleep the night before a big trip.

Most people have that trouble, even when they're not planning how to catch a murderer.

I think the crew are onto me.

The flight attendants have been giving me strange looks ever since we got on the plane.

I saw two of them whispering to each other just now.

'The girl in 58B,' I think one said, 'she's planning to ruthlessly hunt down a French criminal and make the French police look lazy and slack. We'd better alert the French authorities.'

I hope I'm wrong.

I hope they're just staring because of my mouth-organ. I was playing it a bit loudly during takeoff. I needed something to help me relax and you can't dig on a plane.

My worry, but, is that they're staring because of the security-alarm incident.

It wasn't fair. Nobody warned me that a mouth-organ would set off the metal detector at the airport security gate. I'd have put it through the x-ray machine with Dad's belt buckle if they had.

Instead I had to take everything out of my pockets, including the plastic car and the rag doll I've borrowed from Erin's toybox.

Dad gave me a puzzled look when he saw them. He knows I haven't played with dolls for years, and I only play with cars when he wants a race.

I'm hoping he's thinking I've just borrowed them to remind me of Erin. Instead of to help me act out Mum's death for the jury in a French courtroom.

The security guards saw them too, and swapped a look.

I reckon they told the flight attendants.

It'll be tragic if I get stopped now, because everything's gone so well over the last three days.

We drove down to the city without any problems except for one scare when we saw a van behind us. We thought it was Paige Parker but it just turned out to be a nappy service.

The travel agent in the city was really helpful, specially when we gave him a box of apples. And the passport office, where we thought we might have to queue for days, was a breeze. They've got a special counter for handicapped people, and because Dad's finger was in a splint after he shut it in a cupboard door at our motel, we felt OK about using that.

It was the busiest three days of my life. I hardly had time to think, let alone worry about being sprung.

I've only started worrying about that since we've been on the plane.

If only I could tell Dad what I'm planning to do. At least then if the French customs officials handcuff me and try to bundle me on a plane home, he could protest to the Australian embassy.

But I don't want to make him more stressed. He's got enough on his plate as it is, poor bloke. The pressure of being unfairly hounded by the media's really getting to him.

Usually he wears his best clothes when we're going somewhere special. His pink satin shirt with the black guitar on the back and his Viking-on-a-tractor belt buckle.

So far this trip all he's worn are denim work shirts and the World War One belt buckle he only wears when he's depressed.

Usually if he was in a group of three hundred bored people he'd have a sing-song going by now. There's a Carla Tamworth song about a bloke sitting on a rock waiting for his pilot sweetheart to arrive for their wedding. He doesn't know she's crashed and he waits so long that moss grows on his tuxedo. It'd be perfect for a twenty-two-hour flight like this one.

But Dad's just sitting here, flicking through the in-flight magazine.

I offered him a go on the mouth-organ, but he just shook his head and –

Oh no, a flight attendant's bending over and speaking to him.

Is she explaining that I'll have to be sent home at Singapore?

No, she's just asking Dad to tell me not to play my mouth-organ once they start the movie.

Phew, they mustn't be onto me after all.

That's a relief.

Now I can relax for the rest of the flight.

Except for one other little thing that's worrying me.

When we were saying goodbye to Claire and Erin at the airport, Claire whispered something to Dad. She didn't think I heard because I was busy blowing a raspberry on Erin's bottom, but I did.

'Ro's old enough to know the full story,' she whispered to Dad.

The full story about what?

I asked Dad while we were waiting to get on the plane, but he just looked away and mumbled something about showing me the exact place where Mum was killed.

I had the weird feeling he was hiding something.

I hope not.

Perhaps I'm just getting too suspicious after everything that's happened.

Can't be helped.

You need to be a bit suspicious when you're tracking down your mum's killer.

We got through French customs without a hiccup.

OK, one.

On his customs form, under 'Reason For Visit', Dad put 'holiday'. On mine I put 'business'.

It was careless of me, but luckily they just thought I was a dopey kid who didn't understand forms.

Still, I wanted to get out of that airport fast, in case their computer matched my name with Mum's name and they saw I was the daughter of an unsolved hit-and-run victim planning to take the law into her own hands. I know Mum's death was quite a few years ago, but computers can do that sort of thing standing on their heads.

'Airport train station,' said Dad. 'This way.'

I've got Claire's rucksack and Dad's got a

suitcase on wheels so we can move pretty fast.

We're here, I thought, my insides tingling with excitement. We're in France and I'm going to avenge Mum and nothing can stop me now.

Boy, was I wrong.

First, we got lost. Paris airport is like a huge shopping centre. Dad always gets lost in shopping centres, even ones that don't have signs in French.

We bought a French phrase book and found the station.

Then Dad tried to buy tickets.

The bloke in the ticket office couldn't understand what Dad was saying and Dad couldn't understand what the bloke was saying.

Dad said the name of Mum's town all the different ways he could think of, but the ticket bloke just kept frowning.

'Sorry, Tonto,' muttered Dad. 'It's been twelve years since I've said it.'

I handed him the phrase book.

The phrase book didn't have towns.

'Tell you what,' said Dad to the ticket bloke. 'Show me a list of all your towns and I'll see if I can spot it.'

The ticket bloke looked at him blankly.

Dad started thumbing through the phrase book.

I started feeling pretty anxious in case the ticket bloke decided to run a check on us. Train ticket-office computers are almost as powerful as customs ones.

Then I had an idea.

I rummaged in my rucksack until I found the old French press cuttings about Mum. Without letting anyone see them, which wasn't easy because there were about fifty angry people behind us in the queue, I copied down all the words in them that started with capital letters.

I showed my notebook to the ticket bloke, praying that one of the words was the name of the town.

The ticket bloke rolled his eyes and put two tickets on the counter. He said something in a loud voice. It was in French but I got the gist from his hand-movements. He was saying I was smarter than Dad, which I thought was pretty unkind in front of all those other people.

Then he said something else.

I watched his hands closely.

'We've got to change trains in the city,' I said to Dad.

'I knew that,' said Dad grumpily. 'I'm not an idiot. I only did this trip twelve years ago.'

The station we changed at in Paris was the biggest station I've ever seen.

I gaped, even though I've promised myself I won't get distracted from my mission of revenge by tourist sights. There was a roof over the whole station, and the noise of pigeons and trains and French people echoed like something in a dream. And the air smelled fantastic, like apple fritters made with garlic.

Dad brought me down to earth quicker than a sprayed codling moth.

'After we've had a squiz at Mum's grave,' he said, 'we'll go to Euro Disney.'

He pointed to a huge poster of Mickey and Goofey riding on a roller coaster with French writing coming out of their mouths.

I stared at him in panic.

Why would a bloke who's just travelled round the world to his dead wife's grave want to go to Disneyland?

Must be jet-lag.

'Um . . .' I said, trying desperately to make my hands look natural, 'I'm feeling pretty jet-lagged too so I wouldn't mind resting-up in Mum's town for a bit first. Just for a couple of weeks.'

Dad gave me a strange look. I don't know why, I was telling the truth. I hardly slept at all on the plane. Every time I nodded off, I clunked my head on the woman next to me's crossword book. It's OK for Dad, he can sleep anywhere, even on a tractor.

We're on the train now, and I'm staring out the window at the French paddocks. They're even flatter than ours at home. And really dark green, except for the ploughed ones, which are dark brown.

A few minutes ago a thought suddenly hit me.

I'm only a few miles away from Mum.

Maybe the colours just seem darker because of that.

They can do, when you've got tears in your eyes.

Then I had another thought. As far as I can see, the French paddocks are bare of trees. There are a few trees around the houses and villages, but they don't look very friendly.

'Is Mum buried near apple trees?' I asked Dad anxiously a moment ago. I really hoped she was. At least they'd remind her of home.

'No,' said Dad. 'Too wet round here for apple trees. All they can grow round here is turnips.'

That's really crook.

My own dear mum, buried near turnips.

That mongrel driver's gunna pay for that.

It's not fair.

All I needed was a few days.

Once I was on the hit-and-run driver's tail I could have tracked him down really quickly. Specially if he'd panicked and left clues lying around.

I could have had a written confession by Thursday, probably.

Instead all I got was twenty minutes.

Twenty minutes in Mum's town before the police swooped.

Twenty minutes and here I am in the back of a police car.

They probably spotted me and Dad when we came out of the station. We must have looked pretty suspicious, the way we were staring at everything.

Dad was staring at street signs, trying to remember the way to the hotel. He was also glancing anxiously at every passer-by.

At first I couldn't work out why he was doing that. Then I twigged. He must have been worried the locals would recognise him as Mum's husband. And think he'd come back to stir up trouble about her death.

If things turned ugly he couldn't run very fast because a wheel had fallen off his suitcase. That must be why he was trying to hide his face with his jacket collar, which is about as suspicious as a person can look in public, specially when they're wearing cowboy boots in a district that doesn't have any cows.

I can't blame it all on Dad, but. I was probably looking pretty suspicious myself with all the staring I was doing.

I was staring at how narrow the streets are. No wonder people get knocked down here. And you can't even widen these streets because all the houses and shops are made of brick. At home if you want to widen a street you just bung the wood and fibro buildings on the back of a truck and shift them back a bit.

I was staring at the streets for another reason too.

I was wondering which one Mum was killed on.

I kept getting a pang in my chest and it wasn't just the rucksack strap cutting into me.

For a bit I wasn't sure if I really wanted to know.

Then I remembered it was a clue and I had to know.

I was about to ask Dad when he suddenly pointed to a damp-looking grey building.

'Our hotel,' he said.

I don't understand why the police didn't just pick us up on the street. Why did they wait till we were in the hotel? Perhaps they needed to go to the toilet before they arrested us.

I certainly did.

I left Dad at the check-in desk thumbing through the phrase book and went for a pee.

When I sat down I realised how tired I am. I haven't slept for about twenty-six hours. I almost nodded off on the dunny.

I stopped myself, but, and when I got back to the check-in desk Dad wasn't there.

I looked around.

I saw the police car parked outside.

I saw an anxious face peering at me through the car window.

It was Dad.

For a sec I thought I'd nodded off and was having a nightmare.

I hadn't.

This isn't a dream.

We're in a police car and the policeman behind the wheel is driving much too fast down these narrow streets.

He must be taking us to police headquarters.

Well, I won't be blabbing.

They can shine a lamp in my eyes and question me for hours, but it won't do them any good.

All I'll tell them is my name, my address and what class I'm in at school.

Talk about weird.

I mean, I know France is a foreign country, but I wasn't prepared for anything like this.

The police car suddenly stopped outside a brick house with blue shutters on the windows and a hedge that had been carved into shapes of birds and windmills and things.

Jeez, I thought, pretty strange police headquarters.

It got stranger.

The policeman beeped the horn and two people came running out of the house. One was another policeman. He had a moustache and a tummy that wobbled as he ran and a feather duster. The other was a tall woman in normal clothes. I figured she must be a detective. She was wearing an apron, but I've heard how much French people like to cook.

As they got closer to the car, I noticed a really strange thing.

They were both grinning and waving at me and Dad.

They both looked really excited to see us.

All I could think of was that it had been ages since they'd had anyone to interrogate and they'd been getting really bored.

Then Dad got out of the police car and the policeman with the tummy threw his arms round Dad.

The woman detective did the same.

Dad looked a bit taken aback and I got out of the car in case this was a form of police brutality I hadn't come across in Australia.

It wasn't – they were hugging him.

The woman hugged me too, and even though I didn't have a clue what was going on, it felt pretty nice.

'Rowena,' she murmured. 'Little Rowena.'

She let go of me and I stared at her.

Her voice didn't sound like a detective at all. It was so beautiful it made my neck prickle. It was the warmest, softest, gentlest voice I'd ever heard. I wondered if all French people sound like that when they speak English.

'Rowena,' said Dad, 'this is Mr and Mrs Bernard. They're mates of mine.'

Normally I can cope with just about anything Dad comes out with, but today I just stood there staring at Mr and Mrs Bernard like a stunned aphid.

Mates of his?

Mrs Bernard was gazing back at me.

She had tears in her eyes.

'Poor girl,' she murmured. 'Poor, lovely girl.'

I wondered if she meant me.

Mr Bernard was talking excitedly at Dad in French, waving his feather duster. I tried to work out from his feather-duster movements what he was saying. Something about a telephone.

'My husband does not speak English,' Mrs Bernard said to me.

I nodded. My brain was still too scrambled to say anything intelligent.

The policeman who'd driven us was carrying our bags into the house. Mrs Bernard put her arm round my shoulders and gently steered me along the gravel path to the front door.

Mr Bernard was still talking excitedly.

'Alan is saying we are sorry we didn't meet you,' Mrs Bernard said to Dad, 'but when the hotel rang us we were unprepared. Why did you not let us know you are coming? Why the secret hotel?'

I could see Dad didn't know what to say, even in English.

Perhaps Mrs Bernard's voice had got to him too.

'Er . . .' he said, 'um . . . we were gunna surprise you.'

I had a feeling he was making that up, but I didn't dwell on it because suddenly I had something else on my mind.

Something so big and so confusing that I tripped over Mrs Bernard's feet and almost fell into a bush shaped like a car.

I would have done if Mrs Bernard hadn't caught me.

The thing is this.

If Dad is such big mates with the local police, why didn't he get them to track down Mum's killer?

I'm sitting on the bed in the little attic bedroom Mrs Bernard has brought me to and I'm trying to figure it out.

I can't.

When Dad came in to check my bed was comfy and to see if his toothbrush was in my rucksack, I asked him.

He looked away with a pained expression.

At first I thought he hadn't heard me because he'd just remembered he'd used his toothbrush on the plane to polish his boots.

But he had heard me.

All he did, though, was give me a big hug and say, 'Sometimes, Tonto, it's best to let things rest.'

Well, he might think so, but I don't.

I thought about the mystery for ages, which wasn't easy with jet-lag.

If Dad had wanted to, he could have got Mr Bernard and the other local police to check every car in the district for hit-and-run dents.

They could have done it standing on their heads.

Why didn't they?

I didn't know, so I went downstairs to look for clues.

Dad and Mr and Mrs Bernard were in the kitchen. As I came along the passage I heard Dad saying, 'I want to tell her myself.' Then Mrs Bernard said something in French, which was probably her translating for Mr Bernard.

I went into the kitchen and they all stopped talking.

Dad went down on one knee and sang me a quick verse of that haunting Carla Tamworth classic 'I Love You More Than Pickled Onions'.

When he'd finished I was about to ask him what it was he wanted to tell me himself, but Mrs Bernard spoke first and what she said took my breath away, and not just because of her voice.

'We go now to your mother's grave,' she said. 'Yes?'

My guts gave their biggest lurch since our plane hit an air pocket over Afghanistan.

I nodded.

We piled into another police car with Mr Bernard driving this time and soon we were speeding through the narrow streets.

My chest was thumping so hard from fear and excitement that I didn't think about flowers till we were almost out of town.

I prodded Dad and told him.

'Bit late for flowers now,' he said. 'Sorry, Tonto.'

I was stunned. Normally Dad would crawl through wet cement to get flowers for Mum's grave.

Mrs Bernard turned and gave me one of her sad smiles. 'It's not too late,' she said. 'Ro must have flowers.'

She said something to Mr Bernard in French and he slammed on the brakes and did a squealing U-turn through a petrol station. He zoomed back into town and parked on the footpath outside a flower shop.

Inside, Mrs Bernard said lots of things in French to the two young women shop assistants. While she spoke they stared at me, their eyes getting bigger and bigger.

It didn't worry me, I get stared at quite a lot.

I just wanted to buy some flowers and get to my mum's grave.

The assistants must have understood my hand-movements because suddenly they jumped into action and gave me a beautiful bunch.

Then something weird happened.

They wouldn't take any money. Even when Dad took the senior assistant's hand and put some French money into it she just gave it back.

He tried again with Australian money, but she didn't want that either.

I realised what was going on.

They probably hadn't seen a kid before with bits missing from her throat.

'They're being charitable,' I said to Dad.

Dad frowned and turned to Mrs Bernard, who was smiling and nodding. He opened his mouth to explain how Australians don't usually accept charity unless it's absolutely essential because we're used to battling a harsh land with droughts and bushfires and floods and unreliable tractors and pushy TV presenters.

Then I saw him decide it was too complicated to try and explain all this through a translator, even a top one like Mrs Bernard.

Instead he gave me an apologetic shrug.

It was OK, I understood.

Well, I thought I did.

'Ta muchly,' Dad said to the assistants. 'Very nice of you.'

That's what I thought too, at the time.

Mr Bernard got us to the cemetery in about three minutes.

Mum's French cemetery is very different from her Australian one. It's got a wall round it with a gate, probably to keep out local hoons and their dog poo.

I was shaking so much as I followed Mrs Bernard through the gate that I could hardly hold the flowers.

She took me to Mum's grave.

Most of the graveyard is gravel, and most of the graves are grey stone.

Mum's isn't, but.

Mum's is the most beautiful grave I've ever seen.

Her headstone is marble and her grave is covered with really soft dark-green grass, perfectly clipped and edged with more marble.

But it wasn't just the neatness of the grass that made my mouth fall open.

It was the four other bunches of flowers lying on it.

All fresh.

I stared, gobsmacked.

I'd imagined Mum's French grave would be wild and unkempt and I'd be the first person tidying it up and putting flowers on it for twelve years.

Instead it's the best-cared-for grave in the whole cemetery.

I was about to ask Dad what was going on when something else happened. An elderly couple standing at another grave with a poodle looked over and saw us and gave a shout. They hurried over and started shaking Dad's hand and beaming. Dad looked a bit alarmed, probably because the poodle was trying to have sex with his leg. Even though I couldn't understand a word the French people were saying, I could see they were delighted.

Why?

Was Dad being mistaken for a local footy star? Surely not with his crook knees.

Then it hit me.

The reason everyone here is so friendly to Dad.

The reason nobody's bothered to catch the hit-and-run driver.

The thing Dad wanted to tell me himself.

The full story Claire reckoned I should know.

It's this.

Dad must have been offered a deal when Mum was killed.

The local council must have offered Dad a top grave for Mum, serviced regularly, if he agreed not to make them hunt down the hit-and-run driver.

And he accepted.

That's why all the locals are so grateful to him. He's saved them the shame and embarrassment of admitting they've got a ruthless killer in their municipality.

Of course. That's why Dad wanted to sneak into town without anyone knowing we were here.

He was scared a local would blab to me.

He was scared I'd lose all respect for him.

Which is exactly what I'm doing.

Dad, how could you?

How could you let a killer get away with it for a bit of lawn and a few flowers?

That's what I asked myself at the cemetery as I laid my flowers on Mum's grave and it's what I'm still asking back here in Mrs Bernard's attic bedroom.

I haven't asked Dad in person.

I don't want him to know I've twigged.

He might guess what I'm planning to do and try to stop me.

Not that I'd let him.

I'm going to avenge Mum even if it means the local council won't look after her grave any more and I'll have to live here for the rest of my life and mow it myself.

It was morning and Mum was stroking my forehead and talking to me softly in her warm gentle voice with its warm gentle French accent.

French accent?

I opened my eyes.

It wasn't morning, it was night and it wasn't Mum smiling down at me, it was Mrs Bernard.

'Sweet little Rowena,' she whispered.

I wish she wouldn't keep saying that. I'm not little and when I get my hands on a certain local driver I don't plan to be sweet.

'You slept for five hours,' said Mrs Bernard. 'Now you need food.'

It was a kind thought but she was only partly right.

I also needed clues.

'We go to the cafe,' said Mrs Bernard.

My heart gave a skip of excitement.

I jumped out of bed and splashed water on

my face from the bowl so Mrs Bernard wouldn't see my mind racing.

Cafes are good for clues, I was thinking. People gossip in cafes. It's the milkshakes. Sugar loosens tongues as well as teeth, that's what Dad always reckons. In cafes down our way people are always mentioning the names of other people who've been mean to pets or overdressed at the bowling club or driving carelessly.

Hope it's the same here, I thought as I brushed my hair. Hope French cafes are good for clues.

This one was.

Sort of.

Mr Bernard drove us there in about ninety seconds, which was pretty scary because it was round at least twelve corners.

The trip was nowhere near as scary as the cafe itself.

Inside there wasn't a single milkshake.

Just smoke and noise and music.

And people.

About a hundred people, all raising their glasses of wine and beer to us and cheering as we walked in.

I glanced at Dad. He looked as stunned as I felt. But he soon started to relax as people shook his hand and slapped him on the back and yelled at him in excited and happy French.

Probably thanking him for sticking to the deal.

Boy, I thought bitterly as people shook my

hand too, and patted my head, and gave me glasses of mint cordial. Do French people a favour and they never forget it.

Dad hasn't been in this town for twelve years and people were falling over themselves to buy him a drink. We were only away from our town for five years while I was at the special school and when we got back people didn't even remember us.

I wished Sergeant Cleary was in the cafe tonight. He'd soon change his opinion of Dad if he saw how popular Dad is in France. I even thought of ringing him and telling him. Then I remembered I've lost respect for Dad, so I didn't.

Mr and Mrs Bernard steered us through the crowd to a table at the back. We sat down and almost immediately someone put big plates of meat stew in front of us.

I was starving and even though it's not easy eating a meal while about fifty people are staring at you and grinning and your guts are knotted with lack of respect for your father, I gobbled it down.

Right up until I had a thought.

I looked around at the faces and suddenly I wasn't hungry any more.

Any one of those men, I realised, could be the hit-and-run driver.

The men carried on grinning and saying friendly-sounding things.

The meat stuck in my throat.

Mrs Bernard slapped me on the back and anxiously lifted my glass of mint cordial to my lips.

She's a very kind woman, but if she really wanted to help my digestion she would have given me a name, not cordial.

Then, as soon as Dad finished eating, everybody started shouting at him.

Mrs Bernard whispered something to him and he stood up and cleared his throat and did his neck exercises.

That could only mean one thing.

They wanted him to sing.

I was speechless.

Dad's sung to big groups of people heaps of times but tonight was the first time I'd ever seen a group ask him to.

He climbed onto a table in the middle of the cafe and sang the Carla Tamworth song about the bloke with ninety-seven cousins who loves them all dearly even though he can't remember any of their names.

The crowd went wild, even though Dad didn't get many of the notes right.

Then he sang Mum's song.

I realised I was probably in the actual place where Dad had taped Mum singing it all those years ago.

Suddenly my eyes were full of tears.

Which is how I came to turn away, so people wouldn't see.

Which is how I came to spot the man with the black curly hair.

I noticed him at first because he was the only person not standing gazing up at Dad. He was putting his coat on and heading for the door.

Either he's late for something else, I thought, or he's got musical taste.

Then I recognised him.

I'd seen him before, in Australia.

He was the bloke driving down our driveway when I got back home from being locked up at the police station.

What's he doing here?

I yelled at him to wait, but he wasn't looking in my direction so he couldn't see my hands.

As he opened the door several of the people in the cafe waved goodbye.

I struggled through the crowd, but by the time I got to the door and peered up and down the street, he'd gone.

My head spun in the cold night air.

If he's a local, what was he doing at our place in Australia?

I asked Dad on the way back to Mr and Mrs Bernard's.

Dad reckoned I was mistaken.

He reckoned it must have been someone else.

It wasn't, but.

I've been lying here in bed for ages testing my memory and I know I wasn't mistaken.

He's the same bloke I saw in our driveway.

He even had the same suit on tonight.

What's going on?

When I woke up and realised it was really early, I had a listen to Mum's tape. Just a few times so I didn't wear it out.

I'm glad I did. I reckon Mum's voice inspired me. In less than twenty minutes I'd thought up a complete two-part investigation plan.

Part One. Start at the beginning and find the exact spot in town where Mum was knocked down.

Part Two. Try and find a passer-by with a really good memory who'd been walking a pet nearby at the time of Mum's death and could remember the number plate of the car.

OK, Part Two was a bit hopeful, but I'm still glad I thought of it, given what's happened since.

'Dad,' I said at breakfast. 'Where exactly was Mum killed?'

Dad sighed and looked unhappy, though that

might have been because Mrs Bernard had left a dried goat's cheese on the table and Dad had just put the whole thing in his mouth thinking it was a muffin.

'Tonto,' he said, using his hands, 'don't torture yourself.'

I thought that was pretty rich coming from a bloke who was choking to death on his own breakfast.

I poured him a glass of water.

'Rowena,' he continued, 'I want you to stop thinking about Mum's accident, OK?'

I gave him a look I hoped would curdle cheese.

He looked at his hands, which I could see were struggling for the right words.

'She didn't suffer,' he said at last.

There was pain on his face and it wasn't just from the cheese and suddenly I felt sorry for him.

'She heard the car,' continued Dad with trembling hands, 'and tried to get out of the way. She slipped. The car whacked her on the back of the neck. It broke her spinal cord. The doctors said she died instantly. There, now you know.'

I fought back tears.

I had more important things to do than get sad.

'Did you see the car?' I asked.

Dad shook his head. 'It was dark and raining

and I was busy with you,' he said.

The tears wouldn't go away. Not now I was thinking that if I hadn't been there, Dad might have been able to save her.

'We've got to stop this,' said Dad. 'We both need a good cheer up. Tomorrow we'll say goodbye to this dud place and I'll take you to Euro Disney.' He took a deep breath through his nose and gave me a cheesy grin. 'Couple of weeks there and we'll be doing cartwheels back to Australia.'

I didn't argue.

When Dad gets an idea in his head it's like couch grass. Takes weeks to shift.

I haven't got time.

After Dad had gone back to his room for a lie down to finish swallowing the cheese, I tried Mrs Bernard.

'Mrs Bernard,' I wrote, 'do you know which street my mother was killed in?'

Mrs Bernard studied my notebook.

She gave a huge sigh.

For a sec I thought it was because I'd ended a sentence with 'in'. Then Mrs Bernard hugged me to her chest so tight I was worried her bra strap was going to make one of my eyes pop out.

'My poor, poor little Ro,' she said. 'Don't make yourself tortured.'

I realised she'd been talking to Dad. She sat me down and went to the fridge and made me a huge ice-cream sundae with peaches and frozen raspberries and mint syrup.

It was very kind, but I took it as a 'no'.

I tried Mr Bernard.

He was in his workshop out the back, wearing a white singlet and braces, cleaning a rusty old pistol with a cloth. On the workbench were lots of other rusty old pistols and rifles. A few clean ones hung from the roof with some cheeses.

When Mr Bernard saw me he smiled and said something in French. Then he mimed digging.

For a sec I thought he was asking if I was feeling stressed. I was about to tell him I was, but that I didn't have time to dig a sandpit. Then I realised he was telling me the guns had been dug up. From battlefields, I guessed. There were heaps.

Before he could go into lengthy detail about the war, I showed him my notebook.

Mr Bernard looked at it blankly.

I hoped desperately French policemen were trained to read English even if they couldn't speak it.

Mr Bernard shrugged apologetically.

I wished I had a better phrase book. All the phrases in the one I've got are for talking to hairdressers and waiters. You'd think a decent phrase book could translate a simple sentence like, 'Do you know in which street my mother was killed?'

Then I had an idea.

I beckoned to Mr Bernard and he followed me through the house to the front yard.

I pointed to the bush that had been clipped into the shape of a car. Then I pointed to another one that was shaped like a person. I couldn't tell if it was meant to be a man or a woman, but I hoped he'd twig I was talking about Mum.

Mr Bernard frowned, then his face lit up.

He dashed into the house.

Yes, I thought. He's gone to get a map of the accident location. Or maybe even a file with a list of suspects' names in it.

Mr Bernard reappeared, waving a pair of hedge clippers.

My insides sagged like an apple fritter in cold oil.

Then, while I was politely watching Mr Bernard clip a bush into the shape of a kangaroo, it hit me.

Of course. Clippings. Newspaper clippings.

Finally Mr Bernard finished and I thanked him and hurried up to my room. In the phrase book I looked up the French word for street.

Rue.

Then I pulled the old French newspaper clippings about Mum's death out of my rucksack. There, in the first one, I found them. *Rue Victor* and *Rue Amiens*, both in the same sentence.

I checked another one. *Rue Victor* and *Rue Amiens* again.

I could hardly breathe.

Mum must have been killed at the corner of those two streets.

I stuck my head and hands into Dad's room, trying not to look too excited. Dad was cleaning his teeth. I hoped he'd bought a new toothbrush.

'I'm just going for a walk,' I said.

Dad gave me a doubtful look.

'The tourist office might have Euro Disney brochures,' I said.

Dad thought about this, then nodded. 'Don't be long,' he said.

On a notice board in front of the town hall I found a tourist map with a street index.

Rue Victor and Rue Amiens were only a few minutes away.

When I finally arrived here on the corner where they run into each other, possibly on the exact spot Mum was killed, I felt very sad.

And then, when I looked around, very angry.

Yes, Victor and Amiens are narrow streets, and yes it was night when Mum was killed, and yes it was raining.

But there's a street light right over the corner. Not a new one, it's at least fifty years old, so it would have been there on that night. And a pedestrian crossing. And stop signs.

That driver must be a maniac.

My eyes filled with angry tears. Through the blur I noticed a young woman in pink jeans on the opposite corner giving me a strange look. I turned away and found myself staring into the window of a deli.

That's when I saw the most amazing thing I've seen in my life.

The window was full of sausages and meat-loaves and slices of devon and jars of meat sandwich spread. Except that in the middle of the display was a pile of dried dog poo.

The same type of dried dog poo that Dermot Figgis left on Mum's Australian grave.

It couldn't be.

I blinked and pressed my face against the window.

I've got really good eyes. When one bit of you doesn't work, the other bits get extra good, it's a known fact.

I've been staring at that stuff in the deli window for ages now.

It's definitely Dermot's dog poo.

Except sausage shops don't put dog poo in their window, that's also a known fact.

So it can't be dog poo, it must be a type of sausage.

Which is even more amazing.

Why would Dermot Figgis leave two French sausages on my mother's grave?

Before today I thought hit-and-run clues were things like dented bumper bars and bent aerials and people selling their cars for $11.50.

Not dog-poo sausages.

Boy, was I wrong.

But it took me a while to realise it.

I was still staring at the sausage-shop window, trying to remember if Dermot Figgis and his mum had been on holiday to France recently, when a man came out of the shop.

He was wearing a white apron and carrying a big leg of ham that was the same pinky-white colour as his bald head.

With a warm smile and a little bow, he gave me the ham.

I staggered under the weight of it, not knowing what to say.

Then I remembered what Dad's always told

me about taking gifts from strange men, so I gave it back to him.

A woman with a grey hairdo came out of the shop. She was wearing a white apron too and holding a big salami on a string. She kissed me on both cheeks and gave me the salami.

Dad's never said anything about accepting gifts from strange women, but he's pretty strict about no charity so I gave the salami back.

It's incredible.

There must be a shortage of people around here with bits missing. When one comes along, the kind people in this town go bananas.

I realised I'd met the man and woman before. At Mum's cemetery yesterday. And at the cafe last night. They were kind there too. When Dad finished singing they applauded longer than anyone else, despite the fact that they must both be in their fifties and a bit short of energy.

Now they were looking really disappointed that I didn't want their gifts.

I was glad there was one thing I did want from them so I didn't have to disappoint them completely. I pointed to the dog-poo sausages in the window.

Their faces lit up and they led me into the shop.

The man reached into the window, lifted the whole pile of sausages onto a sheet of white paper and held them out to me.

I took one.

I didn't want to do what I was about to do, but I had to be sure.

I sniffed it.

It didn't smell like dog poo.

I rolled it next to my ear.

It didn't sound like dog poo.

I bit a piece off and chewed it.

It was hard and dry and as it crumbled between my teeth, strong flavours filled my mouth.

Salty flavours. Garlicky flavours. Spicy flavours.

None of them were dog-poo flavours.

It was definitely a sausage.

I must have been grinning with relief because the man and the woman both started grinning too.

'Moth-hair,' said the man. For a sec I thought he meant the sausage was made from moth hairs. I wished I hadn't just swallowed some. Then I realised he was saying 'mother'.

'Fav-oo-reet,' he said. I understood. This sausage was his mother's favourite. Then I saw he was pointing to me and my stomach went cold.

He was saying the sausage was *my* mother's favourite.

'Deedoh,' he went on, nodding and smiling. 'Australee.'

The woman gave him an anxious dig with her elbow, but he didn't seem to notice.

I stared, brain churning, as he mimed packing the sausages into a suitcase, climbing onto a plane, flying to Australia, unpacking the sausages and laying them very carefully onto the ground.

'Moth-hair,' he said again. 'Fav-oo-reet.'

With a gasp I realised he was talking about putting the sausages on Mum's grave.

I scribbled 'Deedoh' on my notebook and held it out, pointing to him.

He shook his head. 'Rosh-ay,' he said, pointing to himself and the woman. He took my pencil and wrote it down. He spelled it '*Rocher*'. Then he crossed out 'Deedoh' and wrote '*Didot*'.

Mrs Rocher, who was looking very worried now, nudged him again. Mr Rocher noticed this time and frowned and looked like a man who'd said too much.

My mind was racing.

He was saying that someone called Didot had taken sausages to Australia and put them on Mum's grave.

Suddenly I knew who Didot must be.

The bloke with the curly hair, the one I saw in the cafe last night and in our driveway. He must be Didot. The day I saw him at home was the same day I found the sausages.

But why would a bloke fly halfway round the world and risk smuggling sausages into Australia and leave them on a person's grave? Even if they were that person's favourite?

My eyes must have been bulging with the effort of thinking so hard because Mr and Mrs Rocher were looking at me, concerned.

I gave them a smile to show I was OK.

Then I nearly fainted.

Everything fell into place.

Guilt.

That's why a bloke would go all the way to Australia to leave a person's favourite sausages on her grave.

Guilt at knocking her down with his car.

Twelve years after killing her, he was still trying to make himself feel better.

Got you, I thought.

I would have roared it out if I could.

I'm hurrying to the post office now as fast as I can to get Mr Didot's address. It's not that fast because Mr and Mrs Rocher insisted I take the sausages and the bag's really heavy.

Plus I'm feeling a bit of guilt myself. I'm wondering if what I did to Dermot Figgis's car was a bit much given that he didn't even put dog poo on Mum's grave.

No, I've just decided he still deserved it for mocking the memory of a fine woman.

When all this is over, but, I am going to try to learn to control my temper.

First, though, I've got something much more important to do.

I can see the post office up ahead.

Soon I'll know where Mr Didot lives.

And then I can meet that murdering mongrel face to face.

I was just about to go into the post office when I caught a flash of pink out of the corner of my eye.

Across the street, watching me, was the young woman in the pink jeans who'd been staring at me outside the sausage shop.

I waved.

She ducked behind a parked truck.

I dumped the bag of sausages. This was no time to be loaded down with smallgoods. Then I kept on walking.

After a bit, I glanced back. As I thought, she was following me.

I wasn't worried, but. I've been followed heaps of times. There's a kid in my class, Darryn Peck, who used to follow me with his mates and make dumb comments about my throat.

I'm good at getting rid of people who follow me.

I walked casually for a bit, then ducked into a supermarket.

Supermarkets are good for losing people because they always have a back door leading out to the carpark. At least, Australian ones do.

This one didn't.

I stood in a panic, staring at the fruit and veg display where the back entrance should have been.

If the woman in the pink jeans followed me in I was trapped. She was probably a detective who worked with Mr Bernard. The local council probably had her keeping an eye on me, ready to pounce and arrest me if I got too close to exposing Mum's killer.

I was getting very close.

She wouldn't like that.

I thought I could hear her creeping towards me down the cereals and dry goods aisle, handcuffs at the ready.

I didn't dare turn around.

Not more than halfway.

Which was enough to see a plastic swing door between a display of lightbulbs and a freezer cabinet.

I threw myself at the door and burst into a gloomy corridor and sprinted down it to a storeroom full of boxes.

A man's voice shouted at me in French. I saw a patch of daylight and ran for it, knocking over a box of fruit and stubbing my toe on some tins.

I ducked under a half-open roller door, sprinted down a narrow lane, across a road, into a park, wriggled through some thick bushes, came out into a sort of square, crept between some parked cars and found myself standing in front of a building with big windows.

Through the windows I could see shelves of books.

It looked like a public library.

I didn't hesitate.

I went in.

Nothing looks more suspicious than a person gasping for breath outside a public library. They're obviously either on the run or having an anxiety attack because their library books are six months overdue.

Inside I went straight to the shelf furthest from the door and the window, ducked down behind it and grabbed a book.

I pretended to read it.

It was in French of course, but luckily it had lots of pictures so I didn't have to pretend too hard. They were black and white photos. I stared at them in amazement.

For a sec I thought it was a book about the dangers of using too much spray on paddocks. The photos showed areas of land that were totally and completely wrecked. Just mud and dead cows and splintered trees.

It looked even worse than the paddock Paige Parker had sprayed.

Then I spotted something else in one of the photos. There were trenches in the ground with soldiers in them wearing World War One uniforms.

It wasn't sprays that had wrecked the land, it was war.

Someone tapped me on the shoulder.

I spun round and looked up, panicking.

But it wasn't the detective in the pink jeans, it was a plump lady trying to get past with a librarian's trolley.

I jumped up and got out of the way. The woman smiled and pointed to the photo I'd been looking at.

'*Ici*,' she said.

I didn't know what she meant. I hoped that in France librarians aren't allowed to make arrests on behalf of the local council.

Then I realised from her hand-movements that she was saying the photo had been taken nearby. Locally. Something like that.

I thanked her, put the book back and hurried out of the library and round a couple of corners.

She didn't follow me.

I wandered around lost for a while, then found a street I recognised and hurried back to the post office. I had to find Mum's killer before the detective in pink jeans found me.

I looked around carefully as I approched the post office.

No sign of her.

My bag of sausages was still on the footpath. I grabbed a couple for evidence and hurried into the post office.

There was a public phone booth in the corner with a phone book on a string. I went over to it, heart pounding. Somewhere in that book was the address of the man I'd come round the world to find.

I opened it at the Ds, praying there was only one Didot.

A hand grabbed me by the shoulder.

I froze.

Please, I begged silently. Please let it be the librarian with more information about local World War One battles and not the detective in pink jeans.

I turned round.

It wasn't either of them.

The face looking steadily at me with bloodshot eyes had stubble on it and black curly hair on top.

It was Mr Didot.

I was in shock.

Total and complete shock.

That's the only reason I let Mr Didot lead me out of the post office without kicking him and biting him and letting him have it in the privates with whatever stationery I could lay my hands on.

That's the only reason I let him put me into his car.

It was only when we were driving down the street that my brain started working again and I realised what I'd done.

I'd let him kidnap me.

And now he was going to make sure I couldn't tell anyone he'd killed my mum.

Lock me away somewhere.

Or worse.

I felt sick and weak and panicky, but I knew I mustn't give in to the feeling.

I wondered if Mr Didot's car had central locking. If not, perhaps I could fling the door open and dive out.

If only he wasn't driving so fast. Doesn't anyone in France drive slowly? I asked myself gloomily. Not maniac hit-and-run drivers, that's for sure, I replied bitterly.

Then I noticed something very weird.

The way he was looking at me. With a gentle, concerned expression.

Caring.

I've seen psycho-killer movies at friends' houses and psycho killers often pretend to be gentle and concerned and caring but you can always tell they're faking it.

With Mr Didot I couldn't.

His caring expression looked real.

Well, I wasn't going to be sucked in.

I scribbled angrily in my notebook, ripped the page out and held it in front of his face.

'You killed my mother,' it said, 'and I've got the sausages to prove it.'

He stared at the page, frowned and kept on driving.

At least he wasn't looking concerned and caring any more.

Which would make it easier for me when I had him put away for life.

A few minutes later we pulled into the driveway of a house.

I made a mental note of as many details as I could to help Dad find me if I was able get a message to him. The driveway was gravel. The house was two-storey with a slate roof and white shutters. The window-ledges all had flower pots on them. The flowers were all red.

Blood red.

I forced myself to calm down.

If I got hysterical thinking about the danger I was in, I'd never get a confession out of the killer.

I let Mr Didot lead me into the house. He took me through a living-room full of rich-looking old furniture and into an office with used coffee cups and plates all over the desk.

I decided to go for the direct approach. Dad always does and it usually works for him.

'I confess,' I wrote in my notebook. 'I killed her. Signed . . . . . .' I put dotted lines where I wanted Mr Didot's signature to go, tore out the page and handed it to him.

He stared at it with a blank expression, then went over to the desk and switched on a notebook computer.

I couldn't believe what he did next. He typed the confession into the computer. Yes, I thought, heart pounding. The years of guilt have got too much for him. He's going to sign the confession but he doesn't want it to be in my untidy handwriting.

Boy, was I wrong.

Mr Didot didn't print out the confession.

Instead he reached for the mouse button and clicked on a French flag at the top of the screen. Almost instantly my English words on the screen turned into French words. I stared, amazed. It was a computer program that translated from one language to another.

He looked at the confession on the screen, sighed, looked at me and shook his head.

Then he typed some French, clicked an English flag and it turned into English.

'Mr and Mrs Rocher from the sausage shop rang me and told me you'd probably be thinking I killed your mother,' he'd written. 'I didn't. I was in hospital the night she was killed.'

'Prove it,' I typed and clicked the French flag.

'That's why I've brought you here,' typed Mr Didot.

He opened a drawer in the desk and took out a folder. It was full of forms. He let me look at them. They were all in French, but printed on the top of each one was what looked like the name and address of a hospital.

I noticed the same French word on several of the forms.

Rein.

I typed it into the computer and clicked the English flag.

Kidney.

Mr Didot looked uncomfortable. I wondered if it was because the forms didn't prove a thing. He could be a caterer with a contract to supply food to the hospital, including kidneys.

Mr Didot tore the top off one of the forms and gave it to me.

'The hospital will tell you I was a patient that night,' he typed.

While he was typing I noticed that a photo had fallen out of the folder. I picked it up. It showed a younger Mr Didot in a hospital bed connected to a medical-looking machine. The weird thing was, he was wearing a party hat and grinning. The people crowded round the bed looked like they were having a party. Even the machine was wearing a party hat.

Mr Didot saw I had the photo and snatched it from me. He stuffed it back into the folder and shoved the folder back into the drawer.

He seemed anxious I'd seen it.

I was confused.

Was he making the stuff up about the hospital?

It didn't look like it.

But I wasn't letting him off that easily.

'If you didn't kill Mum,' I typed, 'why did you go to Australia and leave sausages on her grave?'

Mr Didot looked startled. Then he let out a sigh and typed for a long time.

'I knew your father from when he was here

twelve years ago,' he wrote. 'About a month ago, when he first knew the media were investigating the sprays, he wrote to me.'

I stared at the screen. A month ago? That meant Dad knew the media were sniffing around several weeks before I found out. Why didn't he say anything?

He was hoping the whole thing would blow over, probably.

'I'm an industrial chemist,' typed Mr Didot. 'Your dad asked me to check up on the sprays he was using. It is very hard because the chemical companies do not want to answer my questions. I am spending many nights on the Internet.'

I looked at Mr Didot's bloodshot eyes. Either he was telling the truth or he'd been lying awake worrying like guilty killers do on videos.

'Last week I went to Australia,' typed Mr Didot, 'to talk to the TV people. To tell them they cannot accuse your dad without more proof. They wouldn't listen to me. They wouldn't even let me switch my computer on. I did not want the whole trip to be a waste. So I went to your mother's Australian grave to pay my respects. With her favourite food. It is a custom in my family.'

I've known some pretty good liars in my time. Darryn Peck, for example. He had the whole school fooled when he claimed it wasn't him who let off the starting pistol in assembly.

But he didn't fool me.

I looked hard at Mr Didot. He looked back at me steadily with sad, gentle, concerned, bloodshot eyes.

I wanted him to be lying.

I wanted to have found Mum's killer.

But deep in my guts I wasn't sure. His hands hadn't wobbled guiltily once while he was typing.

I let Mr Didot put me back in the car to drive me to Mr and Mrs Bernard's. I felt sick and numb with disappointment.

As we drove past the sausage shop, Mr Rocher came running out carrying a sort of meatloaf wobbling on a plate.

Mr Didot stopped.

Mr Rocher tried to hand me the plate through the window.

Suddenly I couldn't stand it.

I leaped out of the car, pushed past Mr Rocher and ran. Along streets. Across squares. Down alleyways.

Finally I found Mum's cemetery.

The grass on her grave is soft against my face.

But it's not making me feel better. The longer I lie here, the worse I feel.

It's not fair.

I just wish everyone would stop being so nice to me and tell me who killed my mum.

If you want to find out the truth, play a mouth-organ in a cemetery, that's my advice.

I started playing mine to cheer myself up. And to let Mum know I wasn't beaten.

I can only play part of one tune. Dad taught me 'Waltzing Matilda' on the plane over, but we'd only got halfway through when the flight attendant took the mouth-organ away and locked it up till we'd landed.

I was sitting next to the grave, sadly playing half of 'Waltzing Matilda' for about the sixth time, when a small black dog ran up and sat in front of me. It gazed up, panting happily.

I stopped playing.

The dog jumped up and barked.

It wouldn't stop. I decided to try and distract it so I started playing again.

The dog sat down and listened contentedly.

Despite everything that had happened, I

started grinning. A French dog that liked 'Waltzing Matilda'. Weird. Trouble was, every time I grinned I had to stop playing and every time I stopped playing the dog started barking.

After a while I realised someone was standing behind me, watching.

I stood up.

It was an old bloke, even older than Grandad. He was so frail, his clothes looked like they were propping him up.

He was smiling.

'Her favourite tune,' he said, nodding towards the dog. At least I think that's what he said. 'I play the record for her all the time at home.'

I stared at him.

Not because it's unusual to play records to dogs.

Because he was speaking with his hands.

'You speak sign,' I said. Then I stuffed my hands in my pockets. I hate it when they embarrass me by saying really obvious things.

The old bloke's smile faded. 'When I was very young there was a battle near our house. A banana exploded too close. It blew up my ears.'

Some of his hand-movements were a bit different to the ones I know, but I got the gist. I was pleased to see his ears were still in one piece. On the outside, at least.

I pulled my hands out of my pockets. 'How did you know I speak sign?' I asked.

He frowned at me, thinking.

'Fry them with garlic and onions,' he said.

I realised we had a bit of a language problem. I asked him again, making my hand-movements slow and big.

'Ah, I understand,' he said, making his slow and big too. 'How do I know you speak sign? I know much about you Australian visitors. I watch people's lips. I have been hoping to meet you. I love all Australians.'

Boy, I thought. You obviously haven't met Dermot Figgis or Darryn Peck.

The old bloke's face wrinkled into a scowl and for a sec I thought he had.

Then he said, 'Nobody told me about the party at the cafe last night.' He sighed and gave a shrug. 'Perhaps it's because they know that me and Simone go to bed at seven-thirty.' He patted the dog.

'Why do you like Australians?' I asked.

'Come,' he said. 'I will show you.'

He led me out of the cemetery and across a big paddock. It was a long, slow, muddy walk.

Probably the best long, slow, muddy walk I've been on in my life.

While we walked, the old bloke told me how during World War One the town was attacked by a German sausage. That's what I thought he said. Then I realised he'd said German army.

There were French soldiers defending it, he

went on, and English, but mostly Australian.

Suddenly he stopped.

We were at the other side of the paddock. Running along by the fence was a deep trench, too wide to jump across. I could tell it was old from the weeds and rain gullies in the dirt walls. Parts of it had caved in, but other parts were about twenty times as deep as Erin's sandpit at home.

It would have taken some digging.

For a sec I thought the old bloke was going to tell me the town people dug it in the war to work off the stress of being attacked by the Germans.

He didn't.

'Australians dug that,' he said. 'The Australian soldiers who saved the town.'

He had tears on his cheeks.

I didn't blame him. I'd cry too if Australian soldiers saved my mum and dad.

Then it hit me.

Of course.

That's why everyone here's been so kind to me and Dad. They must treat all Aussies that way. To say thanks for saving their town.

I sat down at the edge of the trench, weak with relief.

Dad didn't do a deal with the local council after all. The reason they look after Mum's grave is gratitude for the war.

The dog was licking my face, probably hoping I'd play 'Waltzing Matilda'.

I was so happy I almost did.

Then I remembered a couple of things and my lips went too stiff to get a note out of the mouth-organ even if I'd wanted to.

One, Mum's killer is still at large.

Two, the old bloke's an expert on Australian visitors.

I looked up at him. My hands were shaking but I got them under control.

'Do you know who killed my mother?' I asked.

The old bloke wiped his eyes on a hanky and looked at me for a long time. At first I didn't think he'd understood me. I pulled Erin's rag doll and plastic car out of my pocket and made a little road in the dirt and crashed the car into the doll and knocked her down.

I hated doing it but I had to be sure he understood.

I did it again.

I only stopped when I couldn't see for tears.

I felt something being pressed into my hand. It was the old bloke's hanky. I wiped my eyes and gave it back to him.

He gestured for me to hand him my notebook. I did.

He wrote something and handed it back.

Even before I made out the words I saw it was a name and address. I jumped up and threw my arms round the old bloke and hugged him.

He looked startled, but I think he liked it.

Thank you, my hug said. Thank you, thank you, thank you for finally telling me the name of the man who killed my mum.

I looked at the name and address.

Boy, was I totally and completely wrong.

It's a woman.

I stood by the trench in a daze, dog dribble drying on my face, staring at my notebook.

My brain felt like stewed apple.

I don't remember saying goodbye to the old bloke and the dog. I was too busy getting used to what he'd just told me.

That the person who killed Mum wasn't the stupid, careless, hairy-knuckle cowboy hoon I'd imagined – it was a woman called Michelle Solange.

That felt very weird.

Michelle has always been one of my favourite names.

I had a pet rat once called Michelle.

Stop it, I told myself. Pull yourself together. Because it doesn't make any difference.

If she's Mum's killer, I'm going to bring her to justice. And if I can lay my hands on a decent quantity of rotting apples, I'm going to teach her car a lesson too.

First I went back to Mum's grave to let her know that everything's under control.

Then I went into town to the tourist map. I found the killer's street. It's on the northern edge of town.

I was about to head over there when I remembered Dad. I'd told him I was going for a walk hours ago.

I imagined him sitting by the window at Mr and Mrs Bernard's, pulling threads out of the carpet and chewing them, which is what he usually does when he gets worried sick.

Suddenly I felt really bad.

I'd been really unfair to Dad, thinking he'd done a deal with the council and losing respect for him like that.

He'd probably wanted to expose Mum's killer but had been scared to in case the locals got angry and yelled at him for lowering the tone of the district. Then he'd have had the Australian embassy yelling at him for lowering the popularity of Aussie tourists in the district.

It must be really scary, having people angry and yelling at you when that's all your father ever did.

Poor Dad, I thought.

I decided not to go straight to the killer's house.

I decided to go to Mr and Mrs Bernard's first and give Dad a hug.

I wish now I hadn't.

At Mr and Mrs Bernard's place the kitchen was empty. I couldn't see Dad anywhere. I hoped he wasn't out leading a search party.

Then I heard voices coming from the lounge-room.

I opened the door and stepped in.

And froze.

Sitting on the settee, next to Mrs Bernard, was the young woman in pink jeans. Next to her was Mr Didot. Opposite them were Mr and Mrs Rocher from the sausage shop.

They were all staring at me.

Every single one of them looked awkward and uncomfortable.

I thought it must have been because they were all detectives and I'd just blown their cover as nice, concerned local citizens. Then I noticed they weren't jumping on me and arresting me to stop me getting at Mum's killer.

I was confused.

I took a step back.

None of them moved.

I had to find out what was going on.

I wish now I hadn't. I wish now I'd run out of the house and gone straight to the killer's place.

Instead I grabbed my notebook and wrote in

big letters 'WHO ARE YOU?' and thrust it at the pink-jeans woman. Mrs Bernard looked at it and translated.

The pink-jeans woman stood up and held her arms out as if she was going to hug me.

I hadn't expected that. I took another step back.

The pink-jeans woman opened her mouth to speak. Mrs Bernard grabbed her arm. She said something to the woman in French. The only word I understood was Dad's name.

The pink-jeans woman gave me a sad, worried look and sat back down.

Mr Didot and Mrs and Mrs Rocher were giving me sad, worried looks too.

I wanted to jump on the coffee table and scream 'WHAT'S GOING ON?'

As it turned out I didn't need to.

Mrs Bernard took my hands in hers and stroked them gently.

'Your father is upstairs,' she said. 'He wants to see you.'

My brain was racing as I went upstairs. Why was everyone looking so sad and worried? Had Dad been offered a recording contract by a French CD company? Had the sausages I'd left outside the post office gone mouldy and someone had eaten them and was suing us?

When Dad opened his door I saw it was much worse than that.

Dad had been crying and he only cries at Disney movies or when things are really, really crook.

'Rowena,' he said, 'I've had some rough news.'

He made me sit on the bed and put his arm round me.

My mind was in a panic.

Was someone sick?

Had someone died?

'Claire rang,' he went on. 'She's had a letter from the TV people. They've come up with some more evidence.'

Dad's voice wobbled as he said evidence, which made my guts wobble too.

'Claire faxed the new evidence to her old science teacher at uni,' continued Dad, 'and he reckons it's kosher.'

I didn't know what kosher was, but Dad's strangled voice was enough to give me a knot in the guts bigger than Western Europe.

'Love,' said Dad, 'it looks like the TV people were right about those sprays. The ones I used before you were born. They probably did what the TV people said they did. They probably stuffed your throat up.'

My brain went to stewed apple again.

Dad started crying again.

I sat there numb, while Dad sobbed, 'I'm sorry, I didn't know,' over and over into my hair.

Then he sat up and wiped his tears and gripped my shoulders and put his face close to mine.

And softly started to sing.

He sang one of my favourite songs, 'I Love You More Than Pickled Onions', and he's never sung it with more emotion in his voice, but I didn't want to hear it.

By the end of the first verse I was feeling sick and dizzy.

I pulled away from Dad and told him I needed to lie down, and left him there and came to my room.

It's not fair.

Dads shouldn't do this to kids.

Tell them this sort of news.

No kid wants to feel angry and let down and violent towards her own dad.

Luckily I don't have to.

Luckily I'm using all my anger up on someone else.

A woman who I'll be going to visit in another hour or so, just as soon as I'm sure everyone in the house is asleep.

A woman who has brought misery and sadness and loneliness and grief into the life of an innocent child.

A woman who deserves to die.

The gun was old.

And heavy.

When I lifted it off the wall of Mr Bernard's workshop, I nearly pulled a muscle.

I didn't care.

It was big.

The barrel was long.

It looked like it could shoot a hole in a fridge. Or a cowardly hit-and-run driver.

Which was exactly what I needed.

It even had a convenient strap for slinging it over your shoulder. I slung it over my shoulder. The wooden part smacked against some hanging cheeses.

I snapped my torch off and held my breath, hoping I hadn't woken anyone up.

It didn't sound as though I had.

Then I saw a dark shape behind the workshop door.

One of the good things about having a dud throat is you can't scream with terror and wake the whole street up.

Inside my head, though, I yelled good and loud.

Then I realised it was just a coat.

A big, old, heavy coat hanging inside the door.

It was as thick as a doormat and I nearly dislocated a shoulder getting it on, and as I walked it dragged on the ground behind me.

But it completely covered the gun. I checked in the hall mirror as I crept out of the house. Only really dumb kids carry big guns along streets at two in the morning without hiding them under coats.

Boy, those World War One soldiers must have had serious muscles to carry those guns.

By the time I'd lugged mine about two kilometres down the road towards the killer's place, I felt like I was carrying a sink.

Even the bullet in the coat pocket was starting to feel heavy. There'd been three in the display case on Mr Bernard's wall. I was glad I'd only brought one.

One was all I'd need.

Then I saw it, up ahead, glowing white in the moonlight behind some dark bushes.

The killer's house.

Her bushes weren't carved into any shapes.

She obviously didn't want to draw attention to herself. I didn't blame her. If I'd killed an innocent member of the public, I wouldn't want to win gardening competitions either.

I checked that the number on the gatepost matched the number in my notebook.

It did.

My guts tightened and suddenly the gun didn't feel so heavy.

I crept past the bushes.

There were no lights on in the house.

I tried the front door. It was locked.

I moved as quietly as I could round to the back. Country people hardly ever lock their back doors, it's a known fact. This place was on the edge of town about half a kilometre from any other houses. I hoped the killer thought it was the country.

She didn't. The back door was locked.

OK, I thought, a window.

I can get through really small windows. Once on Dad's birthday I snuck in through our toilet window with his present. A long-handled toilet brush is almost as big as a rifle.

I moved down the other side of the house looking for an open window.

I wish I hadn't done that.

I really wish I hadn't.

Because that's where it happened.

I found a window. It was only open a bit,

but I was able to get my hand in and release the catch and swing it open.

Peering in, I saw a figure asleep in bed. I could just make out a frilly bed cover. And a frilly dressing gown hanging on the wardrobe door.

My heart was thudding like a battlefield.

I took the bullet from the coat pocket.

I looked at it in the moonlight.

This bullet, I thought, is going to get justice for our family.

When I climb through that window, and wake her up, and point the gun at her, and she sees me loading it with a bullet, she'll know I mean business.

With a bit of luck I won't have to pull the trigger and give away that the gun doesn't actually work and the bullet's just a replica.

With a bit of luck she'll write out a confession so fast she'll need a non-skip ballpoint.

That's what was supposed to happen.

Instead, before I even got one leg through the window, the person in bed rolled over so her sleeping face was in a patch of moonlight.

I stared, my brain spinning.

It was a kid.

A girl of about my age.

She couldn't be the killer. She'd only have been a baby when Mum was killed. She wouldn't even have been driving a pram, let alone a car.

I realised I must be looking at the killer's daughter.

I tried desperately to stop the pictures that were crowding into my head.

Me getting a confession from the girl's mother at gunpoint.

A judge reading the confession and sentencing the mother to life in a maximum security prison with no carpets.

The girl growing up without a mum.

Just like me.

That's when I started trembling.

That's when I knew I couldn't do it.

And that's when I heard the vehicle.

I spun round, peering through the bushes at the headlights coming along the road towards the house.

I prayed it wasn't a police car.

It wasn't, it was an ambulance.

I prayed it would drive past.

It didn't, it stopped at the front of the house.

I ran.

The backyard was like an obstacle course with garden furniture and washing and bean poles and about a million compost heaps.

As I darted between them, the big coat flapped around my legs almost tripping me up and the gun cracked me in the knees.

I didn't dare stop and take them off.

At least when I dived over the back fence the

coat helped cushion my fall onto the mud.

As I picked myself up I heard the ambulance door slam. Mr Bernard must have found the gun missing and panicked. He must have called the ambulance.

He and the other police wouldn't be far behind.

A horrible thought stabbed through me. What if stealing a gun is an even bigger crime in France than running someone over?

It could be me who ends up in the maximum security prison.

I kept on running.

I was in a big ploughed paddock with mud furrows shining in the moonlight.

Then the moon went behind a cloud.

I tripped over and sprawled face-down in the muck.

I didn't care.

Darkness was what I wanted. I picked myself up and staggered on. I felt like a big cockroach in that coat, scuttling through the blackness. Glancing anxiously behind to see if they were following me.

They weren't.

Or if they were, they were doing it with much less panting and falling over and scrambling to their feet and mud-spitting than I was.

Then I tripped for the last time.

Instead of my face hitting cold mud again, I

somersaulted forward into empty air.

And landed so hard on my back that even the coat couldn't stop my brain from scrambling.

When I was able to stand up, I looked around.

Walls twice as tall as me towered up on both sides. I ran my hands over them. They were dirt.

I looked up at the strip of moon-hazed sky overhead and realised where I was.

In an old trench like the one the old bloke showed me.

The perfect place to bury a gun.

I started digging, using the barrel of the gun as a crowbar and the wooden end as a spade.

While I dug I thought bitterly about Mum's killer.

It wasn't over. I wasn't going to let her get away with it. I'd just have to wait till her daughter was old enough to do without a mother.

What age was that?

Twenty? Thirty? Seventy?

Be fair, I told myself, it's not the kid's fault her mother's a criminal.

Just like it's not my fault my father's a ratbag.

She's lucky.

At least her mother only damaged someone else.

At least her mother didn't hurt her.

Not like my father.

Not like Kenny the Cowboy.

Not like the fastest spray gun in the western postal district.

Angry tears flooded my eyes but I kept on stabbing the gun blindly into the dirt.

I had to keep digging to make a hole deep enough to bury the evidence.

Except suddenly it wasn't the gun I wanted to bury, it was the mouth-organ jiggling in my coat pocket.

And the elastic-sided boots Dad bought me last birthday.

And the photo of him in my wallet.

Everything that reminds me of him.

I was crying so hard I wasn't watching what I was doing.

The hole I was digging must have been too close to the wall of the trench.

I was swinging the rifle like a pick axe, eyes squeezed tight against the tears and the sadness and the memory of what a good dad I used to think he was.

Then the trench wall started to collapse.

I felt lumps of dirt cannoning into me and stones stinging my face and before I could jump back a dark object started sliding towards me out of the crumbling wall of the trench.

I put my hands up to protect my head and found myself being pushed backwards by rusty metal.

I tried to stay on my feet but the metal thing

kept coming and wet dirt was showering into my face and my feet slipped on stones and I fell onto my back and the thing came sliding down onto my chest.

I waited to be crushed.

I wasn't.

I'm trapped under it, but.

In the moonlight I can see it's a metal cylinder about the size of the water heater we used to have over the bath. Before Claire and Erin came along and we got one outside.

It's so rusty I can't tell what it is.

It could even be a water heater.

Or one of those big gas cylinders people use if they've got a lot of welding or barbecueing to do.

It could be a million things. Give people a hole and they'll dump anything.

Anyway, I'm lying here, half covered in dirt, trapped under it.

Luckily it's still half in the trench wall, sort of balanced, so it's not actually crushing my chest, just pinning me down. Trouble is, both my arms are buried so I can't even try and shift it. And when I try and wriggle, the thing starts to slip and more bits of trench wall collapse.

I've been here for about half an hour already.

I could be here for days.

I don't care, but.

When your mum's dead and your dad's ruined your life, where else is there to go?

What's that noise?

It sounds like a vehicle bouncing across the paddock. Now it's stuck in the mud. I can hear wheels spinning.

The ambulance?

The police?

I don't know if I want them to find me or not.

Is juvenile remand centre worse than being trapped in a trench under a lump of rusty metal?

Wait on, that voice, calling my name.

It's Mrs Bernard.

Why does her voice do this to me? Make my guts tingle. Make my heart skip. Make me not want to be buried alive.

I'll whistle to attract her attention.

My mouth's too dry. Too much dirt in it.

With my arms buried I can't even clap.

It's not fair.

Normally I can cope with not having a voice, even though it means I can't yell and scream and roar at dopey policemen and rude TV cameramen and grouchy grandparents and suspected killers.

But now I need one.

I'm not asking for much. I don't want to tell long complicated jokes. I don't want to quote Shakespeare. I'm not asking for Mum's gift of the gab. I just want to yell a couple of words.

'I'm here.'

Is that too much to ask, Dad?

Now I'm crying again. Oh well, perhaps if I let the tears run into my mouth I'll be able to whistle.

Hang on.

The mouth-organ.

It's in my coat pocket.

If I can just get one hand free.

The left one's no good, it feels like it's trapped under my bum. The right one's better. I can move it under the dirt. Wriggle it into the pocket.

Got it.

Now, get the mouth-organ up to my mouth without causing another avalanche.

Slowly.

Hope this mouth-organ was specially made for war in the trenches. Hope it's a special model with holes that don't clog up with dirt.

I'll give them a suck just in case.

I don't feel up to the first half of 'Waltzing Matilda'. I'll just blow a note. And again. And again.

I think Mrs Bernard's heard it.

Her voice is getting closer. I can see a torch beam flashing.

There she is, peering over the edge of the trench. She's calling down to me. She's forgotten I don't speak French.

Even when I don't understand a word, her voice makes the hairs on my neck stand up. Or it would do if they weren't caked with mud.

Wait on, she's got people with her.

A row of faces, concerned and anxious, staring down at me.

Mr Didot.

Mrs and Mrs Rocher from the sausage shop.

The woman in pink jeans.

Jeez, I've never seen a group of nice people so desperate to help people with bits missing. Even if they're detectives, they're incredibly dedicated. It's 3 a.m. It's starting to rain. And now they're climbing down into the trench.

Please, go easy. If you start a mud slide, we're all history.

They've made it.

Mrs Bernard didn't stop talking all the way down, but at least she switched to English.

'I blame myself, Rowena,' she said. 'I should

have guessed you'd find out who the driver was.'

I wish I could tell her not to be so hard on herself. But I'm still groping in my pocket with my free hand for my notebook.

Mrs Rocher is unwrapping something and holding it out to me.

It's a slice of something with bits in it.

Mr Rocher is reading from an English phrase book.

'Bolled ship's had yelly.'

I think he means boiled sheep's head jelly.

I wish I hadn't worked that out.

Mr Rocher has just dropped the phrase book. He's staring at the metal thing I'm lying under. He's looking horrified. He's yelling at Mrs Bernard. Perhaps it's a bit of his old fridge and he's just remembered he left some duck nostrils in it.

They're all staring at it.

They all look horrifed.

They're all talking to me in French.

I can tell from their hand-movements they don't want me to move. Not even a tiny bit. I think Mr Rocher would prefer it if I didn't even breathe.

The woman in pink jeans is making a frantic call on her mobile phone.

'Be brave, little Ro,' Mrs Bernard is saying. 'Help will be here soon.'

The danger of a mud slide must be even worse than I can see from here.

Mr Didot has got his notebook computer with him. He's switching it on. He's crouching down next to me. He wants me to read the screen.

'Your dad's going to be OK,' it says. 'I've had a reply from the top agricultural chemical lab in Sweden. They checked the amounts of spray your dad was told to use. The amounts were too high. He was told to use too much. It wasn't his fault.'

I'm struggling to digest this.

I think it means that the salesman who sold Dad the spray lied to him about how much he should use.

I think it means that.

I'm finding it a bit hard to concentrate because I'm also watching Mrs Bernard and Mr Rocher's hand-movements and I've just realised why they're whispering so frantically to each other.

The big rusty metal thing I'm lying under.

It's a bomb.

Isn't it amazing how a few seconds can change your life totally and completely for ever?

A bomb can explode.

A car can hit you.

Somebody can tell you something.

And from then on you're never the same.

I'll never be the same, not after what Mrs Bernard has just told me.

I thought what she told me about the bomb was mind-boggling enough.

'It's not a bomb,' she said, stroking my cheek. 'It's a shell.'

'What's the difference?' I typed one-handed on Mr Didot's computer that he was kindly holding for me.

'A bomb comes from a plane,' she said. 'A shell comes from a cannon.'

I could tell there was more.

Mrs Bernard took a deep breath.

'This shell is from World War One,' she continued. 'It is more than eighty years old. It is very fragile. One tiny movement and boom. You must be very still.'

I wished desperately she hadn't used the word boom.

It's really hard to be very still when your whole body's shaking.

I typed on the computer with the tiniest finger movements I could.

'Get out. Get to safety.'

Then, because if they did get out this would be my last chance to write anything, I also typed, 'If I die please bury me with my mum.'

I needn't have bothered.

They didn't get out to safety.

They stayed where they were, looking at me with such care and concern.

I didn't understand.

'Rowena,' said Mrs Bernard softly, 'you are with your mother here.'

I understood that even less.

'She is in all of us,' Mrs Bernard went on.

I thought I understood that. I thought she meant they remembered Mum fondly. I thought they were being sweet and kind and religious.

Boy, was I wrong.

I saw Mrs Bernard exchange glances with the others. Mr Rocher gave a small nod.

Mrs Bernard turned back to me.

'Your mother did a wonderful, generous thing,' said Mrs Bernard. 'Years before she was killed, she instructed that when she died, parts of her body could be given to people who needed them.'

Mrs Bernard pointed to the small group standing around her.

'We are the people who needed them,' she said.

I looked at her, trying to understand.

'Twelve years ago Mr Rocher was almost dead from a heart disease,' said Mrs Bernard gently. 'His heart was finished. Then he was given your mother's heart.'

Mr Rocher gave me a small nod. I'd never seen so much love in the eyes of a bloke I wasn't related to.

Although, my spinning brain tried to tell me, in a way I was.

I wasn't listening to it.

Mrs Bernard was speaking again.

'Edith was blind,' she said, pointing to the woman in pink jeans. 'Then she was given your mother's eyes.'

I stared at Edith.

She stared back at me, her eyes shining in the moonlight.

Except they weren't her eyes.

'Mr Didot,' continued Mrs Bernard, 'was on a kidney machine. Then he was given your mother's kidneys.'

Mr Didot held up his computer.

'Thank you,' said the screen.

I didn't type 'you're welcome'. I was thinking of the party hats in the hospital.

I felt a stab of pain in my chest and it wasn't just the big lump of high explosive pressing on it.

'And I . . .' said Mrs Bernard. She stopped. Her eyes were full of tears. For a second she couldn't speak. Then she did.

'I had an accident,' she said. 'A child was drowning. I dived into the river. There was wire. My throat was damaged. Then I was given your mother's voice.'

For the first time I noticed the small scar on her neck.

I stared at her, numb, for what could have been hours.

At some point she reached out and stroked my face. 'I was lucky,' she said sadly. 'My condition wasn't as serious as yours. The operation was a big risk. Most fail. Mine was a success.'

Suddenly feelings started swirling through my whole body.

I wanted to kill them all.

If you'd told me this morning that I'd want to kill people with bits of my mother in them, I wouldn't have believed you.

But I did.

All I had to do was give the shell a thump.

I probably didn't even have to do that.

My heart was probably thumping enough as it was.

Then there was a yell from above us.

'Hang on, Tonto.'

A figure was tumbling down into the trench in a spray of dirt.

Dad.

'Don't panic,' he yelled. 'I've got it.'

Before anyone could move, he grabbed the shell and tried to wrestle it off me.

Everyone panicked.

Mrs Bernard yelled in French.

I yelled in one-handed English.

Dad wasn't listening. He flung himself down next to me and wriggled into the dirt and tried to push the shell off me. He wasn't very successful. The shell slipped further out of the trench wall, onto us both.

Mrs Bernard and the others put their arms over their faces.

The shell didn't explode.

I saw the veins next to Dad's ears bulging. He was supporting the weight of the shell, stopping it from crushing us.

It wasn't a good time to say what I said next, but I couldn't stop myself.

'Why didn't you tell me?' I yelled at him tearfully with my free hand. It was flying about so furiously it almost bashed the shell.

'Why didn't you tell me about Mum's bits?'

Dad took a deep breath.

He was silent for a while. I started to think he couldn't speak because of the weight of the shell.

He looked sadly at Mrs Bernard and the others. Then he looked back at me and sighed.

'I was ashamed,' he said quietly. 'Ashamed I hadn't saved all of her for you.'

My heart stopped.

Did he mean . . .?

He couldn't. When Mum died I was a small baby. Her throat bits would have been about eight sizes too big for me.

'Mum wanted to give her body to help others,' Dad was saying. 'It was her wish. My wish was you'd think Mum was buried in Australia where you could feel close to her. All of her. For ever.'

I understood.

I shut my eyes.

I remembered how close to her I'd always felt, sitting by her grave in Australia.

My insides went warm, just thinking about it.

Then I realised Dad was still speaking.

'There's another reason I didn't tell you the truth about Mum,' he was saying. 'I . . . I didn't want you to know it was my fault she was killed.'

I turned my head towards Dad in the dirt.

His face was very close to mine.

I stared at him.

He took another deep painful breath. Even though Mrs Bernard's torch was getting a bit dim, I could see the tears in Dad's eyes.

'Mum brought me here to see my grandfather's grave,' he went on, 'so I could understand why my dad's such a ratbag. Him growing up without a dad and all. If Mum hadn't been trying to help my dud family, she wouldn't have been in France and she wouldn't have been killed.'

Over the years I've seen a lot of pain on Dad's face, specially when I catch him watching me when he thinks I'm not looking, but I've never seen as much pain as I saw at that moment.

I felt a stab in my chest. For a sec I thought the shell was slipping more. Then I realised it was a sob.

I knew how he felt.

All those years I'd thought Mum's death had something to do with me being born.

All those years me and Dad had been feeling the same thing and we hadn't known it because we hadn't told each other our side of the story.

'Such a waste,' Dad was saying. 'Her lovely, lovely life wasted and it was my fault.'

I reached out my free hand and put it on his cheek.

Then I took it off so I could tell him.

'Mum's death wasn't your fault,' I said, moving my hand gently in front of his straining, tear-streaked face. 'And it wasn't a waste.'

I looked up at Mrs Bernard, Mr and Mrs Rocher, Mr Didot and Edith, who were peering down at me, faces soft with care and concern.

'That's not a waste,' I said, pointing to them.

I was shocked I'd said it.

But I meant it.

Before I could get my breathing under control, I had another thought.

What Mum wanted could still happen.

Dad could still visit his grandfather's grave. He could still have a chance to understand his dad's side of the story.

If we could get out from under this shell, Mum's mission could still be successful. It wouldn't have ended in vain.

As I turned to Dad to tell him this, I had an incredible feeling.

I was carrying on Mum's mission.

Which means I've got a part of Mum in me too.

Dad was struggling again with the shell.

'Get off her, you mongrel,' he grunted, veins bulging.

I felt the weight lift from my chest and suddenly I was being dragged out from under the rough metal.

Mrs Bernard pulled me to my feet and

wrapped her arms round me and shielded me with her body.

Well, the bits of it that are hers.

Dad groaned and the shell dropped back onto his chest.

The others put their arms over their faces again.

The shell didn't explode.

'Get her somewhere safe,' said Dad. 'Now.'

Before I could get my arms free to talk to him, Mrs Bernard started moving me away down the trench.

Dad looked at me as I went. 'I was wrong,' he said. 'I should have told you the truth about Mum. I stuffed it up.'

I wriggled round in Mrs Bernard's arms to face Dad. I still couldn't get my hands free to reply. In the torchlight I noticed something gleaming in the dirt near his head.

My guts gave a lurch.

It was a skull.

The skull of an old soldier.

It could even be the skull of Dad's grandfather.

Dad saw it. He stared at it sadly.

Then the shell started slipping further out of the trench wall. I wanted to throw myself back under it and stop him being crushed, but Mrs Bernard held me tight.

Dad shifted his body and managed to stop it.

'I know what you're thinking,' he said through clenched teeth. 'I've stuffed everything else up, I'm probably gunna stuff this up as well.'

As Mrs Bernard pulled me away along the trench, my eyes were so full of tears I couldn't see if Dad was speaking to me or the skull.

Why's it taking them so long?

With the amount of gear they've got here, you'd think they'd have him out by now.

If I was the French version of the State Emergency Service and I had cranes and scaffolding and generators and lights and an army of bomb-disposal experts in padded suits, I'd have had Dad out of there hours ago.

OK, I know the shell's so fragile that the slightest bump could blow him and them into the next country.

And I know the edge of the trench is so crumbly that they have to reinforce it before they can get the crane close enough.

And I know the shell's slipped so far out that they daren't try and get scaffolding in next to Dad in case the whole thing comes down on them.

But I still reckon I'd have him out by now.

And then I could get home to bed instead of hanging around behind this security tape having painful thoughts.

Like how, even though I really want to blame Dad for what he did to me with the spray, I'm having trouble doing it.

Because if I had a dad like Dad's, a dad who was always angry and yelling at me and never showed he loved me, I'd probably get sucked in by a friendly, caring, older chemical salesman too.

A salesman who seemed to like me.

A salesman who took me under his wing.

A salesman who wanted to teach me things.

I probably wouldn't notice he was doing all that just to sell me more chemicals either.

I'd probably trust the scumbag just like Dad did.

This is ridiculous.

What are they doing over there?

I've built really complex Lego rescue operations in less time than they're taking over there.

If I climb onto the roof of this four-wheel drive, I can just see Dad down in the trench.

Oh no, the shell's slipped out even more.

Dad's having to support most of the weight of it.

I can see his arms trembling with the effort.

He's giving it everything he's got, but how much longer can he take the weight?

If I was the French version of the State Emergency Service I'd be feeding him onion soup to keep his strength up. And I wouldn't have that ambulance parked where he can see it and get depressed.

Thank God Dad's used to giving things everything he's got.

Like when he first married Mum and started the farm and everyone told him it wouldn't work.

Including the bank, the stock and station agent and his dad.

He showed them, but.

'Every day,' he told me once, 'I'd look at Mum's tummy getting bigger with you, then I'd go out into the paddocks and give it everything I'd got.'

Now I'm crying.

I don't want to because if Mrs Bernard sees me she's liable to get all motherly and take me home.

Oh come on, you blokes, work faster.

He can't last much longer.

He's my dad and I want you to get him out.

I'm yelling encouragement to him, but he can't see my hands from down there.

If only Mum was here to yell with her voice.

Wait a sec, I've had an idea.

Mrs Bernard was brilliant.

For a woman who's never sung in public before, she was amazing.

OK, she got to read the words off my notepad, but she also did a great job with the tune and she's only heard Mum's song a few times and most of those were twelve years ago.

I couldn't even play her the cassette because it's back at the house and I was worried Dad wouldn't hold out that long.

Mrs Bernard's guts must have been in a knot as we walked to the edge of the trench. I know mine were. For a start we weren't even meant to have climbed over the security tape.

When the rescue workers saw us, I was sure they'd make us go back.

They started yelling and pointing, but we just ignored them and started singing.

Mrs Bernard really belted it out and Dad

looked up almost straight away. He frowned at first, then gave the sort of crooked grin people do while they're holding up huge weights.

I made my hand-movements as big as I could so he'd know I was singing too.

Then I heard other voices joining in behind us.

I turned round.

Mr Didot and Edith and Mr and Mrs Rocher had followed us. They were singing as well, peering over Mrs Bernard's shoulder to see the words.

They couldn't pronounce half of them and they were even more out of tune than Dad usually is.

It didn't matter.

By the time we'd got to the chorus bit –

'*I know you love me*
I know you're doing your best,
That's why I'm not angry
You've got my head in an ants' nest.'

– Dad's legs had stopped trembling and his shoulders had straightened up.

Which was just as well because suddenly my shoulders were shaking with sobs.

It was Mrs Bernard's singing that did it.

Even though Mum has been dead twelve years, her voice was still alive.

Helping me save Dad.

And her heart.

And her eyes.

And her kidneys.

I looked up at the singing faces gazing down at me and I knew I was being given the one thing I've always wanted more than Mum's voice.

Her love.

At that moment one of the rescue workers trying to get a nylon crane sling in position slipped and bumped the shell.

The shell slid out further.

Other rescue workers yelled in alarm.

Dad was only just able to hold it. I don't reckon he would have if we hadn't been singing.

Then suddenly the crane sling was in position.

The rescue workers started yelling again, instructions this time.

The crane motor revved, the cable tightened, and slowly, slowly, slowly the shell was lifted off Dad.

He was free.

Bomb disposal experts dragged him up out of the trench.

He was surrounded by people slapping him on the back and kissing him on both cheeks.

I couldn't even get to him.

The truth is, I held back.

I wanted to hug him, but something was stopping me.

What if I put my arms round him and it didn't feel right?

What if even though my brain knew it wasn't his fault about the spray, my guts wouldn't let me forgive him?

What then?

I didn't get a chance to think of an answer.

Suddenly the crowd around Dad fell back.

A woman was walking slowly towards him across the rescue site. She was wearing an ambulance driver's uniform.

The local people all stared at her, and then at Dad, and nudged the non-local rescue workers and told them to shut up.

I felt arms slip round me and hold me tight.

It was Mrs Bernard.

The woman stopped in front of Dad and looked him in the face.

In the bright rescue lights I saw her cheeks were wet with tears.

Mrs Bernard stepped closer to Dad and took me with her.

The woman said something to Dad in French. Mrs Bernard translated.

'My name is Michelle Solange.'

Suddenly I had a knot in my guts the size of Australia, including Tasmania.

The woman spoke again. Mrs Bernard hesitated, then translated.

'I killed your wife.'

Some of the onlookers gasped.

I did inside.

Dad blinked.

Still the woman kept looking straight at him.

'My baby daughter was very sick,' she continued. 'I was rushing her to the hospital. I was in a panic. That's why when I hit your wife I did not stop.'

For the first time she looked at the ground.

'Also,' she said quietly, 'I was scared they would take me away from my daughter.'

She looked at Dad again.

Dad still had no expression on his mud-streaked face, but I could see his eyes were red and I knew it wasn't just because of the time being 4.20 a.m.

'To try to make amends,' said the woman, 'I became an ambulance driver. I have helped save hundreds of road victims. But it is not enough. So I have come to you to say what I should have said twelve years ago.'

Mrs Bernard paused, and I realised it was because her throat was choked with tears.

Finally she whispered the woman's last words. 'I'm sorry.'

There was a long silence. Dad and the woman looked at each other.

Then Dad did a wonderful thing.

He lifted his arms and put them round the woman and held her to him.

I looked at them, two weeping parents who'd both just tried to do their best.

And I knew in my guts I wanted to hug him too.

I did most of my crying at Mum's grave.

Mrs Bernard and Mr Didot and Mr and Mrs Rocher and Edith did a fair bit too, specially when I laid the sausages next to Mum's headstone.

But we did some laughing as well.

And some singing and mouth-organ playing.

Mum would have liked that.

Dad did most of his crying at his grandfather's war grave. He's still doing some now.

I don't blame him.

Standing here among the hundreds of white stone crosses, it's hard not to shed a tear.

A lot of these young Aussie blokes were dads when they were killed in the war. Dads who were just doing their best.

A lot of kids had to grow up without them.

That chemical salesman might even have been one.

I reckon that's pretty sad.

Specially for someone like me who's growing up with one of the world's top dads.

Just now me and Dad had one of the best hugs we've ever had and Dad told me he's planning to do two things when we get back to Australia.

First he's going to put a metal plaque on our biggest apple tree in memory of his grandfather.

Then he's going to go and make his dad a bacon and jam sandwich.

I reckon Mum'll be pretty happy to see that.

She won't be there in person, of course, but I will, so that's almost the same.

And then afterwards I'm going to use my gift of the gab to tell Paige Parker everything that's happened.

And when I do I'll make sure I give this place a special mention.

Because if the TV people want to broadcast the truth about Dad and the sprays and me, they should tell the whole story.

It's only fair.

Also by Morris Gleitzman

'Morris Gleitzman is in dazzling form'
Lindsey Fraser, *Scotsman*

A selected list of titles available from Macmillan Children's Books

The prices shown below are correct at the time of going to press. However, Macmillan Publishers reserves the right to show new retail prices on covers, which may differ from those previously advertised.

Morris Gleitzman		
Belly Flop and Water Wings	978-0-330-44294-7	£5.99
Linda Aronson		
Naturally Rude	978-0-330-48254-4	£5.99
Terence Blacker		
ParentSwap	978-0-330-43741-7	£5.99
Frank Cottrell Boyce		
Framed	978-0-330-43425-6	£5.99
Millions	978-0-330-43331-0	£5.99
Andy Griffiths		
Bumageddon . . . the Final Pongflict	978-0-330-43370-9	£4.99

All Pan Macmillan titles can be ordered from our website, www.panmacmillan.com, or from your local bookshop and are also available by post from:

Bookpost, PO Box 29, Douglas, Isle of Man IM99 1BQ

Credit cards accepted. For details:
Telephone: 01624 677237
Fax: 01624 670923
Email: bookshop@enterprise.net
www.bookpost.co.uk

Free postage and packing in the United Kingdom